STARS SHINE IN YOUR EYES

London Sullivans 2

Bella Andre

STARS SHINE IN YOUR EYES
London Sullivans 2
Malcom Sullivan & Josie Hartwell
© 2024 Bella Andre

Sign up for Bella's New Release Newsletter
bellaandre.com/newsletter
www.BellaAndre.com
Facebook/Meta ~ Instagram ~ Twitter/X
facebook.com/bellaandrefans
instagram.com/bellaandrebooks
twitter.com/bellaandre

A note from Bella

Hello and thank you for reading my books! I have a special place in my heart for London, as many of you know. Some of my very best friends live in London and Bath – and I am lucky enough to have a flat in London with a view of the Thames and the oldest bridge in London!

The London Sullivans series began as my love letter to England with *As Long As I Have You*, and I've realized with this second book in the series, that all of the London-set Sullivans are continued love letters to one of my favorite cities in the world.

This book is very special to me, and I hope it will be special to you too!

Happy reading,
Bella Andre

P.S. While Elderflower Island is my own fictional creation, I have been heavily inspired by Eel Pie Island in southwest London, along with the London Borough of Richmond upon Thames. For those of you who know the area well, thank you for allowing this American writer the license to embellish a few major details here and there throughout my books.

P.P.S. More stories about the London Sullivans are coming soon! Please be sure to sign up for my newsletter (bellaandre.com/newsletter) so that you don't miss out on any new book announcements.

CHAPTER ONE

Josie Hartwell could hardly believe she was in England. It had been an eleven-hour trip from Coeur d'Alene, Idaho, to Heathrow Airport in London. She should be tired after spending hours beside a couple who chattered the entire way, and if there was a crying-baby section, she was in it. However, she was so excited to be in the UK that she didn't feel tired at all.

Instead, she was energized. She couldn't wait to run her first reading retreat at Elderflower Island Books on Elderflower Island. Even the name sounded magical. When she had started her business of creating reading retreats, she had never dreamed that one day it would take her all the way across the Atlantic. She felt so lucky, as though everything she'd been through in her life to get to this point was finally all worth it.

She'd developed an expertise not only in running retreats but in designing spaces in which to hold them. As she and Mari Everett, the owner of Elderflower Island Books, had chatted on email and then, when they got more comfortable, on Zoom, she'd discovered

Mari to be an energetic woman with big plans. She wanted to create a retreat space, and she wanted Josie to design it, then run the first reading retreat. "And more if it works out, which obviously I hope it will," Mari had said.

Josie was excited to see the project through from design to holding the first retreat, so she'd enthusiastically agreed. Mari had booked a flex ticket in case the two weeks ran over, and Josie was careful not to take any bookings too close to the end of her time in the UK. She knew perfectly well that sometimes projects took longer than expected.

For the next two weeks, she was going to be staying on a houseboat on Elderflower Island, in a borough just outside of London. Mari had offered to book a hotel room if she preferred, but the houseboat belonged to her partner Owen's brother, and since Mari was working so hard to launch her bookstore and reading retreats, Josie imagined money was tight. A loaned houseboat would be a lot cheaper than a hotel and, to Josie's mind, so much nicer, so she happily chose the boat. She'd read a little bit online about the area, but she hadn't wanted to do too much research before embarking on the trip. She wanted to experience it all fresh—to see and feel and be amazed by everything in person for the first time.

One thing she noticed as soon as she got to Arrivals

at Heathrow: Everyone looked so cosmopolitan in their trench coats and fashionable boots, with expensive bags swinging from their shoulders. They all walked with such purpose, as though they had important meetings to go to. Or, like the woman who ran into the arms of a man holding flowers, they were meeting a lover whom they hadn't seen for a while. And there was the family waiting for their father to walk out of the baggage claim area, holding a sign that said, DADDY, WE ARE SO HAPPY YOU'RE HOME! Already, England felt welcoming, and Josie hadn't even left the airport yet.

Unlike the lovers reuniting beside her, Josie didn't have anybody waiting for her back in Coeur d'Alene. Her mother had moved from the rainy Pacific Northwest to the Las Vegas area for year-round sun, and Josie's friends were so busy with their kids and husbands that Josie no longer felt like she fit in anywhere. Or with anyone.

Once upon a time, she'd thought she was headed toward wearing a wedding dress and walking down the aisle to recite vows of forever. Maybe she'd even start a family in the not-too-distant future. She'd thought she'd found Prince Charming, her one true love, the man she was supposed to be with. Everything had been so perfect.

Until the day she'd had the biggest shock of her

life... when she'd learned that her boyfriend already had a wife and baby.

Until the day she'd been forced to face the fact that she was nothing more than a mistress who had been lied to in every possible way.

She'd never forget the day she opened the door and found a young, attractive, furious-looking woman holding a baby and accusing her of being a home-wrecker.

No, Josie thought with a shake of her head. That was her past. And this—coming to London to do her dream job—was her future. She was living a different life now. A better life. One where she chose books—both fiction and nonfiction—to help her clients.

Whatever state their personal, physical, or mental affairs might be in, the right book could help. She still could hardly believe that she was making her living by helping others find the books that were right for them, in the same way stories had always helped her through tough times... and now she'd be working in London too!

When her "perfect" relationship had fallen apart, she'd decided that she didn't need or want a man in her life to be happy. She couldn't trust men anymore, and that was fine with her because she was far happier being alone. Happier knowing that she wasn't falling for some fantasy spun by a scumbag masquerading as a good man.

Even two years later, it was difficult not to let herself stew on how badly he'd betrayed both her and his wife. But she refused to let her ex ruin her life or take any more from her than he already had.

If only she could forget his frantic phone messages in which he'd claimed:

1) The situation was more complicated than his wife had made it sound.
2) He would have left his wife if she hadn't gotten pregnant.
3) Josie was the woman he was *truly* in love with, not his wife.

Josie never responded to any of those messages, and within a week of breaking up with him, she got a new phone number so that he couldn't bother her anymore.

Unfortunately, when he couldn't reach her by phone, he had come to her house. She hadn't let him in, though. Instead, she'd sat on the floor with her back against the door, where he couldn't see her and the tears streaming down her cheeks.

Tears because the fairy tale had never been real.

Tears because she hadn't seen from the start what a horrible man he was.

Tears because she'd unwittingly hurt another woman, especially one with a beautiful new baby.

All of that was behind her now, thankfully. Mari Everett, bookstore owner and Josie's new client, was somewhere in Heathrow's Arrivals hall, ready to take Josie to the island. Mari had said she'd be holding a sign with Josie's name on it.

But when Josie got all the way out of the baggage claim area, dragging her heavy suitcases behind her, and looked around at all the signs, she didn't see anybody holding one with her name on it. Nor did she see Mari.

Maybe she'd been held up in traffic? Josie had the woman's phone number, so she could call her, but she figured she would wait a few minutes before seeing if there was a problem.

Josie had always enjoyed people-watching, and standing in the middle of the Arrivals area of one of the biggest airports in the world was a great opportunity. More lovers were reuniting to her left. A mother and son were greeting each other a little awkwardly. A businessman was heading off to continue building his empire, great purpose in each step.

Ever since Josie was a child, she had created lives for people inside her head. Her mother had always fondly said that it was what came of reading so much. Her mother had assumed that one day Josie would become a writer. But although Josie could spend all day reading, she had never had the patience to sit in a chair and type for hours, day after day. She adored writers, of course. But she would always stand firmly on the reading side of books.

Her gaze landed on a man in a well-tailored suit. As he was turned slightly to one side, she could tell that he was on the phone and that he looked irritated. He also, she couldn't help but notice, cut a fine figure. He might wear a bespoke Italian suit and handmade loafers, but the body beneath the fine threads looked like it just got off the rugby field. His thousand-dollar haircut looked ruffled, as though he ran his big hands through it when he was frustrated. In fact, he looked a lot more like an athlete than a business tycoon, whatever his wardrobe said.

Just because she had no interest in seriously dating anyone or getting married, she was still a warm-blooded woman. She could appreciate a good-looking man when she saw one.

She wondered what his story was. Was he a highflier in the corporate world, and a deal that he was trying to save was going bad? Or was he here to meet someone flying in from, say, Australia, with whom he was going to begin working? Or was he here to meet one of the beautiful British blondes in their sleek pencil skirts and impossibly high heels?

Just then, he turned so that she could see his face... and her heart stopped, along with her breath. As though he felt her staring, he glanced up, and his blue-gray eyes rested on her for a second. She glanced away, hoping he hadn't caught her staring at his square-jawed face or the strong nose that was even more attractive for having been broken at one time.

This man reminded her of a boy she'd once known, a British exchange student named Malcolm Sullivan, who had come to Coeur d'Alene for his senior year of high school. *Everyone* had had a crush on him. The British accent alone would have been enough, but his good looks and his slightly wicked smile had sent all of the girls at her high school over the edge. No surprise, he'd dated the most popular girl in school—the cheerleader, the class president, and, unfortunately, one of the mean girls.

No. It couldn't be him. What were the chances that she'd see a guy she went to high school with at Heathrow Airport?

Still, the sight of him took her back.

Josie had always been a bookworm, reading a book even as she went from class to class and definitely during lunch breaks. Back in high school, she'd had big glasses too. Brianna Sterling had made Josie a target right from freshman year. Bumbling Bookworm was what Brianna and her friends had called her. Then it just got shortened to Worm.

Josie had acted like it hadn't bothered her, but of course it had. And through it all, Malcolm hadn't seemed to know that Josie existed.

Why would he? She was two years behind him in school, and she certainly wasn't going to any of the parties or dances that he was invited to. The only reason she'd gone to prom was because another senior that she was friendly with—and who also loved to read—had asked her to be his date. Although Josie guessed he had a bit of a crush on her, and she didn't want to lead him on, she'd agreed to go. Just so she could see what a school dance was like before she graduated.

In some ways, it had been better than she thought. The hotel ballroom the prom committee had booked was better than a decorated gym would have been. It was also fun dressing up and going to a fancy dinner with her date, even if they were both pretty awkward and didn't really know what to say to each other. At least, until they started talking about their favorite books.

In other ways, however, prom was *way* worse than anything she had imagined. Because when she looked at the couples dancing close, some of them kissing before they were pulled apart by the chaperones, it was hard to ignore the longing inside for someone who made her heart race. For someone she could laugh with and also spend time reading with, side by side on a comfy couch. It also hadn't been great when her date made a move to kiss her. She hadn't reacted quickly enough, so his wet lips and tongue found their way not only inside her mouth, but all over her cheeks too. She remembered pulling away and making a quick excuse about having to go to the bathroom.

Rather than going to the bathroom, however, she went outside the hotel to a private area down by a pretty little garden with a flower-covered pergola where she guessed they hosted weddings.

By that point in the evening, she didn't want to go back inside. The music was too loud. Her high heels were hurting her feet. The ballroom was starting to smell like sweaty teenagers. And she really, *really* didn't want to risk her date kissing her again.

That was when Malcolm Sullivan suddenly appeared. And that was also when everything changed. A few moments with her British crush gave her both her highest high and her lowest low.

All this time later, nearly fifteen years since Malcolm had kissed her—and she could still remember every detail of the kiss as though it had happened yesterday.

In any case, there was no way this man in the airport could be him. Seriously, what were the odds that one of the first people she'd see after landing in London would be Malcolm Sullivan? Or that so many years later, she'd recognize the boy she'd kissed so long ago?

Clearly, her tired, overstimulated imagination was playing tricks on her. She had never forgotten the way he'd drawn her into his arms, looked deeply into her eyes, then kissed her. For a few perfect moments, she'd felt safe and perfect and alive and beautiful in his arms.

Until it had all come crashing down when she learned the kiss was a prank. He'd mocked her for thinking the kiss was heartfelt by telling her he'd done it on a dare. That cruel joke had nearly destroyed her fifteen-year-old heart.

She'd told herself a million times over the years that she'd surely built up their kiss in her memory as being way better than it had been. Heck, she'd been fifteen years old. What fifteen-year-old being kissed by a British dreamboat wouldn't have thought that he was *everything*? Except he *definitely* hadn't been a dreamboat in the end. Not by a long shot.

But as the man shoved his phone into his pocket, and she could see his face better, it grew harder and harder to convince herself that he wasn't Malcolm Sullivan. The height was correct, and though he'd filled out more, his body had the same athletic grace. His face was even more attractive, with a few laugh lines around the eyes.

She rubbed a hand over her own eyes. Jet lag. She probably should have slept more on the plane, but she'd been reading such a good book by a British author named Tasmina Perry that she hadn't slept much at all.

Her exhaustion was the only thing that could explain it. Still, she couldn't take her eyes off the man as he took a folded piece of paper out of his pocket, glanced at his watch as though he really had better things to do, unfolded the paper, and held it toward the stream of incoming arrivals.

JOSIE HARTWELL.

Her gasp was loud enough that several people looked her way. The Malcolm Sullivan lookalike was there to pick her up. How could this be? Where was Mari?

Josie fumbled for her phone in her carry-on bag and realized it was still on airplane mode, so if Mari had tried to get ahold of her, Josie wouldn't have gotten her message. Of course, as soon as she took it off airplane mode, a series of text messages came flying in from Mari, who apologized profusely for being unable to pick her up. Her helper at the bookshop had called in sick, and she had a Mathilda Westcott fan group coming that afternoon, so she couldn't close the store and come to the airport. Mari explained that her partner's brother Malcolm would come get Josie, which she hoped would be okay because it was his houseboat that Josie would be staying in. Mari suggested that he could even help her get settled before bringing her by the bookstore.

Josie took a deep breath. She wouldn't let herself treat this as a disaster. The name of Mari's boyfriend's brother was Malcolm. So this *had* to be Malcolm Sullivan standing there, looking impatient. She got the feeling he was usually the one being greeted at airports by drivers with signs, not being the driver.

Okay. Calm down. It was no big deal that Malcolm Sullivan was picking her up… and that she was also going to be staying on *his* houseboat! There was no way he'd remember her. Not a forgettable fifteen-year-old called Worm.

Planting a big smile on her face, she walked toward him. "Hi. I believe you're here to pick me up in place of Mari Everett."

He had been holding the sign with one hand and scrolling through his phone with the other. He glanced up at her as though annoyed that she'd interrupted his web browsing. She almost found herself apologizing for disturbing him, but since he was here to pick her up, she worked to keep the smile firmly planted on her face, her lips almost wobbling from how much she was trying to look happy.

There was no hint of recognition in his eyes. She'd

been right. He didn't remember her at all. Even though it felt weird that he didn't seem to recognize her, she was grateful.

He shoved his phone into his pocket. "Yes, Mari called at the last second and asked me to give you a lift." He looked at the two enormous suitcases behind her. "You don't travel light, do you?"

Perhaps if he hadn't seemed quite so grumpy, she would have explained that only one of the bags had clothes in it. The other was full of books. Even though she was here to work with a bookstore owner, and also knew that there were a zillion bookstores throughout London, she still carried certain books with her everywhere, the way a craftsman might carry their own tools to do a job. These books were all precious to her for one reason or another, and she knew better than anyone that they could help a person heal.

But at this very moment, she couldn't find her voice. Not now that she'd heard his. It was lower than she remembered, because he was a man now rather than a boy on the verge of manhood. But she no longer had one single doubt that this was Malcolm Sullivan in the flesh, the foreign exchange student who'd rocked her world... and then broken her heart. All in a single night.

His eyes narrowed as he waited for her to speak, and she knew she was making a terrible first impression. Or rather, a terrible first impression fifteen years after they'd last seen each other.

"We know each other," she blurted. Wait. Where had that come from? What was wrong with her jet-lagged brain?

He appeared astonished at this news.

Okay, so she no longer wore thick glasses, had grown several inches since high school, dressed better, and had changed her name from Josephine to Josie. So she could understand why he might not be able to connect her with that random girl he'd kissed back in Coeur d'Alene so many years ago.

And yet, she was so flabbergasted to come face to face with him again, she couldn't stop herself from saying, "We knew each other in high school. You were the foreign exchange student from England. You dated Brianna Sterling. The cheerleader. And at the prom, when I was a sophomore, we—"

Oh no. Really? She had almost brought up the kiss that had begun like heaven and ended like hell within the first sixty seconds of speaking with him?

Josie was doubly mortified when recognition finally came into his eyes… along with what looked like horror at seeing her again after all these years.

"I didn't realize you were the person Mari was going to be working with." He obviously didn't think this was good news.

It was a tiny bit gratifying that he seemed as stunned as she was. As though he'd woken up in an alternate reality where the random girl he'd kissed and then dissed back in high school was not only standing in front of him, but was also about to move onto his houseboat for a few weeks.

At a loss for something better to say, she opted for, "Thanks for coming to pick me up. I literally just saw Mari's texts saying that she couldn't get away from the store."

Just like that, he snapped into action. Without asking, he took hold of one of her suitcases and headed for the elevators that led to the parking garage. Despite his grumpy demeanor, it was lovely of him to help, even if she wished he'd grabbed the heaviest bag instead.

"It's not a long drive to the island," he said over his shoulder, carrying her bag as though it weighed nothing, "so if traffic's not bad, we should be on Elderflower Island in about twenty-five minutes."

She tried to follow at his pace, but her bag was so *heavy*. She was breaking into a sweat, and even though her suitcase was on wheels, she felt like she was dragging a block of concrete through the crowded airport.

When he finally realized just how far behind she'd fallen, he waited until she caught up. "How heavy is your bag?"

"It's all books," she explained. "So it's really, really heavy."

He frowned again. "You brought books with you when you're going to be working out of a bookstore?"

Anything she said to explain the situation at this moment would surely come out wrong. "I did."

He shrugged as if it wasn't his business anyway and frankly, he didn't care. "It will be faster if I take both bags."

Before she could say that she could handle the books just fine on her own—especially when that was clearly *not* the case—he rolled both suitcases toward the elevator, leaving her with only her carry-on.

Despite what a physical relief it was to not have to roll the bag, she couldn't help but feel that she was giving him the upper hand. And after what he'd done to her in high school, even if it was fifteen years ago, there was a part of her that couldn't stand the idea of letting him get the upper hand with her ever again.

Which was why she said, "I can handle it," and then proceeded to wrestle the bag back from him.

It would have been funny, she supposed, if the two of them grappling over a suitcase and blocking the entrance to the elevator hadn't been so ridiculous.

Finally, he all but shoved the bag back at her. "If you want it that badly, it's all yours," he said, dialing his Mr. Cranky act up to eleven.

And yet... cranky or not, he was still the best-looking man she'd ever set eyes on. Not to mention that his deep voice and charming-as-hell British accent still felt like red wine flowing through her veins.

Every feminine part of her that had gone dormant these past two years felt like it had just sparked back to life. Like someone had plugged her into a sensual wall socket, and now her battery was fully charged, ready and raring to go.

No, she silently reprimanded herself in a firm voice. *No. No. No.*

She was not here to sample another one of Malcolm's kisses, no matter how amazing it had been when she was a teenager. Frankly, she wasn't here to sample *anyone's* kisses. She was here to help Mari set up a reading retreat on Elderflower Island—and also to have a wonderful time sightseeing in London for the next two weeks.

Seeing Malcolm again was nothing more than a very weird bump in the road. Unfortunately, it was made worse because she was going to be staying on his houseboat. But how could Josie have known that Mari's partner's brother's houseboat belonged to Malcolm Sullivan?

Staying on a houseboat on the Thames had seemed like a lovely option. But now she wasn't so sure it was a good idea. Not if Malcolm was going to be popping in at random times throughout the day for the next two weeks, scowling at her every time she left a cup on the counter or a dirty dish in the sink.

"Mari says the houseboat I'll be staying on is yours?"

He nodded, not looking at her as he pulled his car keys out of his pocket and beeped them at a very fancy car. One that didn't look like it had a trunk big enough for her massive suitcases.

"I sometimes stay on it when I've been visiting with family and friends on the island and don't feel like heading back to my flat in central London. But I haven't used it much at all in the past couple of years." He shot her a sidelong glance. "You didn't think I'd be staying there with you, did you?"

She planted another big fake smile on her face before saying, "No, of course not," in what she hoped was a convincing voice. "I just didn't realize the houseboat belonged to you until today."

"You should be comfortable enough on it," he said. "Although you should know that it doesn't have the latest gadgets or even a TV, so if you don't like it, there are plenty of nearby inns or flat rentals you could book into."

Wow, it had barely taken him any time at all to propose that she stay elsewhere. Had she offended him in some way? Because it felt like her entire presence was offensive to him at the moment. Then again, even before he'd known who she was, that was the vibe he'd been giving off. Like he was too busy and too important to take a break from negotiating some zillion-dollar deal to pick someone up at an airport.

"I'm sure it will be great," she said in as positive a voice as she could manage. "I've never stayed on a houseboat before. But every time I've read a book about someone who lives on one, it has sounded so romantic. And I don't need a TV. I have books."

She wasn't completely positive, but did his lip curl a little bit at the word *romantic*? Honestly, it was enough to make her laugh, and though she did manage to keep her laughter in, the smile on her lips was finally genuine.

This whole situation was just too ridiculous. Almost as though she were still on the plane, trying to sleep in an uncomfortable seat while having weird 30,000-mile-high dreams. If this hadn't actually been her life, it would have been the perfect plot for a novel: A cranky Englishman and a fish-out-of-water American who'd kissed once when they were teenagers come face to face again without any warning.

If you couldn't laugh, what could you do? The only time she let herself cry was when she was reading a beautifully sad story. But in her real life? Nope, she refused to be a crier. She was a get-on-with-it-er.

She was about to ask him if he had been back to Coeur d'Alene—basically looking for any kind of small talk to fill the uncomfortable silence in the car—when his phone rang.

"I have to get this," he said.

"No worries. Just pretend I'm not here."

"Genevieve, what's the latest?" For the next twenty-five minutes, he talked in business-speak. Next year's projections, something quotas, import duties... Pretty much the only words she understood were *New Zealand*.

She had no idea what he was talking about, so she closed her eyes, letting his lovely accent and the movement of the car lull her into a dream state.

Malcolm Sullivan.

Who would have thought she'd ever see him again?

CHAPTER TWO

Malcolm parked in the space allocated for his houseboat and turned off the ignition. Beside him, Josie was sleeping in the passenger seat, her head leaning against the window, one leg tucked up beneath the other.

He decided it would be best to let her sleep for a few more moments. He needed time to not only figure out how this balls-up had happened in the first place, but also how to best deal with it. Especially given that he hadn't exactly been his most charming self so far today.

Since that moment in Mari's bookstore when he'd received a call letting him know that a deal he'd been chasing for a decade—and had all but given up on—was in play, he'd been working toward the biggest deal of his career. He didn't need more money—he could never spend all he already had and gave a great deal to charity. However, there was a sense of satisfaction in knowing he could turn a local brand into a global leader. His second-in-command, Genevieve (call her Jenny and be prepared to lose a body part), had been working even more tirelessly than he on the deal and had hit a snag. Genevieve Duvall didn't often come to him, only when she was truly stuck. But she'd come to him this morning with news that the brand owner was having second thoughts.

"They don't want to grow too fast," she told him. "I explained that we've done the research and they are ready, but let's face it, the wonder boy who invented House in a Box is more interested in saving the world than in reading financial projections."

"Can't he see that we're helping him save the world?" Malcolm exploded in frustration.

"Apparently not," she replied in crisp tones that barely covered her own annoyance.

His workday had started badly and quickly become worse. The CEO and owner of House in a Box (and the man who held far too many roles there) was feeling under pressure. "I'm sorry, mate," he said in his thick Kiwi accent, "but I don't want to grow too fast so we crash and burn." Then he'd abruptly ended the call, as there was some emergency he had to deal with.

Kieran Taylor had too few staff. It was one of the things Malcolm, Genevieve, and their team would fix. What Kieran also had was a brilliant concept—small-footprint, eco-friendly homes that could be shipped in a box and put together for a price that was lower than most garages cost to build. He was a visionary who wanted to help overpopulated cities, poor people who hadn't previously been able to dream of owning their own home, and even people who wanted to put a home in their backyard for their aging parents or grown-up kids.

Malcolm had every intention of making House in a Box a global brand, and he shared Kieran's vision of genuinely helping people and the planet into the bargain. He had a feeling he'd be jumping on a plane to Christchurch before he was much older. Both he and Genevieve, who'd busted her butt pulling in investors to help Kieran take his vision global.

For pride's sake, and for Genevieve, he didn't want to see this deal fail at the last second.

And then Mari had called from the bookstore, pleading with him to pick up a woman named Josie at the airport and take her to his houseboat. He'd been happy to lend the houseboat—he rarely had time to go there these days—but did he have to play chauffeur too? Didn't she know that his days at the office started at six in the morning and usually ended more than fourteen hours later? But when she'd explained that she'd already tried every other person in his family and that he was her very last resort before calling an impersonal car service to do the pickup, that had grated too. Why was he the last on her call list?

Of course, he knew precisely why. Mari not only

knew how busy he was, she also knew that he could be a grumpy git at the best of times.

He ran a hand over his face, the ridiculously low number of hours he had been sleeping lately finally catching up with him. He was lucky that he never needed much sleep. Even for him, however, the four hours he'd been getting each night during the past week weren't cutting it.

It should have been a good thing that he had a vacation to Thailand to look forward to, but even that was a mess. All because the woman he was supposed to go to Thailand with... Well, to put it bluntly, he wasn't sure he even wanted to have dinner with her anymore, let alone spend a week in a foreign country with her.

It wasn't that Katrina wasn't beautiful, because she was quite possibly one of the most stunning women he'd ever dated. Unfortunately, it turned out that he needed more than looks to keep from being bored, a lesson he had learned—or rather had failed to learn—from one relationship to the next.

A part of him wondered if he should just suck it up and make it through the week in Thailand before telling Katrina that he thought there was someone better out there for her. You know, the whole "it's not you, it's me" speech.

But frankly, he wasn't sure he'd make it through

the flight to Thailand with her vacuous conversation, let alone a week on a beach. Inevitably, he'd want to parasail or trek through the jungle, and she'd complain that he wasn't spending enough time with her, even though she'd be spending all of her time in a bikini on a chaise longue, scrolling through her social media feeds and posting pictures intended to make everyone who followed her jealous.

If she would read a book on the beachfront lounger, that wouldn't seem nearly as bad. But no one he dated ever seemed to read. It was a pity, because when Malcolm wasn't at the office, or hanging out with his family, the one thing he liked to do was read. Books about military history and business, mostly, along with a few novels.

In deep contrast to all of the women he had dated over the years, Josie had packed an entire suitcase with books. And the truth was that he didn't remember much about her from high school beyond two things.

She'd always been reading.

And he had kissed her.

A kiss he had wanted to apologize for ever since.

Not actually the kiss, which had been surprisingly good as far as he could remember through his beer goggles. It was what had come after.

Oh man. *After.*

It hadn't been pretty.

For so many years afterward, he'd thought about trying to look her up so that he could apologize. But he never had. Because what could he have said to her beyond, *I was that British bloke in high school who completely messed with you at the prom, and I've felt bad about it ever since.*

There was nothing he could say to make up for what he'd done, and it seemed more cruel to bring it up again. At least, that's what he told himself at two a.m. on nights when he couldn't sleep and the memories came back, making him feel like the biggest arsehole in the world.

Josie stirred, and since he didn't want her to think he'd been staring at her like some weird stalker while she slept, he got out of the car and went to lift her luggage out of the backseat, which was the only place in his sports car where her bags would fit. He drove a vehicle meant for racing down the *autobahn*, not picking up people at the airport.

She stirred again as he pulled out the suitcases, then yawned and rubbed her eyes, looking around as though she had no clue where she was. Transatlantic flights could be brutal, especially if you weren't a good plane sleeper. He'd always had a knack for dropping off when he needed to, which was handy with all the business travel that came with his job. It would be nice, he suddenly found himself thinking, to travel for pleasure instead of business, at least once in a while.

Which was exactly what his upcoming trip to Thailand was supposed to be about. Just relaxing. But though he intellectually understood the concept of relaxation, it didn't mean he was great at putting it into practice. Already, he knew what he'd be doing in Thailand. Not parasailing or trekking through any jungles. Instead of having any kind of adventures at all, he'd be on his computer dealing with email, or on a video call, or on his phone with someone back at the office or a new client he wanted to land.

The only time he didn't do those three things was during meals with his family. His mother, Penny, had no tolerance for anyone being on the phone while they were together as a family, unless it was an emergency.

The one time he'd told her it was an emergency (it wasn't), she'd taken the phone out of his hand and said, "This is Malcolm's mother. Right now, he should be enjoying this meal with his family. He will call you back later." Then she'd hung up and tucked his phone into her pocket for the rest of the evening.

Clearly, it was better for everyone if he simply respected his mother's wishes. She was as kind a woman as they came, always ready with a smile and a laugh, always prepared to help you any way she could. But if you crossed her or made her angry?

Well, let's just say it was best not to get on the

wrong side of Penny Sullivan.

"Sorry, I didn't mean to fall asleep," Josie said as she got out of the car, yawning again. As she stretched her arms over her head, her sweater and jeans conformed to her body in an accidentally sexy way.

He should've looked away. Hell, he was *trying* to look away. But she had a stunning figure. She wasn't overly thin like most of the women he went out with. Instead, Josie had curves in all the places he liked to see them.

Yet again, he tried to connect the adult Josie with the teenage Josephine he'd kissed at prom. She must've been fifteen at the time? And he was pretty sure she'd had glasses back then.

He never should have kissed her that night. But when the group he'd gone to the prom with had brought booze—and plenty of it—Malcolm had felt compelled to keep up with their partying. He grimaced, remembering being seventeen, drunk, and stupid as a brick.

Stupider.

Josie's voice stopped his silent reminiscing. "The weather is beautiful here. I thought England was supposed to be rainy and dreary."

"It's a little white lie all Londoners agree upon in order to keep too many people from flooding into town," he said with a smile that he hoped didn't look as false as it felt. "Sure, there are days where it will be pissing down rain, but we get plenty of blue skies too. Particularly in the morning."

As he dealt with her bags, he actively tried to be less cranky and more friendly. He'd all but bitten off her head at the airport. It wasn't her fault that his business was having issues, or that he'd fallen out of like with his girlfriend, or even that he and Josie had undealt-with past history.

He grabbed both of her suitcases before she could stop him and walked down the narrow path to his houseboat. "What are you helping Mari with?" He vaguely recalled Mari had said something about Josie being a book consultant, but he wasn't sure what that meant.

"I'm here to help Mari set up a reading retreat."

Her unexpected reply stopped him in his tracks. "A reading retreat? What's that?"

She must not have seen him stop, because she plowed straight into both him and the suitcases. Letting go of her luggage, he spun around to catch her before she tumbled back, inadvertently bringing her face close to his, her chest pressed against his.

He shouldn't have noticed how good she felt, but it was impossible not to.

We're a perfect fit.

As he belatedly became aware of the instinctive

thought, he abruptly let her go.

"I must be more tired than I thought," she said. "Sorry for barreling into you like that."

"It was my fault." He gestured for her to walk ahead of him. "My houseboat is at the end of this lane. Make a right along the towpath, and it's the fourth houseboat, white with black trim."

As she walked in front of him, his eyes strayed to her hips. Jesus, what was wrong with him? He was acting like a teenager again, almost as though being with her had somehow tapped into the seventeen-year old who couldn't keep it in his pants.

It wasn't like he went without. He wouldn't use the word *player* to describe himself, although he suspected his sister Alice might. She disapproved of his behavior, even though he rarely had one-night stands, choosing instead to sleep with women he had dated for a while. Well, a week or two, at least.

Then again, Alice seemed to have this notion of true love. A notion that Mari and Owen had only solidified. Stars in her eyes. That's what his little sister had. He hoped she got everything she wanted in life, and he was always ready to help her out if she needed it.

Realizing Mari hadn't answered his question, he asked again, "Tell me what a reading retreat is."

"It's a vacation where all you have to do is read."

Though he couldn't see her face as she walked in front of him, he could hear the pleasure in her voice. "If you want to read all day, perfect. If you want to read part of the day and do something else for part of it, that's great too. But books are the center of the retreat. I don't allow phones or laptops during retreat hours, which can be difficult for some people at first, but then they get used to being able to concentrate on the books and their own feelings. It's magical."

He couldn't imagine being unplugged for as long as an hour, never mind a full day. As he moved beside her on the towpath, he finally saw her smile. She really was beautiful, especially when a smile was lighting up her whole face… because she was talking about books.

"It's a tremendously nourishing experience," she continued. "Though I occasionally work one on one with a client, the bulk of my work is running retreats and helping businesses, mostly hotels, set up rooms, both inside and out, with wonderful reading nooks all over. I help them stock their in-house libraries. And I also work directly with their guests as a bibliotherapist to help create lists of books that they'll love."

"I've never heard that word before. *Bibliotherapist*."

"I didn't invent it," she said, as though he might be trying to give her credit for coming up with the entire idea. "There are trained therapists who work one on one with clients with depression, anxiety, PTSD, and so on, and part of the therapy is reading fiction, nonfiction, and poetry to help them work through their issues. But when I stumbled on the concept of reading retreats and went to one that made a huge difference in my life and how happy I felt, that was when I realized I wanted to switch careers from freelance editor to bibliotherapist. The one that I went to a few years ago was in Vancouver, not far from Coeur d'Alene. In any case, that's probably more than you want to know. It's just that once I get started talking about books, I find it hard to stop."

She gave him another smile, one that made his heart beat a little bit faster. "It's a really interesting concept, Josie." He could see how reading retreats would be a great add-on at hotels around the world, in addition to the spa and adventure packages that already existed. He filed that away in the back of his mind to mention to his cousin Brandon, who owned the SLVN international hotels.

"Is this it?" She stopped in front of his houseboat, and he nodded. "Oh, it's lovely," she said. "And the name—*River Star*... Did you come up with that?"

"Whenever I'm here, I always find myself up on the roof deck gazing at the stars," he explained. "The name just seemed to fit."

"It's the *perfect* name," she enthused. "I can't wait to see the stars from the roof deck!"

She was clearly delighted by his houseboat. So different from the last woman he'd brought here, whose lip had curled as she said, "We're not actually staying on this old boat, are we?"

"I can't believe I get to stay on a houseboat for two weeks!" Josie gave a little clap, obviously thrilled with it, but then turned to ask, "Are you sure you're not going to need it? I feel bad putting you out of your home, even if it's one you only use sporadically."

He shook his head. "I can't imagine a scenario where I'd need it for the next two weeks. You're more than welcome to stay, Josie. For as long as you'd like, in case your trip here ends up being longer." Still wanting to make up for being a jerk at the airport, he added, "And I apologize for being short with you when I picked you up. It's been a bit of a day, with a deal potentially going sideways."

"I was wondering if that's what might have happened. Even before I knew you were there to pick me up, when I saw you, that was one of the scenarios that popped into my head."

"Scenarios?"

Her cheeks pinkened. "I have this habit of making up stories about the lives of strangers. In airports, at the grocery store, in a bookstore."

"That's got to have something to do with all the books you read," he noted. "Does this mean you're a writer too?"

She shook her head. "I write when I have to—mostly emails, the shorter the better. But I far prefer spending hours reading rather than writing. Or talking to my clients about books. We start with the reading list, and then we talk about what they've read and how it's helped them, and maybe we pick a few more titles."

He laughed. "I like short emails too. That's the beautiful thing about my line of business. I can send one-sentence emails, and everyone assumes I'm too busy to write more."

"Wow. What kind of business do you run?"

He paused, trying to explain in simple terms what he did. He'd never found a simple explanation for his work. "I find businesses that are ready to expand globally and put them together with money. The latest one's a New Zealand–based business. They have a line of small-footprint, eco-friendly homes that come packed like flat-pack furniture. Easy enough for anyone with decent DIY skills to assemble. Then they bring in a plumber and electrician to finish off the home. It's been phenomenally successful in Australia and New Zealand and begs to be a global brand. I'm talking to finance partners in Hong Kong and New York, putting together the money, then my firm will help take the products worldwide. That's just one of many projects I have on the go. It's exciting, and stressful, and I'm never bored."

"Just busy all the time?"

"I suppose I am," he said as he unlocked the door to the houseboat, then handed her the key. "Welcome home. Why don't you go in and take a look around while I bring in your suitcases? I won't need to go to the gym after lugging the one stuffed with books, that's for sure."

"Sorry," she said again.

"No apologies necessary. It's all part of my airport-pickup service," he said with a grin that almost felt out of place on his face. It had been a long time since he'd felt like smiling.

The moment she walked inside, she gushed, "Oh my gosh, this is better than anything I could've imagined! It's like an apartment inside. I wouldn't have guessed. So charming and cozy." She peered out one of the windows, clearly delighted. "Seeing the river right outside your window is extraordinary." She turned back to him. "How do you ever bring yourself to leave?"

Looking at it through her eyes made Malcolm feel as though he was seeing his boat for the first time. He remembered when he'd bought it. He'd been in his early twenties, and the boat had been *this close* to ending up in a dump somewhere. He and his brothers and father and sisters—whoever was available—would come over and help him rebuild it. Both Malcom and his family had put their heart and soul into the *River Star*. Malcolm had hand-sourced all the tiles in the kitchen and bathroom and around the woodstove from eclectic sellers throughout London. Even the soft furnishings had been something he'd been very particular about, knowing exactly what the ambience of a riverboat should be. He'd found exactly what he wanted in Cornwall—deep blue fabric with small seashells printed on it. Seafaring, but comfortable too.

Those first few years, he'd lived on the boat full time. He'd go to flea markets and source pottery and glassware from local artisans. That was when he began thinking about helping small-business owners reach wider markets. Using his degree in business, he'd begun putting together franchises, helping business owners find financing and international markets. Now he helped business all over the world grow their markets. Over time, he'd become so successful that he'd barely found time to leave his office in central London. When he did, it had been too much of a slog to come back to the houseboat late at night. So he'd bought himself a place in Clerkenwell, in the business district of London, then upgraded several times over the years to bigger and grander places with even better views. His current penthouse had a view of St. Paul's Cathedral with the Thames in the background. And he rarely, if ever, came back to his boat.

A tug of regret yanked at him. Regret that didn't make any sense. He had everything. More money than Croesus. Everything he touched turned to gold. Even today's deal would be one he'd surely pull together in the end. The business owner, the investors, and he would make a sizable profit. His business was great, and so was his personal life. He dated the most beautiful women in London and had some good friends. He had a great family.

And yet, the regret was still there. A sense that maybe the path he'd ended up on wasn't exactly the right path for him after all.

Finally, he answered Josie's question. "This boat was a labor of love. It was ready for the junkyard when I bought it, and I fixed it up with the help of my family. For several years, I did live on it full time, until the commute to my office got to be too much on a daily basis."

"If it truly was ready for the junkyard when you got it, then you did an amazing job bringing it back to life. It feels so much bigger inside than I could have imagined."

"You're right that it's one of the bigger ones, with two beds and two bathrooms. When I lived here full time, I liked having family and friends stay over. And there was always room on the couch. But, like I said earlier, the roof deck is where the boat really shines."

"It's a dream to get to stay here, Malcolm. Thank you so much. I know I'm going to love every single second of it."

"You're very welcome, although perhaps we should talk tomorrow after you've spent a night here, and see if you're still as pleased. The hot water can be a little tricky sometimes, and if the jet lag doesn't get you, the birds will have you up at the crack of dawn."

"Waking up with birds will make it even better," she said with a very happy grin.

It struck him that she was remarkably easygoing, especially after the terrible welcome he'd given her at the airport.

Malcolm had never dated an easygoing woman. Suddenly, he found himself wondering if he had been searching out the wrong kind of woman all along. His sister Alice certainly thought so—she'd hated every single one of his girlfriends over the years. He assumed that was because Alice had nothing in common with his posh, polished girlfriends, given that she spent 24/7 covered in dirt and mulch out in the garden. But now he wondered if she simply had a better girlfriend radar than he did.

Alice worked at Kew Gardens, her dream job. Still, like him, she was looking toward her next step. Everyone in the family knew that her ultimate dream was to manage her own large garden. Something similar to the extensive and amazing gardens at Sissinghurst in Kent.

It was a dream he'd love to help her with. He often joked that he'd happily give her the *seed money* to buy a plot of land to grow her dream into reality. But Alice was quite stubborn about getting things done on her own merit, and he respected that. It always felt good to put your own blood, sweat, and tears into things. At the same time, asking for help wasn't a bad thing either.

Especially given that if there was one thing the Sullivans were good at, it was pitching in for one another... and also poking their noses into one another's business, whether they lived in California or Australia or England.

Malcolm had always counted himself very fortunate to have the unconditional acceptance and open arms of his family. Regardless of what else was going on in his life, he always knew his family, both near and far, would be there for him.

Josie yawned again, and he decided he'd better give her a quick tour of the boat before she fell asleep on her feet. "The tour won't take long. Here's the lounge. The woodstove is fairly easy to light and will warm up the entire space nicely." He pointed out the printed instructions he'd taped near the stove for people other than himself who needed to light it. "The galley—" He gestured to the attached space that had a small peninsula jutting into it. "—is tiny, but it does the job. The fridge is also small, but comparable to what you'd find in a lot of flats. It just means you'll have to stock up on fresh fruit and veg more often than you would in the States. And as I said earlier, the hot water can be a little tricky, but if you do a little dance to the gods when you turn on the water heater, hopefully you'll be okay."

She did a funny little tap dance in front of him. "Will this do?"

He laughed, surprised at how easily it came when he hadn't been in a laughing mood lately. "It should do nicely. Now, if you'll head down the hallway, you'll see the guest bedroom on the right. It's barely bigger than a coat closet, but will sleep two people in a pinch. And the bathrooms are back to back beyond that, the smaller bathroom for the lounge and the guest room and then a separate one for the primary suite." He put the words *primary suite* in air quotes, acknowledging that it was a very tiny space.

The main bedroom contained a double bed with a top-of-the-line mattress, because while he didn't mind being in close quarters, he insisted on sleeping comfortably. There were built-in wardrobes, built-in bedside tables, and not much else. The linens were cheerful and from the Cornish Drapery Company, one of the first companies he'd franchised.

She laughed and said, "I bet those build-a-house-from-a-box homes are about this size. And yet, it has everything."

He hadn't even thought about that and liked her fresh take on his latest venture. "You're right." Then he turned to her. "Too small?" He might as well do some market research while he had someone who was about to spend two weeks in a small space.

"It's the perfect size, and I love it," she said. "Every last inch of it. Especially the living room. With all those windows, the chair in the corner is the perfect little reading nook. In fact, this whole boat is the perfect reading nook. Now you've got me wanting to start reading retreats on boats all over. Wouldn't it be amazing if people could be floating down a river while reading?"

He nodded. "Sounds good to me." Then he said, "While I bring in your bags, why don't you head up to the roof deck, where we'll finish the grand tour?"

A few minutes later, they were stepping back out and around to the top. He loved the view from his houseboat—you could see Richmond Bridge from nearly every window.

"This is absolutely stunning," Josie said. "I'm going to want to move here at the end of two weeks." She took a few more moments to look all around her, doing a quick three-sixty. "Heck, I've only been here a few minutes, and I already want to move here."

"I was lucky to get this boat. The good ones sell really quickly, but fortunately I have a mate who keeps his eye on the market, and I was able to buy it before it officially went on sale, even though it was a wreck. In other words," he added, "I had to do my own little dance to the gods to get it."

She smiled. "Let's see it. I danced—now it's your turn."

Normally, he wouldn't have been so silly, but she was right—since she had already done her dance, he owed her one of his own. He did a not-bad version of a soft-shoe dance.

Her laughter bubbled out and across the water. "That was excellent," she said in a teasing voice. "Fred Astaire has nothing on you."

"Ginger Rogers has nothing on you either."

He found himself unable to look away from her… and he wasn't positive, but quite a large part of him felt as if she was having just as hard a time looking away from him.

Belatedly realizing that the moment was more loaded than he had intended, he forced his gaze from hers, then gestured to the teak seating. "This is a great place to come out and have morning coffee, or watch the sunset, or just hang out and watch the boats, rowers, stand-up paddleboarders, and kayakers."

She turned away from the view to look directly at him. "Really, Malcolm, thank you for this."

"It's my pleasure, Josie."

He felt, again, that he should say something about what had happened in high school. But he didn't know exactly what to say, or how to say it. And he didn't want to ruin the easy camaraderie they'd found over his houseboat. Plus, she was clearly terribly jet-lagged, and in his pocket, his phone kept buzzing every thirty seconds.

He promised himself that if he saw her again during her trip, he would say something.

"Is Mari expecting you at the store right away? Or do you have time for a nap?"

"And here I thought I had successfully hidden my fatigue."

"Those transatlantic flights can be rough," he said. "You might find that an hour of sleep in a proper bed right after you've arrived will set you up nicely to get you through until it's time to actually go to bed."

"I'm sure you're right," she said, "but I don't think I can wait that long to meet Mari and see the bookstore. Hopefully, the excitement will beat out the jet lag."

"In that case, why don't we walk over together?"

"Thank you for offering, but you don't have to do that. I'm sure I can find my way. I know you're busy."

"No, it's fine. I'd like to stretch my legs a bit more before I get back in the car and fight traffic in the city. And on our way, if you're hungry, we could pick up a snack at the Elderflower Café. If one of the owners is in, I'll introduce you. There's a nice little community here on Elderflower Island."

"That would be great." She paused for a moment. "The thing is, I'd love to change out of my traveling clothes and maybe even hop in the shower to refresh myself after the flight. I don't want to hold you up, but I'd love the company."

"No problem," he said. "I'll wait on the roof deck for you. Take your time." He held up his phone. "We both know this will keep me busy until you're ready."

She grimaced. "Okay, but I'll still try to make it quick."

As soon as she disappeared from the roof and he looked at his phone, he saw that in the last thirty minutes, a dozen emails and voicemails had come in. He had two personal assistants, but everybody always tried to reach him directly. His PAs dealt with the bulk of the email and voice messages, but he did like to scan through the messages every now and then, just to make sure nothing was being missed. Sure enough, New Zealand was calling. He had a good feeling that the deal was back on. He returned Kieran's call.

And yet, for all the work that he had to do, he

couldn't stop thinking about Josie on the deck below, stripping off her clothes and getting into the shower. Seriously, he was like a randy seventeen-year-old all over again today. Except this time he didn't have the excuse of wanting to kiss her because he was drunk. Nope, this time he simply wanted her.

Malcolm shook his head. He had no business wanting Josie, for so many reasons. First off, he hadn't yet broken it off with Katrina. But even more important, he was exactly the wrong match for a woman like Josie. A woman who was sweet and nice and lived her life in the world of books.

With great effort, he forced his brain away from the thought of Josie in the shower with warm water and bubbles rippling over her smooth skin. Instead, he got down to business assuring Kieran Taylor that everything was going to work out and tried to ignore the fact that even as he did, there was a part of his brain—and his body—that was still hyperfocused on Josie.

CHAPTER THREE

Elderflower Island was absolutely beautiful. Malcolm pointed out the tearoom, several of the boutiques, the old concert hall where so many massive rock 'n' roll careers had begun, the manor house and grounds where locals walked their dogs and laid out blankets on sunny days to sun themselves or savor a picnic. He showed her where the stand-up paddleboarding group met at least once a week to take their boards out on the river. He took her into the Elderflower Café, where she met the owner, Jacob, a large and cheerful man with a bushy beard and a big personality.

"It's good to see you back on the island," Jacob said to Malcolm after they shook hands. "We miss you."

"Good to be back," Malcolm admitted. "Are your sausage rolls still the best in London?"

"Naturally," Jacob said. "But don't even think about franchising my baked goods all over the world. I prefer to keep my business local."

Malcolm grinned. "Then I can simply enjoy your food and not worry about how it would sell in San

Francisco."

"Obviously, my sausage rolls would sell brilliantly in San Francisco," he said with a twinkle in his eye. He passed one to Josie on a square of parchment paper. "Don't you agree?"

She bit into the flaky pastry and then the fragrant, spicy meat filling, and as the flavors hit her tongue, she nodded enthusiastically.

Malcolm bought them both sausage rolls and two teas to go. Then they sat in the manor house grounds and enjoyed the people-watching. It was so good to sit in the warm sun and breathe fresh air after being cooped up in a plane for so long. Josie felt almost as though she were in a dream, which she attributed to jet lag. Though, when she glanced at the gorgeous guy beside her, munching on a sausage roll and drinking tea from a paper cup while wearing a designer suit—more gorgeous now than he'd been fifteen years ago—it was no wonder she felt like she was in a dream.

After a friendly dog had happily taken the last bite of her sausage roll and licked her hand clean into the bargain, she felt ready to face anything.

They disposed of their garbage in a nearby container and then headed for the bookstore.

She felt like she was floating on air. Though they'd gotten off to a rocky start in the airport, he was obviously trying hard to make it up to her by being charming and friendly. Also, she couldn't deny that her companion was magnetically handsome.

Of course, he was completely out of her league. He'd made that perfectly clear in high school, and now that he'd matured, he'd obviously become extremely successful. He had an air of wealth about him, and considering the way he gave crisp instructions over the phone, he had a staff of minions at his beck and call. Besides, even if she'd thought she might have a chance with him, she'd sworn off men forever.

But that didn't mean there wasn't a little part of her still thrilled by being with Malcolm Sullivan today.

Okay, so her exhaustion from the flight was clearly playing into her emotions. But the truth was, she was having a wonderful time with him. He hadn't said anything about what had happened in high school—and he certainly hadn't apologized—but perhaps that was for the best. There was no point in stirring up an old hornet's nest. High school was a million years ago. They had both been teenagers, and most teenagers did super dumb stuff. Especially in front of their peers. He surely hadn't meant what he'd said to her at prom. And even if he had—well, what did it matter after all these years? The best thing was to focus on how thrilled she was to be on Elderflower Island, how much fun it was going to be to stay on his houseboat, and how they'd even shared a couple of laughs today, especially after his dance on the roof of his boat.

He pointed out the pub, and then she spotted Mari's bookstore across the street, on the riverside. The painted sign above the door said ELDERFLOWER ISLAND BOOKS, and she could see a window full of titles she'd no doubt want to read. As she drew closer, she saw that the building dated back to 1883. Excitement filled her at the idea of meeting the woman she'd been emailing with for a couple of months now. Mari had explained that she'd inherited the bookshop and was looking for new ways to add value. When she read a blog post Josie had written about her work, Mari had contacted her, and they'd soon begun chatting like old friends about the books they'd loved and new releases they couldn't wait to read. Then, finally, Mari had asked if she could hire Josie to come to London to help her create a space where she'd hold reading retreats. Naturally, Josie would lead the first one.

She hadn't stopped to think about it, but had enthusiastically agreed. She'd set up reading retreat spaces in a couple of hotels, a spa, and a library, so she felt confident in her ability to give Mari exactly what she wanted.

"Wow. I absolutely love it," she told Malcolm. She felt like a broken record, but it was true. She was loving everything she'd seen since she'd landed. The only thing she hadn't loved was when Malcolm had been so grumpy, and she'd realized that her past had possibly come back to haunt her. But as she'd just told herself, there was no point in getting in a funk over bad memories of things that had happened a long time ago.

"This is exactly the way I've always pictured a British bookshop," she continued. "With ivy growing down old stone walls and pretty window displays crammed with books." She sighed. "I have a feeling I'll need yet another suitcase when it's time to go home."

"It even comes with a black cat that sleeps on the counter after Mari lets it in in the morning," Malcolm informed her.

Grinning from ear to ear, Josie said, "I'll have to take pictures of that so I don't forget it after I'm gone."

She already knew she was going to miss Elderflower Island when she left. It wasn't practical to even dream of staying, so she wouldn't waste her time lamenting that.

The door opened, and a pretty woman with a tumble of auburn hair and a huge smile stepped out. "Josie. I'm Mari. Welcome. I'm so glad you're here. It's wonderful to finally meet you in person."

When Mari opened her arms, it felt perfectly normal for Josie to walk into them. As two major bibliophiles, it was like greeting a long-lost friend, all because they shared a love of books.

"I'm so happy to be here, Mari. I love absolutely

everything about the island so far. Malcolm's houseboat. How gorgeous the island is. The sausage roll I ate from the Elderflower Café. The classic British pub across the street. And, best of all, your bookstore."

Mari beamed. "I love all those things too. Now come inside. You must be exhausted after your trip." Mari gestured for Malcolm to come in too. "Can you stay a few minutes for a cup of tea, or do you need to rush back to the city?"

"I could do with a quick cuppa," he replied. Since they'd just finished tea, Josie imagined he wanted to visit with Mari for a few minutes.

"Thanks again, Malcolm, for picking Josie up," Mari said. "Things got out of control so quickly in the store today. When Grace called in sick, there really was no way I could leave." She glanced toward an older woman who was chatting with a customer. "Clare fills in when I'm stuck, but she couldn't come earlier, and besides, she doesn't know books, so I had to be here."

"Were Gran's fans happy?" Malcolm asked.

Mari looked over at a group of people visible in a separate part of the bookstore. "I added on a special room for Mathilda Westcott fans," Mari explained to Josie. "There are all sorts of interesting mementos from her career, even things like dolls that were made by a fan for each of the main characters in her books. And it's also a great place for them to meet. This is the unofficial headquarters of the Mathilda Westcott Appreciation Society, and they do support the shop, so I always like to make sure the meetings run smoothly."

Josie looked from Mari to Malcolm. "Wait... Your grandmother is *Mathilda Westcott*?"

He grinned. "Gran's a handful, but I don't know what any of us would do without her. She writes pretty good books too."

Josie felt like she'd stepped into Alice's Wonderland. "Wow. I can't believe you're related to her. I'm feeling starstruck. She's my number one favorite mystery author. And I love mysteries."

Mari laughed. "I felt the same way when I first got to meet her. She is absolutely delightful, and I know she's going to love meeting you. I've spoken to her about your reading retreats, and she's very curious about how it all works. I imagine she'll want to be one of the first people to book a spot once we've got it all set up and running."

Josie swallowed. "I feel like the bar just got set way higher. I use her books in my reading retreats. There's a true lesson in seeing how Camilla Fernsby finds the truth in small details. I feel like we could all do more of that in our lives. Plus, no matter how complicated the plot seems, everything works out in the end."

"That's so true," Mari said.

Josie put a hand to her belly. "But I think I'd be a

nervous wreck if I actually met her."

Malcolm shook his head. "Don't worry about impressing her. Despite the fact that she's famous worldwide, she's still just Gran. With that said, if she does terrify you, I'll ask her to tone it down."

Josie laughed. "I'll do my best not to be terrified."

She took a moment to do a slow spin in the middle of the bookstore, taking in the floor-to-ceiling shelves of books, the throw rugs covering most of the old wooden floor, the comfortable velvet and leather seats strewn throughout the space. Then she took a big deep breath, inhaling from her toes all the way up to the top of her head before sighing with happiness.

"There's nothing better than the smell of a bookstore."

"I couldn't agree more," Mari replied. "I knew we were going to get along famously. Now what would you like—builder's tea that'll strip the paint off your insides, or something lighter, like chamomile or peppermint?"

"I was thinking it might be wise to take a little nap in a bit, so peppermint or chamomile would probably be better."

Malcolm pulled his buzzing phone out of his pocket and scowled at the screen as he read. "Dammit, looks like I don't have time for that cup of tea after all." He jammed his phone back in his pocket before turning to Josie. "Let me know if there are any issues with the boat. I left my number on the galley counter. Sorry to drop you off and run, but if I'm going to salvage this deal, it looks like I'd better do it straightaway. Are you sure you'll be okay?"

"Oh, absolutely, you should go. Thank you again, for everything. I'll treat your houseboat like it's my own. Even better." But he was already heading out the door, phone to his ear as soon as he closed it behind him, and she wasn't sure he'd heard anything she'd said.

Mari came back with two pottery mugs. "Where did Malcolm go?"

"He's having issues with a deal."

Mari handed Josie one mug and kept the other for herself. "He'll pull it off. He always does. But I don't envy him. I've never seen anybody work as hard as he does. Not even my father, who owns his own accountancy in California. It's crazy the hours he puts in and the stress that he has to deal with. I honestly don't know how he does it."

"He took a work call in the car, and it was like he was speaking a foreign language. Actually, it put me to sleep."

Mari laughed at that, but then grew serious. "I just hope he's happy. I'm not trying to be nosy, but I've come to know the Sullivans so well since I moved to

London and started dating Owen that I find myself worrying about all of them from time to time. Maybe it's just that I am so blissfully happy now, and I want the same for everyone."

Josie smiled at the woman she already considered a friend. "I can't wait to hear more about the marvelous Owen Sullivan."

"That's good, because I have a hard time not talking about him. You'll have to tell me when to put a lid on it if it gets boring."

"Are you kidding? There's nothing I like better than tales of true love. Even if I find them more believable in fiction."

"I used to feel that way too. I never thought I would find that kind of love for myself."

"It's wonderful that you did," Josie said. "I'm really happy for you."

"I can't wait for you to meet Owen. He's smart and kind and loves books as much as we do. He's also pretty easy on the eyes. Well, you met Malcolm, so you can imagine."

If Owen was half as gorgeous as Malcolm Sullivan, he'd be up there with the best-looking guys Josie had ever seen.

"Anyway, enough about my love life," Mari said. "Sit down while there's a little lull before more customers or Mathilda Westcott fans come in. Tell me how your flight was."

"It was great. I probably should've slept, but I was so excited about coming to Elderflower Island to work with you. And I was on the last half of Tasmina Perry's latest."

"I couldn't put that book down either," Mari said. "I won't keep you too long so that you can take a nap, but be forewarned—don't sleep for more than an hour, or you won't sleep tonight. I went through that myself. I live upstairs, so you know where to find me if you need anything."

"I love how you're actually living the fantasy in your home above the bookstore that you own!"

"Every day, I have to pinch myself," Mari agreed with a smile. "It's not that there aren't plenty of difficult aspects about owning and running a bookstore, especially in a country that I didn't grow up in. But with the help of Owen and his family, and all of the other welcoming people on Elderflower Island, it's been so much easier for me than it would otherwise have been. Especially because I came here after my estranged father died and willed his store and home to me out of the blue."

"Wow, it sounds like you have a lot of stories to tell."

"I do, and I'm sure you'll hear them all soon enough, but for right now, I'd love to know more about you. How did you get the idea to set up reading retreats as a profession? I read what you said on your website, and of course we talked about it on Zoom and over email, but I can't help but wonder, was there some sort of incident or pivotal moment one day that made you want to completely change your career?"

Josie was silent for a moment as she sipped her tea. "Just like in a novel, there was definitely an inciting incident."

"I don't mean to pry, so you can tell me to butt out—"

Josie shook her head. "It's not prying. It's important backstory, where you need to know why the heroine is behaving the way she is."

"Ah, I love someone who talks about real life with genre-fiction vocabulary."

They both grinned at that. But then Josie's smile faded. "I thought I was in love. I thought I had the rest of my happy-ever-after planned out. Perfect guy. Perfect life. Get married. Have children. White picket fence." She paused for a moment. "And then one day, there was a knock on the door."

Mari grimaced. "An unexpected knock on the door is rarely ever good in a novel, or in real life, is it?"

Josie sighed. "You can say that again. A woman I'd never seen before was standing on my front porch, holding a six-month-old baby girl."

"Your boyfriend's wife and daughter, I presume?"

Josie nodded. "Every time I've read books with that storyline, I always questioned, how could the woman not know that the man she was dating had a whole other life? I mean, how could anybody be that blind? How could someone be that lost inside their own fantasies that they couldn't see what was right there in front of them?"

She took another sip of tea, as though that would help settle her stormy emotions. Even after all this time, simply talking about her boyfriend's betrayal riled her up.

"But once it happened to me, I suddenly understood how we believe the people we love. He worked as a salesman, and he was always on the road. Or so I thought, anyway. I would see him once, maybe twice a week when he was in town. And he always told me how he was getting ready to switch jobs so that he could settle down with me. He frequently told me I was the love of his life and had made him rethink his career and his goals. And of course, dumb me, I rolled out the red carpet whenever he was in town. He had gone to an Ivy League school on the East Coast and wore sharp suits and took me out to the fanciest restaurants we had in Coeur d'Alene. I felt so lucky that he chose to be with me when he could have stayed in Boston and been with anybody else." She rolled her eyes. "What a fool I was—he had."

"You can't blame yourself," Mari insisted. "You are neither dumb nor a fool. From what you're saying, it sounds like he did everything he could to set up the narrative that you were his one and only. I don't know anybody who wouldn't be fooled by a plausible story told by someone they love." She put her hand on Josie's shoulder for a moment, then said, "I'm really sorry you went through all of that."

"I am too." Josie sighed. "Coming out of such a screwed-up relationship makes me feel like I'll never be able to trust a man again. Because no matter how great he seems on the surface, how can I trust he isn't telling me a pack of lies?"

Mari didn't reply for a moment. "I could say a bunch of platitudes about how not everybody is a liar and how there are a lot of great guys out there, but while both of those things are true, that doesn't negate what you've been through. Nor do I blame you for being suspicious the next time you're on the verge of being in a relationship with someone."

Josie shook her head at that. "Nope. There are not going to be any verges or budding relationships. I am perfectly happy being footloose and fancy-free. And although I know this might sound strange, telling you my horrible relationship story is actually a very long-winded way of explaining why and how I started to put on reading retreats." She paused to take another sip of tea. "I was so beat up inside over what happened that I couldn't find solace in anything. Not until my mother came to my house, carrying a suitcase full of books. Turned out that she had booked me into a hotel for a week. Her prescription for me, in the hopes that it might help me find some joy again, was to just do nothing but sit and read for a week."

"Your mom sounds great."

"She is. And she was right. I was a freelance editor at the time, and I still do some work for my favorite clients here and there, but I was so down over finding out that I'd been duped by a married man that I didn't even think I could concentrate on a single book. And maybe I wouldn't have been able to if my mother hadn't done such a great job of choosing books that she knew would make me happy. There were several Mathilda Westcotts in there, of course," she told Mari with a small smile. "Along with some of my old favorites. It was a curated list of novels about women who had bad things happen to them, yet who overcame hardship to thrive. *Gone With the Wind*, *Jane Eyre*, of course. *Rebecca* by Daphne du Maurier, *The Color Purple* by Alice Walker, and a stack of others, including some newer titles too."

She stopped speaking for a moment as she thought back to that week inside her head *and* her heart. "Sure, there were love stories running through some of the novels, but in every case, the woman at the center of the story triumphed through her own wits and hard work. It was a message I really needed to hear.

"I went into that hotel stay as one person and came out as another. I was sad and dejected at the beginning of the week, and though things obviously didn't completely heal while I was reading, so much did. Coincidentally, that was when I found an article about two women who were putting on reading retreats in Vancouver. It got me thinking about whether I might be able to do that too. So I reached out to them and asked how they set them up. They were so kind to share their hard-won knowledge with me, because like any book lover, all they wanted was to spread the love of books. The best part was when they invited me to come and experience a reading retreat for myself." She took another sip of tea, then said, "So that's what brought me to creating reading retreats. Heartbreak and betrayal. Just like all good stories, right?" When Mari nodded, Josie added, "Everybody has a story. I know I'm not unique in having gone through something difficult."

"No," Mari said, "you're not."

Josie felt her heart go out to the other woman, even though she didn't know her story yet. All she knew was that Mari still clearly felt pain over it. "Your story was difficult, too, wasn't it?"

"Yes, and it wasn't cut and dried," Mari confirmed. "In a nutshell, my father left me and my mother when I was three, because he had a problem with alcohol. My mother put up with him until the day he was supposed to be watching me, but he left the door wide open, and I managed to get out of our apartment. I was found crossing a busy road in Santa Monica." She shuddered as though she could still feel the terror of a small child in such a terrible situation. "The sad thing was, I think I knew that he loved my mom and me, but he loved alcohol more."

"That sounds like it must've been really hard for all of you."

"It was, and I never heard from him again. Not until the day a lawyer called and told me that my father had left me his bookshop and the flat above it. It was a real shock. I knew he lived in England and had a bookstore, and a big part of me had always secretly wanted to come here and see where he lived and get to know him. But while I never did get the chance to know him in person, everyone on the island has told me so many stories about him—not only that he stopped drinking, but also how kind and gentle he was—that I truly felt like I was getting to know him after all." She paused for a moment before adding, "And then I found the books he'd written."

Josie's eyebrows rose at that new piece of information. "Did you know he was a writer?"

"I had no idea. I only knew that he lived on Elderflower Island and owned the bookshop, because of research I'd done on the internet as a teenager. But no one knew he was writing. No one except Mathilda Westcott." Josie smiled then. "He never tried to get them published while he was alive, but the stories are wonderful, so I pursued publication on his behalf. Kind of a way for us to be together, I suppose. Actually, I just got the very first copies from the publisher today, and I've been dying to show someone."

Mari walked over to a cardboard box on the counter by the store's cash register. She pulled out a hardcover children's picture book. "My father wrote stories about the two of us. About things we did before he left and things he must have wished that we had done as I grew up. When I found his journals with the stories and illustrations, I knew they needed to be read by more than just me. Fortunately, Owen works in publishing, and he was able to connect me with a fantastic children's picture book publisher. These are the very first copies of *Mars at the Beach*." She hugged the book to her, glowing with happiness, before handing it to Josie. "If this book does well, there's an entire series of them. Like *Flying Kites With Mars* and *Playing Conkers With Mars*." Her voice grew husky.

"Mars was his pet name for me. He even named the black cat who comes in and out of here Mars. It's like a whole series of activities he'd have loved to do with me that we never did, so he wrote and illustrated these beautiful books."

"I'm honored to be the first to see your father's book." Josie looked down at the charming illustration on the cover—a father and daughter building a sandcastle. "He was a good illustrator too. You don't mind if I take a few minutes to read it?"

"Of course not. That's what I live for. Later, we'll talk about the space I've got to set up reading retreats in, but I need to go send a couple of quick emails anyway. So why don't you enjoy reading for a while, and I'll check back with you in a bit?"

It felt so perfect, Josie thought, curling up on this cozy leather armchair and getting to read a story that was so precious to someone she had just met. Soon, she was completely enthralled by the story. While the book never used the word *divorce*, it was clear Mars and her father didn't live in the same house, but shared a special bond. They built sandcastles and skimmed stones on the water, and then the sun got low, and it was time for Mars to go home. Her final line was, "See you again soon, Dad."

After hearing Mari's history with her father, Josie's eyes prickled with tears.

The story was sweet, the illustrations were adorable, and she loved every page of the book. If she had a child, she would love to read this to them at night. She could imagine a child whose parents had split up would find a lot of comfort in a book like this.

Her chest squeezed, but she briskly told herself that there was no reason to feel that pain. *No men* didn't have to mean *no children*. She could have a kid entirely on her own if that's what she wanted. After all, she was bold and brave and out living life on her own terms, wasn't she?

A few customers came in, and Josie took the opportunity to read the book again slowly and really savor it the second time. When she finished, she decided it was time to get on her feet, stretch, and then browse this lovely bookshop. She was happily looking through shelves and making notes of a few titles that she thought Mari might like to order for the retreat, when an older woman said, "Excuse me? Would you happen to know if this is any good?"

Josie glanced at the book she held. It was a nice-looking coffee-table book about the history of the domestic cat. However, when she saw the woman's red-rimmed eyes and the air of dejection about her, she didn't think this was a lady who wanted to read about the history of cats. Taking a guess, she asked, "Did you recently lose your cat?"

"How could you possibly know that?" The woman sounded stunned. Then she nodded slowly, and a tear slid down her cheek. "His name was Buttons. I know I shouldn't be so silly over a cat, but you see, after I lost my husband, Buttons was all I had left." She reached into the pocket of her cardigan and pulled out a damp tissue, dabbing at her eyes.

Josie's heart went out to the woman. "I'm so very sorry for your loss," she said softly. Then she led her to a couch, where they sat. "I would like to recommend several books that you might like to read. Nothing will bring back your husband or Buttons, but reading about those who have also suffered a loss can be helpful."

At that moment, a black cat slipped in the door on the heels of a customer, paused to peer around the bookstore, and then strolled over to where Josie and the customer were sitting and jumped up to sit beside them. Josie knew that animals sometimes had a strong sense of human emotions, and this cat obviously sensed that the lady needed comfort.

The woman stroked the black cat. "Oh, aren't you a beauty?" The cat nudged her and then promptly curled up in her lap.

Josie overheard one of the ladies, presumably from the Mathilda Westcott Appreciation Society, say, "Look, that's Mars. He's in the Bookshop on the River mysteries that Mathilda Westcott wrote. Of course, she renamed him Cocoa, but everyone knows Mars was the model."

"This is a very famous cat," Josie told her new friend. "I'm Josie, by the way."

"Emily Soames," the woman answered, still giving Mars all her attention.

"When did you lose Buttons?"

"Only last week," she said on a sniff. "And Bernard—that was my husband—passed away six months ago. It's all been such a shock."

"Let me pull some books that you might find helpful." Josie was so pleased she'd toured the bookshop and had discovered some of her favorite titles on the shelves. There were others in her suitcase, but that was on the houseboat. She'd manage. She chose four titles and returned to where Emily was looking better for spending time with Mars.

"If you read these books, see if they make you feel better, or at least help you understand that grief has stages and it won't always be this painful." First, she handed Emily *On Grief and Grieving: Finding the Meaning of Grief Through the Five Stages of Loss* by Elisabeth Kübler-Ross and David Kessler. "This will help you realize your reactions are normal and part of the healing process. I learned so much from this book about grief, large and small."

Emily nodded and accepted the book.

"The second book I'd recommend is *A Grief Observed* by C.S. Lewis. The author documents losing his wife, and the book is both beautifully written and intensely personal." Then she added two more. "And this is Mathilda Westcott's first Bookshop on the River mystery, *Miss Fernsby Investigates*. Her bookshop is based on this one, and the cat the sleuth sometimes talks to when she's solving a crime is called Cocoa, but according to one of the Mathilda Westcott fans, he's based on Mars here." Josie was fairly certain that Emily was a little hearing impaired and hadn't heard the woman telling her friend about the cat. "My advice is to have a nice cup of cocoa while you read the book. And for something completely different, try T.S. Eliot's *Old Possum's Book of Practical Cats*." She presented the slim volume with the colorful cover. "They are fun, light poems all about cats. I'm sure you'll see Buttons in there somewhere. Andrew Lloyd Webber was inspired by these poems to write the musical *Cats*."

"Why, these are all lovely, Josie," Emily told her. "I can't thank you enough. I'll take all of them, and if I come this way again, I hope you'll be working so we can discuss the books."

Josie smiled. "I don't actually work here, but Mari, who owns the bookstore, will always be able to get hold of me if you'd like to talk."

With a final pat to Mars, Emily Soames got up and

took her books to the register. Only then did Josie become aware that Mari was standing off to one side. She came forward now and said, "I think I just overheard a bibliotherapy session."

They both glanced to where Emily was chatting with Clare as she rang up her books. "It was a short one, but yes, that's what I do."

"I loved how kind you were. She's so much happier now, and I can imagine we could help a lot of people if we incorporated personalized book recommendations." Her eyes were shining. "I know you've barely got off the plane and I already have your plate piled high with things to do, but could you maybe come in one or two afternoons while you're here? People who want personal recommendations for themselves or a friend could spend an hour with you. If we don't have the books you think they should read, we could order them. What do you think?"

Josie laughed. "I think you're one of the most energetic people I've ever met." She loved how enthusiastically Mari was embracing her new role as a bookseller. Then she leaned closer, feeling Mars purr against her thigh. "And I'd love to."

Then Mari picked up her father's children's story. "What did you think?"

"I absolutely love it! Every word, every drawing, the storyline. This is going to go on my must-read list for people who come to the retreats and are divorcing or are already divorced with children."

Mari beamed. "The publisher has high hopes for it. They want me to do some press as well, though I'm not completely sure how I feel about telling my story to the world once the first book officially releases on Thursday." She swallowed, her skin going slightly pale. "The big launch party is only a few days away, and the PR team working with the book has already set up several interviews."

"Just do what's right for you and forget about the rest," Josie said. "If you want to talk about your past and your story with people, great. And if you want your story to be something that only you and the people you love know, then that's perfectly okay too."

"You sound exactly like Owen."

"I'm going to take that as a great compliment," Josie said with a grin. "I look forward to meeting him. And if you want to talk anything through at any point in the future, people have told me I'm a good listener."

"I can already tell that you are," Mari said. "Now, since I know exactly how it feels to get off a plane from the US a mere hour or two ago, you're probably at the point where you could simply close your eyes and fall asleep."

"I'll admit that it wouldn't be too hard to fall asleep right on this sofa."

"I'm getting ready to close up in about a half hour. If you want to look around the shop for a while, how about I make you dinner upstairs? We won't talk shop until tomorrow, but we can at least get to know each other better. And then Owen and I can walk you back to the houseboat so that you can get some much needed shut-eye."

"That sounds perfect." For the next thirty minutes, Josie had a wonderful time continuing to pore through the books in Mari's store, both old and new. She chatted with some of the Mathilda Westcott fans, sharing some of her favorite books in the series. To her delight, the Mathilda Westcott section was decorated exactly like the amateur sleuth's living room, where she often puzzled over clues. One of the fans let on that there was talk of a TV series being made about the books and that it would probably be filmed right here at Elderflower Island Books.

As Mari began to close the shop, the cat jumped up on the counter beside the cash register as though it was his customary spot, then closed his eyes and went to sleep.

Josie then happily went upstairs to Mari's charming second-story flat. The large windows looked out on the river, and the wood-planked floor had obviously experienced plenty of footsteps in the last two hundred years. The roast chicken dinner Mari made was delicious. Owen Sullivan joined them, and Josie had to admit he was very easy on the eyes. It was lovely to see the devoted way he gazed at Mari and the heat that arced between them when their gazes met.

Owen was very sweet, and handsome, but he didn't make her heart flutter like his brother Malcolm did.

The only awkward moment came when Owen mentioned that one of his brothers had done a foreign exchange program in Coeur d'Alene. "You didn't happen to know Malcolm Sullivan then, did you?" He'd said it as a joke, as though the likelihood of them having ever met was nil.

For a moment, Josie didn't know what to say. She and Malcolm hadn't discussed what they were going to tell his family about them having known each other. But she figured the easiest thing to do was to tell the truth.

"Actually, it's kind of a funny story. I do know your brother." Both Mari and Owen looked shocked by this revelation. "I was as surprised as both of you obviously are. When I saw him waiting to pick me up at the airport, I was sure my eyes were deceiving me. Because what are the odds?"

"Wow," Mari said. "It just goes to show how small the world really is."

"Were you in the same year at school?" Owen

asked.

"I was two years behind. And I didn't really know him. I mean, everybody knew about the British exchange student, but it's not like we ever talked the whole year. Only once at the very end, and that was just for a few minutes."

She could feel her cheeks going pink. Because she and Malcolm hadn't talked. They'd kissed, a kiss that had felt like all of her dreams rolled up into pure beauty and pleasure.

And then he'd casually crushed her to smithereens with a few harsh words.

As though Owen could read a little of what she was thinking, he said, "I hope he wasn't an arsehole."

Josie laughed at his assumption that his brother had been rude. Then she shook her head. "Like I said, I didn't really know him back then." Desperate to change the subject, she said, "I love his houseboat. It will be such a treat to stay on it for the next two weeks."

"I remember helping him rebuild it," Owen said. "He loved working on that thing. For a while there, I thought that was what he might decide to do for a living—just chuck in the financial world and rebuild houseboats. But that wasn't his path. I guess the allure of all the cash and power in his world of international big-money deals was too much for him to resist."

To Josie, it didn't seem as though Owen was judging his brother. Instead, it was more that he seemed a little worried about whether his brother was truly happy.

Josie suddenly yawned, a yawn so big her jaw popped. "Sorry about that. I don't mean to be rude. I guess now that I have a full belly from that delicious meal, all the blood has rushed from my head to my stomach, and I'm completely ready to nod off."

Mari pushed back from the table. "In that case, why don't we walk you back to the houseboat? I was so exhausted the first day I got here that Owen found me curled up on that couch, fast asleep while he cleaned up the mess my father had made of the flat all around me."

"Let me help you clean up after dinner first," Josie offered.

"Nope," Owen insisted. "Mari and I can take care of that later. Right now, our only goal is to get you to bed so that you can regain a few of those hours of sleep you lost changing time zones."

The three of them headed out a few minutes later. As they walked to the houseboat, Elderflower Island was even more beautiful in the moonlight. "It's so pretty here. Do you ever get used to it?"

"I haven't," Mari said. "I'm constantly astounded by how beautiful this island and London are." She sighed, her hand held comfortably in Owen's. "And I come from California, which is incredibly beautiful, but somehow this is home."

"I feel the same way," Owen said. "I grew up over in St. Margarets, just across the river. I've been to a lot of amazing places, but this island is where I always want to come home to. Especially now that Mari is here."

They were so sweet together, and Josie couldn't help but hope that one day she might find a man like Owen, who actually cared about her and was honest and had a big heart.

Wait, she'd sworn off men forever, hadn't she?

But a small part of her admitted that maybe there might be a decent, good man in her future. Maybe.

At the door to Malcolm's houseboat, Mari gave Josie a hug. "I can't wait to get started tomorrow. How about I swing by the houseboat and grab you at nine a.m.?"

"Fantastic. See you tomorrow morning. And thank you so much for dinner and the great company."

Exhaustion fell over Josie as she stepped inside the boat. Stopping only to brush her teeth and slip into pajamas, she walked astern and crawled into bed. The sheets smelled fresh, and the bed was warm and toasty.

For a moment, she imagined Malcolm sleeping beneath these same covers, naked and incredibly sexy. Her blood heated for a moment, but then exhaustion took over, and she was down for the count.

CHAPTER FOUR

Malcolm should have been thrilled. He'd stopped the deal going south. By the skin of his teeth, but what mattered was that it was done. The deal was back on track and destined to be a big winner in his portfolio. He and Genevieve had worked their butts off to reassure Kieran. He only hoped they wouldn't have to fly to New Zealand to finally close the deal.

All he could think about, however, was Josie. Was she settling in all right? Had she gone to take a nap? Or was she having dinner with Mari and Owen?

It was surprisingly easy to imagine himself sitting at Mari's kitchen table with the three of them, even though he rarely had a chance to do that. He was always working.

Thankfully, he'd saved this deal right before heading off on a week's break. His executive assistant, a stern and serious older woman named Mabel, who he knew had a secret soft spot for him, asked him if he really intended to not work for an entire week.

Her question had been rhetorical, of course. They

both knew he'd be chained to his laptop and cell phone wherever he happened to be, like he always was in London.

Now, he was waiting at the bar of what was currently the most exclusive restaurant in Notting Hill. Katrina had told him she would meet him there because she was coming from an appointment in Milan, the center of the fashion world. She was an entrepreneur with her own new fashion house, which made sense, as she had come out of the industry as a model.

How many models had he dated? He couldn't count all of them on two hands. Drinking his vodka martini, he couldn't help but feel like a cliché—the billionaire businessman with the model girlfriends.

What's more, all of his recent late nights at the office, working on the deal he'd just closed, had finally caught up with him. He usually didn't need as much sleep as everyone else, but right at this moment, he felt as though he had jet lag. The thought of crawling into his cozy bed on his houseboat filled him with surprising longing. And he couldn't honestly deny that picturing Josie there with him wasn't making it seem even more attractive a possibility…

A part of him felt guilty for having thoughts about Josie while he was still with Katrina. But he had a feeling this would be their last night together once he told her he wouldn't be going to Thailand with her. Partly because he wasn't ready to get serious about anyone. But also because seeing Josie again had sparked a feeling inside that he now realized Katrina had never inspired, regardless of her flawless outer beauty.

Katrina was certain that her new business would be a huge success. He hoped it would be, and he wished nothing but the best for her. But they'd taken their relationship as far as it could go. Tonight would be the end of it. And he had a feeling Katrina might not take it well. Which was why he had chosen to end things in a public place, to up the odds of her not scratching his eyes out in fury.

Yet again, his thoughts went back to Josie. She seemed like such a gentle soul, and even when she'd recognized him as the jackass who had treated her so poorly back in high school, she still seemed to go out of her way to make the best of things. On top of that, she had clearly created a career that she cared deeply about. A job that made her excited to wake up in the morning.

Picking up his martini glass and watching the liquor roll like a wave inside it, he thought about his own career. It wasn't that he didn't like being an entrepreneur who put together franchises. His work was usually interesting, like an ongoing game of chess where you never knew what would be on the board the next time you looked at it, because every deal was different.

He wouldn't use the word *passion*, though, to describe his feelings about his career. He used to be hungry for nothing more than the next deal, just to know he was winning and climbing higher and higher in the business world.

But that had gone stale a while ago.

The atmosphere around him changed suddenly. He knew Katrina had entered by the hush in the room as everyone craned their necks to stare at her. She hadn't been on a runway for five years, but she hadn't lost any of the magnetism or beauty that had made her a top model.

With a sigh, he put his drink down and turned to her just as she said, "I had a hell of a day. Bloody manufacturers. Why can't they follow simple directions for a simple little black dress?" She didn't wait for him to respond before signaling the bartender. "A cosmopolitan."

The bartender barely remembered how to do his job, he was so busy drooling over Katrina. And he certainly didn't seem to have noticed that she had left the word *please* off her drink order.

Malcolm studied her in what felt like a scientific way. Yes, there was no denying that she was stunningly beautiful. But when he really looked closely, it was abundantly clear that she was missing that special glow—the light that Josie had. One that came from the inside. One that came from saying *please* and *thank you*. One that came from someone who didn't expect the world to shower her with riches and adoration simply because genetics had given her a face and body that were the epitome of today's version of beauty.

He tried to shake the thoughts about Josie out of his head. After all, he was here with his girlfriend, even if she wouldn't be for much longer. While he wasn't going gaga over her like every other man in the room, he didn't feel right about disrespecting her. After all, he'd been brought up to treat everyone with respect, no matter who they were or where they came from. And apart from that horrible night at the high school dance in Coeur d'Alene, Idaho, there weren't many times where he could look back and wish that he had behaved better.

Katrina narrowed her gaze on him, almost as though she could read his mind and knew that she wasn't having her desired effect on him. He found himself suddenly thinking about their sex life. How she would pose, as if she always wanted to present only her perfect angles to him.

But sex shouldn't be about perfect angles. It should be about having a damn good time and forgetting everything else.

Thinking back, he wasn't sure they had ever had that good a time together.

"You look like you have something on your mind," she noted.

He shrugged. "A big deal almost fell through, but thankfully, I pulled it off at the eleventh hour." He picked up his drink and downed the rest of it, gesturing to the bartender for another.

She rolled her eyes. "You're king of the business world. What would it matter if you lost a deal?" She didn't wait for his response. "Not that you ever would. Everybody kowtows to you, the great Malcolm Sullivan." She put the word *great* in air quotes, already angry with him about something, even before the breaking-up part of their evening. "The whole world is always at your feet."

Yes, he thought as they both got their drinks and the maître d' approached to take them to their table, there was definitely a bitter edge to her tonight. Almost as though she sensed impending doom. He brightened inside. Maybe she was planning to break up with him. That would be a sweet relief.

They were led to a table in the middle of the room, the prime spot to see and be seen. But Malcolm was sick of always having to be on what felt like a stage. What he wouldn't have given just to be seated in a quiet corner. To have a conversation without everybody looking. To sit and listen in on other people's conversations. Or to just quietly eat his meal and drink his drink without anyone giving a damn who he was or what he could do for them.

He almost laughed out loud at his thoughts. Between his attitude at the airport and his current mood, he was certain playing the grumpy-git card today. His mother would tell him off, and rightly so, while his father would suggest he go for a run to let off some steam.

That was exactly what he'd do tonight. After dinner, he'd go back to his place to change into his running clothes, and then he'd hit the dark streets of London as hard and fast as he could. Until there were no more thoughts, just the press of breath moving in and out of his lungs and his heartbeat pounding like a bass drum in his ears.

"I still need to pack for Thailand," Katrina said after they'd ordered.

She's chosen a plate of undressed greens topped with a tiny piece of something vegan. He'd ordered a steak, which had prompted a very disapproving look. She wanted him to be vegan. He respected vegans, whatever their reasons for eating that way, but he didn't want to be one.

"Are you packed?" she asked.

He paused before answering. He didn't relish this part. Even though Katrina had a hard edge to her, her emotions were as real as anyone's. His mother had raised him to care about other people's feelings, even if sometimes it didn't seem like he did.

"About Thailand—"

She cut him off, irritation already written all over her face. "Are you canceling the night before we are supposed to leave?"

"You'll have a better time without me."

Her artificially plump mouth tightened, and her brow would have furrowed if not for her regular Botox injections. "Don't I mean anything to you? I thought this trip signified a change in our relationship."

"When we booked it," he said slowly, "I thought that might be the case. But you can do better than me."

Her nostrils flared. "You son of a bitch. Stringing me along. Letting me think you were serious when I could have been with anyone."

"I am sorry, Katrina."

"I don't care if you're sorry. I don't need your apologies."

"I can transfer my ticket over to one of your girlfriends, if that would help at all."

She was silent for a long moment. "Actually, I will take you up on that offer. But the ticket won't be for one of my girlfriends." Her eyes were like daggers as she said, with no small measure of satisfaction, "You can transfer it into my lover's name."

He nearly laughed at that point. He hadn't expected her to bring up a lover, hadn't actually guessed that she'd been seeing anyone but him for the past couple of months. But at the same time, he wasn't particularly surprised. After all, he wasn't around much. He canceled their dates frequently for work. He didn't care about the world of fashion. And she'd made it clear that spending time with his family wasn't high on her priority list. All of which meant they had very little in common.

"Do I know him?"

Her smile grew even more self-satisfied. "The hot-shot new lawyer I brought onto my team from America is a demon in bed."

Again, it took great self-control not to laugh. But although she was clearly trying to get a rise out of him, he understood that laughter wasn't the reaction she was looking for.

"Sure," he said. "I can put his name on the ticket. Happy to do it."

Her eyes widened at his easy acquiescence, then narrowed again as she put her hands flat on the tabletop and leaned in. "You really don't care about me, do you?"

"I've had a good time with you," he replied as gently as he could, "and I'm sorry if I've let you down along the way."

"Let me down along the way?" Her voice pitched higher with every word she spoke. "I've never had *anyone* cancel on me as much as you! And I've never had anyone pay me as little attention as you do! You're a billionaire, and Smith Sullivan is your cousin, so there were some sacrifices I was willing to make, if only to have him attend our wedding." She shoved her chair back as if to storm out, then paused. "Actually, before I go, I want you to call the airline and get that change made."

He called the global concierge who took care of these things for him. Five minutes later, it was done. Katrina and her new lover were going to have a great time together in Thailand on Malcolm's dime.

As soon as he put down his phone, his now ex-girlfriend stood. She picked up her drink, and he saw the intent in her gaze a beat before the cool, sticky liquid of her untouched cosmopolitan splashed all over him.

This time, he let himself laugh. At which point, she picked up *his* drink and doused him with that one too.

Without needing to look around the room, he knew that everyone in the restaurant was enjoying the show. And this was the perfect cherry on top. Malcolm Sullivan, London billionaire, with not one, but *two* drinks splashed in his face.

He wouldn't be surprised to see a photo gracing the tabloids tomorrow.

Katrina stalked out of the restaurant just as the waiter appeared with Malcolm's steak and her salad. "Sir, here are your meals." He put them down before asking, "Is there anything else I can do to be of assistance?"

"How about a towel?"

To the man's credit, he barely even blinked. "Of course. Happy to be of service."

Twenty minutes later, Malcolm left the restaurant, pleasantly full from a damn good piece of red meat. In lieu of taking a taxi, he decided to walk to his flat. There was a slight breeze, but it was a nice London night. Elderflower Island was his favorite place, but central London wasn't half bad. Endless amounts of history. Plenty of outdoor space. River sports. Great proximity to the rest of Europe. Top-notch restaurants and shops.

In any case, he was looking forward to getting back to his flat and showering off the sticky drinks that had dried on his skin and hair.

When he rounded the corner to his building, he was surprised to see a host of maintenance trucks. Several of his neighbors were grumbling on the sidewalk.

Ralph, the doorman, walked over to him. "Mr. Sullivan, I'm afraid I have bad news. I tried to call you several times, but there was no response."

Malcolm had been ignoring his buzzing phone in his pocket, figuring it was probably Katrina calling to curse him out again. "What happened?"

"The building flooded. In fact, it's bad enough that I won't be able to let you into your flat tonight."

Malcolm's eyebrows finally went up. "I can't get inside?"

Ralph shook his head. "Not until the water company has determined exactly what it is that's flooded and if it is clean water or—" The man cleared his throat, not needing to finish the sentence for his intent to be perfectly clear.

Malcolm laughed again. What else could he do, given how this night was shaping up? Even though he could smell the cosmopolitan on his skin and hair, and he'd just found out his flat was flooded, he felt wonderful. Katrina was out of his life. The fact that she'd been cheating on him took away any guilt he'd harbored about calling things off with her. "Thanks for letting me know. I'd appreciate it if you could give me a ring once you know more."

"Thank you for being so understanding about it all, Mr. Sullivan."

Malcolm glanced over at a younger couple who

looked to be raising quite a fuss with the building's manager. "Having trouble with the others?"

"I'm afraid I can't say," Ralph said. But he did raise his eyebrows as if to confirm that yes, they were having quite a bit of trouble with some of the other tenants in the building.

"Don't let it get to you, Ralph. It's not your fault. And good luck."

"You too, sir."

Malcolm headed back toward the river. The simplest thing to do would be to call his global concierge again and arrange for a hotel room and some new clothes to be delivered to it, along with a laptop so that he could log in for work.

But he wasn't in the mood for a fancy hotel. Not tonight. No, tonight the only place he wanted to be was his houseboat, even if he knew there was no way he could spend the night with Josie there.

He did, however, have some extra clothes and shoes on the boat. He could crash in his grandmother's back cottage, where Owen lived. Especially since he knew Owen rarely slept there anymore now that he and Mari were together.

Just the thought of going to Elderflower Island tonight put a spring in his step. He arranged for a driver and two minutes later was in the backseat, heading out of central London toward the island.

"My wife, she loves Elderflower Island," the driver said. "She's always getting on me about buying a cottage there. Not that I could afford it."

"Things on the island are pretty pricey," Malcolm said. "I'm lucky that I've been able to spend time there since I was a child. My grandmother has a cottage near the boathouse."

"You lucky sod," the driver said, grinning at him in the rearview mirror.

"I am lucky," Malcolm agreed.

It was good to be reminded of that. Everything he had, everything he did, was because he had chosen it. Tonight, he'd made one big choice already—to change his relationship status from half a power couple to single. And then he'd made another choice—to leave central London for Elderflower Island. Both excellent choices, if he did say so himself.

Malcolm settled back into the seat and enjoyed the knowledge that he'd be in his favorite place within the hour.

CHAPTER FIVE

There was a knock on the door. Who could it possibly be?

Jose had come back to the houseboat after dinner and promptly fallen asleep. And then three hours later, she woke up. Wide awake. It was morning in Idaho. Her body was awake and raring to go. Even though she could tell that she was still exhausted, sleep was evading her. So she got out of the comfortable bed and went into the galley to brew herself a cup of tea. Thankfully, Malcolm, or maybe Mari, had stocked the fridge, so she was just looking into what she could make for a midnight snack.

She'd unpacked and opened her suitcase of books, looking for the perfect comfort read to go with her snack. While she was reviewing her books, she pulled one out, feeling instinctively it was right for Malcolm. She wasn't certain he'd thank her for the broad hint that he worked too much, but she set the book aside anyway. Maybe she'd give it to him if the moment felt right.

And then she heard the knock.

Part of her was a little nervous, wondering who it could be. She was in a foreign country, and it was well after dark. But at the same time, Elderflower Island seemed so safe to her. And she got the sense that this houseboat community was also extremely close. Perhaps it was a neighbor looking to borrow a cup of sugar for some late-night baking...

Still, her heart was pounding. Maybe, though, that was because, as Mari had said, a knock on the door was rarely a great thing. Especially after dark. She zipped up the sweatshirt she had put on over her pajamas—a jersey tank top and jogger pants. She didn't have a bra on, but hopefully the sweatshirt was thick enough that whoever was out there wouldn't notice. She took her phone with her in case she needed to summon help. Then she peeked out the window beside the door.

She was surprised to find Malcolm standing there. Also relieved that he was someone she knew.

She opened the door and said, "Hi! Is everything okay?"

He was dressed in the same suit and dress shirt he'd worn earlier, though his hair and clothes looked a little sticky. Which didn't make any sense. Then again, it didn't really make any sense that he was here tonight either, when he had a flat in central London that he'd told her was his primary residence.

"I'm sorry to bother you, but the light was on, so I hoped you'd still be up. Everything's fine," he said, "apart from the fact that I can't get into my flat because it's flooded."

She moved aside as things started to make sense. "Come on in. I've just got some hot water boiling. I can make you a cup of tea, and you can tell me more about the situation."

"That's great, thanks. The water company doesn't yet know what was in the pipes that burst."

"That sounds slightly ominous," she said as she walked into the galley. Not having a bra on felt really conspicuous now, but what was she going to do? Excuse herself to go put one on? That would be even weirder. No, she'd just have to hope he didn't notice. Besides, he wouldn't care. As he'd made abundantly clear years ago, she wasn't his type.

He shrugged. "I'm sure they'll sort it out. I was actually on the way to my grandmother's cottage to see about crashing in her back unit. But when I saw the light was on, I thought I would swing by to grab some clothes and another pair of shoes. I hope you don't mind my intruding."

"It's your boat, so you couldn't possibly be intruding."

"I'll just pick up some spare clothes, have a cup of tea, and get out of your way."

Before she could think better of it, she suggested, "There's a second bedroom here. Why don't you stay?" Just the thought of sharing the space with him made her heart pound a little harder.

But he shook his head. "I wouldn't want you to feel uncomfortable."

Again, she spoke before she could really think things through. "I am one hundred percent okay with you staying on your own boat. In fact, I insist you do." Just because their one and only kiss was still hanging over them, and he was so ridiculously good-looking, didn't mean she was going to kick him out of his own home.

Finally, he nodded. "Okay, I appreciate that. I'll be gone first thing in the morning."

"I think you should just stay until you can get back into your flat. Whenever they finish—" She used air quotes. "—cleaning it up." She grimaced again. "Sorry, probably shouldn't be joking about it."

He grinned. "No, I laughed when I heard. What else can you do? Some of my neighbors weren't too pleased, but it's only a flat filled with things, all of which can be replaced."

Well, that was interesting. She wouldn't have thought that highflying Malcolm Sullivan would be so easygoing about his likely expensive apartment and expensive furniture and expensive clothes being ruined.

"What kind of tea would you like?" And then she gave him a slightly apologetic smile. "Sorry, I'm acting like it's my kitchen. It's your kitchen—galley—and you can pick out the tea you want."

"I'm glad that you feel completely at home so quickly." But he did go choose a teabag for himself.

She chose mint, hoping that the lack of caffeine would help her nod off. "I was just about to make something to eat, a midnight breakfast-in-my-time-zone meal. Do you want something?"

He looked pleased by the suggestion. "What are you going to make?"

Although Malcolm was probably used to five-star restaurants with snooty maître d's and overpriced drinks, she said, "Looks like I have the makings for grilled cheese sandwiches on board."

"We call them toasted cheese sandwiches here," he said. "And toasted cheese sandwiches are my favorite."

"Didn't you eat dinner?" She wondered if she should try to cook something more substantial.

But he said, "I did, in fact. I had a steak, but I cannot resist a toasted cheese sandwich."

"Awesome. Two toasted cheese sandwiches coming up. Unless you'd like more than one?"

"I already had dinner, so one's good." He pulled his shirt away from his body. "I hope you don't mind my heading into the back to change while you make our midnight snack. A couple of drinks were thrown at me tonight."

She cocked her head. "I don't mind at all, as long as when you get back, you fill me in on the whole story."

He laughed again. "Will do."

Once he left the room and she heard the door to the second bedroom close behind him, she let out a long breath. It was getting easier to act like he hadn't crushed her heart and soul when she was fifteen. It helped that he was no longer cranky and seemed to be in better spirits, despite the fact that he seemed to have gone from one disaster to another tonight. But there was still that voice in her head that told her not to trust him because he had hurt her so badly before. The voice that told her men were all scum. That she had abundant proof. And yet, even as that voice was shouting its warnings, some instinct inside whispered that she should ignore it and just let herself enjoy being around Malcolm. Because when he wasn't being snappish, he was actually really nice company.

She was so lost in her thoughts that she almost burned the sandwiches. Instead, fortunately, they turned out perfectly—crispy on the outside, especially where some of the cheese had melted onto the edges of the bread. She could smell the salty butter and the fresh loaf of bread that she had cut just minutes earlier. Her mouth watered. This wasn't her normal breakfast, nor did she usually have a midnight snack, but it seemed to fit all the bills. She had just finished putting the sandwiches on plates when Malcolm reemerged.

"That smells amazing."

"I hope it will be."

He nodded toward the roof. "What do you say we grab a couple of rugs to wrap up in and sit on the rooftop deck? It's a nice night."

"The rooftop deck sounds great, but you want us to wrap up in rugs?"

"Sorry, I forgot you call them blankets in the States."

"Oh yeah, blankets equal rugs here. I read that in a book recently. And a tank top is called a vest, right?"

He nodded. "You're practically British now."

"Practically," she joked back.

They grabbed a couple of thick blankets from the arms of the seating in the living room—or as he called it, the lounge—and headed up the narrow stairs to the rooftop deck.

She sighed, gazing up at the stars twinkling in the clear sky. A crescent moon added to the romance. "It is a beautiful night. Honestly, I don't know how you ever leave this houseboat. I know I said it earlier, but every second I spend on it just gets better and better."

An owl hooted, and they could hear the rustle of an animal prowling around in the night, maybe a cat in the bushes on the other side of the towpath.

He picked up his sandwich and bit into it. "Toasted cheese sandwich perfection," he exclaimed. He took another bite, saying, "If you weren't so busy with your bibliotherapy and reading retreats, I'd say you should open a popup shop and sell these." He leaned back. "Then I'd take your franchise global, and you'd be the official toasted-cheese-sandwich queen."

She felt all glowy inside from his compliment. "Thanks. They turned out well. I almost burned them, but that extra handful of seconds in the pan made them even crisper."

They smiled at each other, the moon above them.

Then suddenly, the air between them seemed to change, and she felt a little shy, ducking her head to eat her sandwich.

Malcolm had brought their cups of tea while she carried up the plates, and she took a sip as she looked out over the river illuminated by the moon.

"Josie, there's something I've been meaning to say to you. Something I've wanted to say for a long time."

She almost spit out her tea. She knew what was coming, and she did not want to go there, not back to that awful night when she was so enjoying this one. "You don't have to say anything. It's ancient history. We were just kids." She was pleased at how breezy she sounded, like his words hadn't crushed her teenage heart.

"I do. I have to apologize. We might have been kids, but I was the worst kind of teenager. I was thoughtless and hurtful. What I did, what I said, was absolutely unacceptable. Also, it had nothing to do with you."

Her chest ached just from having him bring up the whole sorry scenario again. She really didn't like thinking about it. And she really didn't want to talk about it. "Thanks for the apology, but—"

"No, please, hear me out. I'm not telling you this to make excuses, but I do want you to know more about what happened. Why I did what I did. And I also want you to know that it was a wake-up call for me." His expression was serious enough that she decided that she would hear him out, even if talking about it was painful.

"Okay, I'm listening."

"Right. Good." Now he stalled, but she waited, letting the silence build. Finally, he said, "I have to go back from that year. My father—he was a driver on the Tube. A really cool job for your father to have when you're a little boy. I was a hero at school. But there are parts of the job that are hard. People who hurt themselves by accident, or deliberately, on the tracks. No one really thinks about what the driver sees. No one thinks about what he goes through when he's unable to save someone. Or worse, thinking back to whether he could've stopped in time if he had done something differently." He swallowed. "He saw and experienced things that traumatized him."

She'd never thought about the dark side of being a Tube driver. "How did your father deal with all that?"

"He volunteers to help with PTSD over at the Transport for London offices now. But back then, when I was seventeen, he was in the thick of it. Still driving. And one day, a child fell on the tracks." He closed his eyes, going silent for a moment. "He couldn't save her. I was the first person to find out what happened. I found him at home, with a bottle of whiskey, sobbing. I can still hear him crying out, asking why. Begging for forgiveness.

"He saw me there, in the doorway. It was terrifying. I'd never seen my father be anything but strong and infallible. I put my arms around him, and he cried. And I knew that his passion, driving these trains, trains that he had loved since he was a boy—I knew it would never be the same for him. That he could never find that joy again. Other people had died on his watch, but never a child. He was almost incoherent, but I could make out him saying, what if it had been one of us when we were children? What if they had had to call him and my mother and say that we were gone?"

He picked up his cup of tea and took a drink. She

said, "If this is too hard, you don't have to talk about it." She wanted to reach out, put a hand over his, but they didn't know each other well, and she didn't want to overstep.

"No, it's something I need to say. I've never talked to anybody about this before, but you deserve to know the full truth behind why I was such an arsehole to you. As I said, it won't excuse what I did, but hopefully the story will make you realize my behavior had nothing to do with you."

He collected his thoughts for a moment before continuing. "I applied for the exchange program not long after that. I didn't know how to process what my father had been through, his grief, or what lingered beyond. Because he was diagnosed with PTSD after that, and I felt so helpless, like I hadn't done enough to help him that afternoon, and I still didn't know how to help him. I'd always wanted to go to America, and this was my chance to escape. Escape the pain and the darkness that seemed to hover over our house during that period. Over our family. All that year, I was running, running from feeling anything. That's why I hooked up with the group that I did. The parties, the alcohol—it all helped to numb my feelings and give me something to focus on. I don't think any of us were actually friends, but it didn't matter. I didn't care. I just didn't want to think about my dad, not being able to help, being useless to him when he'd done so much for me and the rest of us. And so that night, at the prom, I'd been drinking, as usual. But more even than before, because I knew I was headed back to the UK soon. And I was afraid of the state that I'd find my father in, if he'd recovered at all. My mother said he was doing a lot better, but she hadn't been there in those first moments. She hadn't heard him crying out, lost and on his knees, begging for forgiveness." He glanced over at her. "I know he wouldn't mind me telling you this now, because I've heard him tell this story many, many times to try to help people who have been in the same situation, to let them know they're not alone."

He lifted his teacup to take a sip, but it was empty. "Hell, I need something stronger for this. I'll be right back."

He headed down the stairs, and she put a hand over her heart. His poor father. And poor Malcolm too. He'd been a teenager who had wanted so badly to take his father's pain away, but he hadn't known how. No one could have done that for his father. Likely only therapy and time would've done it. For some reason, her mind flicked back to Emily Soames and the books she'd recommended for grief. Emily's grief was deep and painful, but it was also straightforward. What Malcolm's father had been through was complicated. Trauma, shock, grief, and self-blame. What an awful combination.

Malcolm came up with a bottle of clear liquid and two glasses. "This is a botanical gin. A friend of mine in the Surrey Hills distills it." He poured them each a glass, a rather hefty one by her measure. He threw his head back and downed his gin in one swallow, then refilled his glass. "When that girl I was dating—Lord, I can't even remember her name."

"Brianna Sterling," Josie said. He might have forgotten Brianna, but Josie never would. Not the girl who'd christened her Worm.

"Right. When Brianna dared me to kiss you... I knew it was wrong. Not because there was anything wrong at all with kissing you," he clarified, "but because we didn't know each other. And she and I were dating. Teenagers daring each other to do things is always stupid. I knew it. I could hear my mother's voice in my head, telling me that I was raised better than that. That I was raised better than my behavior had indicated that whole year. But I didn't say no. Instead, I let my whole twisted-up teenage self walk up to you outside and pull you into my arms without even asking if it was okay to kiss you."

He let out a harsh breath. "I'm sorry, Josie. Truly sorry. Especially about what I said after, when she came out, when she pretended that she had caught us kissing, when she acted like she hadn't orchestrated the whole thing, and when I said those horrible words." He didn't have to say them now for her to hear them.

I was just screwing around with her, Brie. Do you think I would actually want to make out with some random sophomore? You know I have higher standards than that.

"I won't ask you to forgive me. I don't think I deserve it. But I can say I'm sorry anyway."

Jose was on the verge of tears. It was so emotional to have the boy who had done that to her sitting in front of her now, bringing it all up again. But she didn't need to cry this time. Didn't need to go dashing off in a flood of tears the way she had before. She was a grown woman, and she had recovered from that horrible night. Still, his words helped ease the old scar.

"Worse things have happened to people," she said softly.

"I know, but you still didn't deserve to be treated that way." He took another drink from his glass. "The next morning when I woke up, I knew that I was finally done with it all. Done with the partying. Done with the drinking. Done with acting like a dick. I want you to know I've never done anything like that again, never said anything like that to anyone or treated anybody's feelings as callously as I did yours. And though I'm sure some of my exes might disagree," he added with a wry smile, "I never intend to hurt anybody."

She let out a massive sigh. "Thanks for letting me

know. It does help a little to know what you were going through and what made you act that way." She shook her head, taking a sip of gin, which burned all the way down. "I'm not going to lie. I did feel pretty bad for a while after that. But I got over it a long time ago." She thought about it and realized that even then, books had helped her. "I felt the falseness in your words somehow. And it made no sense for you to act that way. The story didn't make sense, so when I stopped feeling humiliated, I was able to realize that what you did could have been done to anyone." She made a face. "But Brianna really did have it in for me."

"If you ask me," Malcolm said, "she was jealous of you."

Shock gently punched her in the stomach. "Jealous? Brianna? Of me?"

"Sure. You were so smart. Focused. Maybe it wasn't cool to love books, but you didn't need other people's adoration the way she did. I think that's why she targeted you."

She very much liked his interpretation of what had happened. She grinned at him suddenly. "You know what my company's called?"

He shook his head.

"The Bookworm. I have Brianna to thank for that."

He chuckled. "I lost touch with that crowd years ago, but I'll wager you've made more of your life than any of the cool kids." He paused and then said, "I noticed, you know. You always seemed so happy, and the way you'd walk around with a book all the time—I found it charming. So I'm even more sorry I did that awful thing."

"Truthfully, it doesn't matter. And I think now that we've cleared the air, why don't we both agree to move on? We're not kids anymore. And it's water under the bridge." Which seemed like the perfect phrase, given that they were floating on a river with one of London's bridges visible from where they sat.

"I'd like that. I'd like that very much. Thanks for giving me a chance to be less of an arsehole the second time we've met." Then he made a wry face. "Although I wasn't much better at the airport, was I?"

She shook her head. "Not really."

"I was just so shocked to see you again. And ashamed. It's no excuse, and I won't hurt you again. I promise."

"You'd better not," she said, but she said it lightly.

Their eyes caught and held, and she gave a little shiver even though she was wrapped in a warm blanket. It was so tempting to spend all night under the stars with Malcolm, to keep talking and sharing. But she knew better. Knew that she needed to keep him in the friend zone.

At the very least, she needed to keep her *own* head

in the friend zone, because she very much doubted that he was looking to kiss her a second time. "I guess we should head back downstairs so you aren't too tired for work in the morning. I'm assuming you have an early start, with all those deals you have cooking?"

"Nope, no work for me tomorrow. I'm on holiday. I was supposed to be heading to Thailand." Then he sighed. "But I'll likely be busy with this New Zealand deal anyway."

She cocked her head. "You're not going to Thailand because…"

"For the same reason I showed up smelling like a cosmopolitan. The woman I was going with is going with someone else now. Turns out she's been shagging her new hire."

A spurt of laughter was surprised out of her. She couldn't imagine a woman choosing anyone else if they could have Malcolm. And he clearly wasn't brokenhearted. "Oh no, sorry, finding that out must have been hard."

"No, it was fine. I realized we weren't meant to be together anyway. I'm sure she'll be much happier with him. With anybody but me, actually. I was a lot more upset over the House in a Box deal nearly going south than over losing a woman. I guess that pretty much defines me as a workaholic."

She'd thought about giving him a book if the moment was right, and this seemed like the perfect moment. "Just a second," she said, standing. "I have something for you."

He looked utterly surprised, and she got the strangest feeling that he was usually the one giving gifts and less often the one receiving them. She ran down and fetched the book she'd chosen for him.

"As a professional bibliotherapist, I'm prescribing a treatment for this workaholism of yours." She said it in a teasing tone, but she truly felt that Malcolm needed to read the old but still very relevant wisdom.

He accepted the book, and she said, in case he couldn't read the cover in the dim light, "It's *Walden* by Thoreau. I usually suggest this as an antidote to stress caused by overwork. But the lessons are good for all of us."

He opened the cover and flipped through the pages, though it was too dark to read. "Thank you, Josie. I didn't expect to be your first patient."

She smiled at him. "First, you aren't. I recommended some titles to a woman today in Mari's bookshop, and second, I don't consider the people I work with as patients. They're clients. Or fellow bookworms."

A moment passed, friendly, peaceful. Then he stood. "I should let you go to sleep, since I'm sure Mari plans to pick your brain bright and early tomorrow for her reading retreat."

Josie nodded as they collected their blankets and empty cups and plates. "That's the plan. I'm really excited." She yawned. "And actually, even though I woke up just before you got here, convinced I'd never be able to get back to sleep, I think I might be able to now."

"Finding out that he's put you to sleep isn't good for a guy's ego," he teased. "I normally don't have that effect on women."

She laughed, but it was a slightly awkward sound. Not sure what she was supposed to say to what sounded a lot like flirting, she said, "Okay, well then, good night. I'll see you in the morning."

"Good night, Josie. Sleep well."

She headed into the back bedroom, feeling a little flushed and overheated, considering that they'd been outside in the cool night air. That was what being around Malcolm Sullivan did to her. Heated her up all over. She put her cool hands on her warm cheeks. She had to stop thinking of him like that. Like a sexy, available man. Okay, so as of tonight it sounded like he was available. And he was completely sexy. But he wasn't for her. No man was, especially not one who was charismatic and wealthy like her last boyfriend. Men were all dogs, she reminded herself as she slipped under the covers. Except that dogs were loyal.

CHAPTER SIX

Malcolm had a hell of a time falling sleep. He couldn't stop thinking about how soft and warm and wonderfully curvy Josie looked in her pajamas. A gentleman wouldn't have noticed she had nothing on underneath. As much as his mother had tried to raise him to be a gentleman, she'd failed on that front. He'd been unable to *not* notice. He had only broken up with his girlfriend an hour before, and yet, he found himself consumed with thoughts of Josie. The sound of her laughter. The way her smile lit up her face. The smell of her faint vanilla scent whenever he got close enough.

And the emotion in her eyes when she listened to him tell her about his father's difficult past, and also when he apologized to her for treating her so badly in high school. Normally, he would pull out his laptop and phone and deal with some business matters before bed. He couldn't think of the last time he hadn't checked in on work before going to sleep. But he didn't feel like it tonight. He'd liked sitting up on the rooftop deck of his boat, staring up at the stars, listening to the owls hoot. He hadn't done that in a long time. If he wasn't working, he was going to some fancy gala or fundraiser, or sitting in the most expensive seats at a must-see show, or attending a new restaurant opening.

He rarely spent an evening relaxing, even with his family. More and more over the years, he'd taken to working every spare moment, his commitments leaving less and less time to enjoy life. Sure, he still got out for a hard run along the Thames most days, and he lifted weights three times a week, but those were things he did for maintenance. He couldn't remember the last time he'd played football or rugby, games he used to love. No time. He exercised to stay fit, the way he ate because he was hungry and not because he really enjoyed the food he put in his mouth.

Though he'd thoroughly enjoyed the toasted cheese sandwich tonight, even more than the perfectly cooked high-priced steak. Josie was not only beautiful and cheerful, she could also make a mean midnight snack. He couldn't imagine any of his exes cooking, especially not something laden with cheese and butter and carbohydrates. Which said a great deal about his taste in women, he realized. Josie was refreshing.

He felt a huge weight lifted now that he'd finally done what he should have done fifteen years ago. He'd apologized to a young woman he'd hurt badly. She'd tried to pretend his behavior hadn't affected her much, but he'd seen the deep hurt in her pretty hazel eyes. He imagined a cocky young man treating one of his sisters that way, and he knew he'd want to take the blighter apart. Still, he'd finally apologized, and now, perhaps, they could move on.

And maybe he could stop thinking about kissing her again.

She'd given him a book. When was the last time someone had given him a gift for no particular reason? It wasn't his birthday or Christmas. She'd offered him a book she believed might help him. Was he so much of a workaholic that a woman who helped people work through their issues thought he needed her help?

He'd flipped through *Walden* and been struck by this line: *Let us first be as simple and well as nature.*

Had Malcolm been so caught up in business that he'd missed out on the finest things in life? The simplest?

Again, he thought about how much he'd enjoyed sitting out on the roof deck with Josie, enjoying the night. It didn't get much simpler than that. Or more pleasurable.

Finally, he drifted off, waking a handful of hours later to birds chirping outside and light pouring in through the window of the houseboat's second bedroom, which he'd never slept in before. The quality of light on the river was totally different from the light in the city. It was no wonder that so many painters had been inspired by this stretch of the river.

He stretched and then realized he could smell freshly brewed coffee. *Josie is here.*

The thought filled him with warmth. It was nice knowing she was close by, somehow. Usually, he couldn't wait to be left alone in his own flat, where he could focus on his computers and his phone calls. But he felt quite the opposite this morning.

He dug through the clothes he kept on the boat and threw on a pair of sweatpants and a long-sleeved T-shirt, padding out on bare feet. "Good morning."

She wasn't wearing her pajamas anymore, unfortunately, but she still looked great in black trousers that floated around her legs and cinched at the waist, and a white fitted top. "Good morning. I wasn't sure if you preferred coffee or tea, but I brewed some coffee. I can make you tea, though, if you want."

"Coffee's better than okay. I may never let you leave."

Her face flushed, and she ducked her head out of his line of vision as she poured them two cups. "Milk or sugar?"

"Both."

She looked at him in surprise. "I was sure you were going to say you take it black."

He smiled at her. "I've always had a weakness for

sweet things."

His flirting was clearly making her uncomfortable, based on that nervous laugh she gave and the fact that when she poured the milk, some of it sloshed over the edge. "I'm not sure who stocked the fridge, but thank you if it was you. I had granola for breakfast, but there's plenty more and fruit in the bowl." She babbled on, and he sort of enjoyed knowing he was the cause of her discomfort. "Mari and I are going to look at the space she's found for the reading retreats today. She should be here soon."

"That sounds interesting."

They sipped, and he discovered she made a mean cup of coffee.

There was a knock on the door. "That must be Mari," Josie said with what seemed like relief as she went to open it. Sure enough, Mari stood there looking full of energy.

"Hi, I hope I'm not too early."

Josie smiled. "No, this is perfect timing."

The two women hugged, obviously already friends even though Josie had only arrived yesterday.

Then Mari caught sight of him and faltered. "Oh… Malc… what are you doing here?"

He got up and gave the woman he was sure was soon to be his sister-in-law a hug. "It's a bit of a long story, but suffice it to say I couldn't stay in my flat last night, and Josie was kind enough to let me crash here."

Mari's eyes narrowed slightly. "Couldn't you have stayed at Mathilda's? Or in Owen's cottage?"

He could have stayed at a number of places, including any of the top hotels in London, but something had pulled him here to the island. He hadn't even planned to stay on the houseboat, had simply come by to get some spare clothes.

"That was the plan, but then one thing led to another, and I ended up here."

"It was no big deal," Josie clarified. "We shared grilled cheese sandwiches on the rooftop deck, and then we both hit the sack. It's really handy that there are two bedrooms." She couldn't have been more clear about the state of their relationship unless she had said, *Don't worry, I didn't sleep with him.*

"Okay then, but aren't you supposed to be at work, Malcolm?" Mari asked, still clearly trying to piece things together.

"I was supposed to be heading to Thailand on vacation today, but things ended with Katrina, so I won't be going with her and her new lover."

Mari's eyes got big. "New lover? When did you guys break up?"

"Around nine last night." Before Mari could ask, he said, "It's for the best for everyone. In fact," he added suddenly, "since I'm free, if you don't mind, I'd like to tag along and see the space that you're planning to use for the reading retreats."

Mari looked at Josie. "Would that be all right with you?"

Josie paused ever so slightly before nodding. "Sure, that'd be great."

Mari shot him a look. "Okay, then. Can you be ready to leave in ten minutes?"

He picked up his mug and headed into the back. "I'll take a quick shower and be right out."

He found himself whistling in the shower as he lathered up. It was funny how much he was looking forward to checking out the retreat locations with the two women. He wasn't normally anywhere near this cheerful before heading into the office. In fact, it was interesting that he had no urge whatsoever to even check his email. If he had gone to Thailand, he would have worked during the entire trip there, during the bulk of the time in Thailand, and during the entire trip back. But here he was, with no plans, just letting work slide. In fact, between Genevieve and Mabel and the rest of the staff, they could handle most of the work for the next couple of weeks. Unless there was a clear emergency, he'd let the staff he paid so well do their jobs.

Ten minutes later, after Malcolm grabbed an apple from the fruit bowl for breakfast, they were headed out along the towpath toward the center of the island.

* * *

"Pemberton House was once the hub of the island," Malcolm explained. "It's a sad story, but it was owned for hundreds of years by the Pemberton family. By tradition, the eldest son was always named Vincent. In the late 1930s, a young and dashing Vincent Pemberton met and married the love of his life. There are pictures in the local archives of the wedding and the parties they used to throw. They had a child, a son, naturally named Vincent. Then war broke out."

Josie was getting a bad feeling about where this story was going. Malcolm had a real gift as a storyteller, and Josie felt herself becoming invested in these people who'd lived here long ago.

"Vincent joined the Royal Air Force and tragically, was killed defending his country. After his plane went down, his widow was distraught, as you can imagine. After the war, she took young Vincent to America, to Chicago I believe, where she had friends. Anyway, she met an American, married him, and never came back."

"But how sad to leave this beautiful house."

Mari and Josie gazed at the empty manor house that seemed bereft without a family to call it home. "I can imagine leaving here and never coming back if anything happened to Owen," Mari said.

Malcolm continued, "There's a firm of lawyers who've looked after Pemberton House and outbuildings ever since. At some point, the family agreed to open the grounds to the public, but otherwise it's been left empty."

Mari took up the tale. "When I read about you, Josie, and got the idea to hold a reading retreat here, I immediately thought of the cottages. It was Malcolm who made it happen."

Josie felt her interest perk up even more. "Really? What did Malcolm do?"

"Very little," Malcolm said.

But Mari just smiled at him. "He knows one of the top lawyers in the firm. You'll find Malcolm knows a lot of influential people in London. Anyway, he persuaded them to get in touch with the owner of Pemberton House and see if I could rent the cottages. To my absolute delight, they agreed, and the rent is affordable. I got the feeling it was more of a favor than anything."

"But that's wonderful." Josie was still staring at the manor house. "But who could own such an amazing house and not want to live in it?"

Malcolm replied, "Not everyone wants to live in a historic home with old plumbing and creaky floors and windows that let in the rain."

"Then maybe they should sell the property to

someone who *would* want to."

"I imagine they will at some point, if no one in the family ever comes back," Malcolm said.

They resumed walking, and behind the big house was a row of adorable cottages.

Mari said, "I was also able to rent the garden space, in addition to the cottages, for the reading retreats. So we'll be looking at all of that today, and I'm really hoping you can transform the cottages into a really wonderful space for people to come and get away from it all with a book."

"A manor house—it's so thrilling." Josie smiled at Malcolm. "We Americans, we're wowed by stuff like this."

"We Brits are pretty thrilled by it too," Malcolm said, then turned to Mari. "I don't believe the cottages have been occupied in decades. Have you been inside?"

"I have," Mari said, "and there is definitely a reason why I'm able to afford the lease. They are in worse shape than Elderflower Island Books was when I took it over, but not too much worse. I took them as is so I could lease them quickly and at a good rate. They need a thorough clean and some cosmetic stuff that I'm sure we can deal with, mostly a scrub and some paint. Fiona's got a friend who's a home stager, and she's organized couches and chairs and tables that we can rent. If it's successful, I'll invest in permanent furniture, but for now, I just want to see if they work."

Malcolm had a feeling he'd be swapping his Brioni suits and laptop for coveralls and a paintbrush in the near future. Oddly, the idea didn't put him off at all. In fact, he was excited by the prospect. He'd spent so much of his life in a suit, chasing investors, organizing deals, sitting in boardrooms, that he craved physical labor.

Mari continued, "I love the idea of the reading retreats taking place on the grounds of Pemberton House. It's so romantic. Plus, it's so close to the bookshop."

It sounded like Mari had her heart set on these buildings, so between him and his brother and the rest of his family, they'd do whatever it took to make the project work for her. They'd already helped her turn the dilapidated bookshop around after her father died, so it seemed natural for the family to pitch in and fix up some outbuildings.

"I'm sure it will all be great," Josie said, positive as always.

Mari smiled gratefully at her, obviously appreciating the boost of enthusiasm. "Here we are," she announced as they reached the string of attached cottages.

Josie exclaimed, "These are amazing!"

He tried to see them through her eyes and could

see the charm. Though on a much smaller scale, the cottages matched the Pemberton House with its exterior of old gray stone, soaring roof, and big windows. The manor had clearly been built by someone who understood proportion and grandeur. The cottages were more intimate, probably built for the staff, but featuring the same gray stone, pretty windows, and slate roofs.

Mari got out a large black iron key that looked like it must be original, and opened the main door.

As she pushed it open, she invited the others inside. Josie gasped again, but this time it wasn't a good, happy gasp. It was a horrified one.

"I know," Mari said. "It looks pretty bad, but I think after a good cleaning, it will be so much better."

Malcolm suspected it wasn't going to be as simple as giving the place a good once-over with a broom and a sponge. It seemed as though this cottage, and probably the others, had become the junk rooms for the manor house. Broken furniture, bits of china, and even a carriage wheel crowded the space. Everything was filthy, and the place smelled dank. He bet there were mice in the cupboards and bats in the attic.

"I think you're going to need to do a little more than just cleaning," he said in as gentle a voice as he could. "Let's see the rest of the place, and then we can assess the situation."

"I'll definitely need to get rid of the junk," Mari admitted, "but I think some of it might be salvageable."

Josie went to a window and wrestled it open, letting in light and air, which helped. A bit.

Malcolm kept his comments to himself as they toured the space. There was a lot of work to be done, and if Mari owned the buildings instead of leasing them, he'd want to do some renovations. Mari looked more and more worried as they made their way through the other cottages. It wasn't the materials that would cost so much. A good scrub and some paint would do wonders. It was the labor. If Mari wanted to hold a reading retreat next week, she'd need labor, and plenty of it. Malcolm knew where the labor would be coming from.

He put his hand on her shoulder. "Don't worry. We'll all help you with this. I know my way around a tool belt and paintbrush, and I find myself with a free week on my hands." His thoughts flicked briefly to Thailand. Beaches, jungles, sunsets, fine hotels. And oddly, he realized he'd rather be here painting walls so that Josie and Mari could host a reading retreat than holidaying in style with Katrina.

Mari smiled at him gratefully, then shook her head. "You work all the time as it is. I can't ask you to help me clean up these cottages."

"Honestly, it'll be a fun project." He found himself

looking forward to something that didn't involve a computer, or a meeting over drinks, or a flight to another country. "It really would be my pleasure to help you, Mari." *And an excuse to spend more time close to Josie*, said a voice in the back of his head.

"Of course, I'm happy to help too," Josie said. "The house I grew up in was an old Victorian that always needed work." She flexed her hands. "I'm pretty handy."

"You're so sweet to offer," Mari said, "but that's not what you came here to do. I want you to choose the books and lead the retreat. You didn't come here to paint walls and take broken tables to the dump." She caught her lower lip between her teeth and appeared troubled. "I let my enthusiasm get away from me. I can't imagine we'll be ready to host a reading retreat before you have to fly home."

Josie looked at Malcolm with a silent but clear question in her eyes. *If we work on these cottages, can we get this off the ground for Mari?*

He gave her a tiny nod, and she turned back to Mari with a smile. "Actually, I think this makes the project even more exciting. I've never been quite this much on the ground floor of a project before. Heck, it'll be like the heroine of a great story who finds herself in a foreign land, helping to bring a historic property back to life."

Mari laughed. "You mean a gothic castle. Well, if both of you are sure—"

"I am," both Josie and Malcolm said at the same time.

Just then, Mari's phone rang—the ringtone the chorus of a Beatles love song. She blushed. "That's Owen. Do you mind if I take it?"

"Go ahead," Josie said.

"Hi, Owen. What's up?"

Malcolm watched Mari's eyes light up. He'd seen a huge change in his brother ever since he and Mari had started dating. Where Owen had been too serious for many years, Mari seemed to have lightened his whole personality. And it was obvious that his brother had done the same for Mari, given how devastated she'd been by the death of her father.

Mari went to the corner of the room and spoke softly while Malcolm moved closer to the walls to see how much needed doing before they were ready to paint.

Josie turned slowly in a circle as though she were on a stage about to deliver a soliloquy.

When Mari ended the call, her eyes were huge. "You'll never guess what Owen just told me! The *London Bookseller* wrote an amazing piece about the bookshop and our Mathilda Westcott connection. It's the entire front page of the mystery section. I had no idea anybody was even thinking of doing a piece about it. He's sending me a copy, but he says Mathilda was interviewed and raved about the shop, especially the re-creation of the living room where her fictional sleuth works. I can't believe she didn't mention the interview."

"She wanted to surprise you," Malcolm guessed.

"Congratulations," Josie said. "That's fantastic news."

"It really is. Your shop is going to become even more popular in the very near future," Malcolm said.

"I don't know. Does an article in the paper make that much of a difference?" Mari asked.

Before Malcolm could respond, her phone rang again. This time, it was her shop assistant, Grace Whitmore, calling. It wasn't too difficult to figure out what was being said, and Mari confirmed it when she hung up. "Grace says there's a line outside the shop already, even before we opened." She sighed. "Seems Mathilda decided to announce an impromptu book signing. I guess that article really did make a difference." She glanced at them both. "I really need to get back to the shop. It's too much for Grace to handle on her own."

"We've got this, Mari," Malcolm told her. "Go back to the store and sell books to all those customers."

Mari looked at Josie. "Is that okay with you? I

didn't intend to leave you all by yourself on your first day here."

"Absolutely, you should go back to the shop. And don't worry, I'm not alone. Malcolm's going to stay to help, remember?"

Mari put her hands to her cheeks. "Yes, sorry. I'm just feeling sort of flustered by this news." She gave them both a hug and then hurried off in the direction of the shop.

"Looks like we'd better get these cottages fixed up quick. Now that the bookstore is suddenly so famous, the reading retreats are sure to become extremely popular too," Malcolm said.

Josie nodded. "I agree. I think Mari's absolutely wonderful, and I want to help her any way I can. Should we just begin a thorough inventory of the cottages and everything in them? And then we can compare notes and work out what needs to be done?"

He nodded. "That was precisely what I was going to suggest."

She gave him another one of those sunny smiles, and though it made his heartbeat pick up, he needed to focus on the task at hand. He'd always been brilliant at focusing, no matter the distractions. But he'd never known anyone quite like Josie. And though he would never call her a distraction, it was certainly true that he hadn't been able to completely focus since he'd picked her up at the airport. She was always somewhere in his head. He couldn't stop thinking of her. Thinking of her in a way that he had never thought about another woman. He was attracted to her—frankly, more attracted to her than he could remember being to anyone else. But it was more than that.

He also truly liked being around her. He was interested in what she had to say. And he was interested in her story and how she'd come to be who she was today. He found himself wondering what had shaped her. What did she love? What was she afraid of? What had her childhood been like?

All questions that, honestly, he'd never really had about any of the women who had come before her.

CHAPTER SEVEN

During the next several hours, Josie seemed to discover a new treasure around every corner. Whether it was the blue and white cups and saucers hidden in the very back of a dingy kitchen cupboard, whose hallmark identified them as Royal Crown Derby and which Malcolm said were very collectible, or a dining chair with the family crest hand embroidered on the seat cushion in what had once surely been a lovely dining room, or very dusty old tomes on even dustier shelves in what she hoped they would transform back into a beautiful library.

Although there was a lot of work to be done, she could see how gorgeous the space would be when it was cleared out and thoroughly cleaned and then filled with books to read and cozy nooks to read them in. The cottages seemed solid. But more than that, the soul of the structures was still there. She knew from the feeling she got in these three interconnected cottages just outside the walled garden that there had been happiness here. Of course, there had been sorrows too—that was life—but on the whole, she would guess the laughter had outweighed the tears. She couldn't wait to help bring the cottages back to life.

"This is going to be my favorite reading retreat so far. I just know it."

Malcolm looked up from his phone, where he'd been making a list of supplies, surprise on his face. "Are you sure about that?"

She nodded. "I'm positive. I know there's work to be done, but it really is cosmetic. And I think Mari's idea to transform these cottages for a reading retreat is very doable. Among the three, the bedrooms will be able to sleep a dozen people, depending on the configuration. Just think, a dozen people every week finding joy again. Finding love. Becoming whole again. Or just taking a much-needed break for the first time in a long time."

He didn't reply for a long moment. Finally, he said, "How do you do it? How do you always see everything in such a positive light?"

"I ... I guess I didn't know that I did."

"You do. You're always smiling. Even when some grumpy jackass picks you up at the airport, you don't let it rattle you. I show up in the middle of the night smelling like booze, and you're okay with it. Mari brings you into a project where it turns out you are going to be dealing with cobwebs and broken bits of old furniture before you can bring in books and readers. And still, you never stop smiling. You never stop seeing how great everything is going to be."

It was quite possibly the nicest thing anybody had ever said to her. Even when she thought she'd been in love, her ex had never said anything even close to that nice or complimentary. And more than that, she felt as though Malcolm was showing her a fresh window into herself.

"Well, thank you. And you just... You made me feel really good, not just because of all the lovely compliments, but because hearing you say that makes me realize I'm really resilient."

His eyebrows rose at the word *resilient*. She might've said too much. She didn't want to go into the whole sob story about what had happened to her. She'd told Mari, and that had felt right, but talking to Malcolm about her recent heartbreak felt different somehow. Like it would create an even deeper intimacy between them, an intimacy that frankly scared her. Not just because of what had happened in high school—they'd already washed that water under the bridge. But more because, as she'd said to Mari, she didn't think she could trust a man anymore. If she couldn't trust a man, how could she ever be truly intimate with him?

In any case, she said, "Well, we're certainly going

to have a busy week or two, aren't we?"

"We are. It's a good thing I've booked a holiday, but I'm thinking a week away from the office isn't going to be sufficient. I'm going to need at least two if we're going to be reading-retreat ready."

"Are you sure you want to do menial labor?" Josie hadn't forgotten that he worked practically 24/7, and could likely hire people to do things like cleaning out old cottages.

"I am looking forward to getting my hands dirty for a change, and I'm fortunate to have contacts in every industry and trade you can imagine. What I and my siblings don't know how to do, we'll hire out."

"But what about your work?"

"The office will be fine without me. If they're not, it means I haven't done my job well enough training my staff." He paused. "Funny, that's the first time that's occurred to me. I hire excellent people and train them well. I should trust them more. In fact, I should have been taking a lot more holidays over the years." He looked sad as he said, "Instead, I've always insisted on being involved in every decision, every deal. I need to learn to let go."

She found herself wondering if what had happened with his father when he was a teenager had impacted more than just the way he'd behaved in high school. Had it colored the rest of his life as well? Had it driven his choices? And could the effect of his father's tragedy have somehow turned Malcolm into a workaholic?

Or had he been born a workaholic in the same way she'd been born a bookworm? She found she had more and more questions about Malcolm and his life with every minute they spent together.

His phone had been pinging with incoming messages all day, but though he checked them periodically, he hadn't shown much interest. Then he got a message that made him smile and turn to Josie.

"What do you say we have afternoon tea with my grandmother?"

She was stunned by the sudden question. "Mathilda Westcott? Really? I'm starved, and I would love to meet her, but I hate to impose."

"Oh, it's no imposition, trust me. More like a command. We've been summoned, but I just thought I'd phrase it as a question to be polite. I imagine Gran's feeling very pleased with herself for bringing so much business to Mari's store, and I'm sure she sold a large number of her own titles. No doubt, Mari's got her interested enough in you that she wants to meet you."

"Wow, summoned by Mathilda Westcott. I could pinch myself." She actually did, making him laugh.

"We need a little time for all of this to digest anyway, and we worked through lunch, so why don't we lock up? We can come back in the morning, ready to get down to work. The first thing I'll do is haul out the broken furniture and rubbish, then we'll be able to start cleaning and painting."

She agreed, and they set to closing up the cottages. She already felt a connection to these rooms and could see them in her mind's eye, revitalized and welcoming. She couldn't wait to come back in the morning.

As they walked out, she gestured at the stone walls beside the cottages. "This is the walled garden?"

"A sadly neglected one. I've seen paintings of it from decades ago when it was flourishing. They grew everything from flowers to vegetables to healing herbs. It truly was a sight to behold. I know my sister Alice would give anything to be able to bring it back to life."

"Is she a big gardener?"

"The biggest. She's actually a professional horticulturalist and currently works at Kew Gardens. She got her degree there, and when you meet her, you'll discover she's always covered in mud, or worse."

Josie smiled, hearing the affection in his tone. "I've always loved spending time in gardens," she said. "I'm afraid I don't have much of a green thumb, though, so I'm not going to be of any use at all here. Although it would be really nice to neaten up the cottage gardens for the reading retreats. Do you think your sister might be able to lend a hand, or at least give us some ideas on what direction to take with them?"

"Just by asking that question, I promise you're going to be Alice's new favorite person. Like I said, it's long been her dream to be able to work on the manor house grounds. But there haven't been available funds for it and from the council, and she's been busy building up her own qualifications at Kew these past years. I'll talk to her about it tonight, in case Mari hasn't got to her yet."

"How many siblings do you have?" Again, the more she knew about Malcolm, the more she wanted to know. When he spoke about his sister Alice, it was obvious how much he loved her.

"Well, Alice is the baby of the family. We all look after her, even though she swears she doesn't need it. And truthfully, she doesn't. She's very focused on what she does. I'm sure she does get up to some trouble, but just makes sure that none of us are aware of it, lest we try to stop her fun. You've already met Owen—he's the oldest. As you probably know, he runs my grandmother's publishing business, which is more than a full-time job, but she doesn't trust anyone but family to do it, so he has gladly taken it all on."

"I think it's great that her books are all in the family like this. And now with Mari having the bookstore and creating the dedicated space for her books and fan mementos, it's like the circle just keeps expanding."

"Expanding to include you, as I'm sure you'll find

out very shortly when you meet Gran. I'm next in line, and then my brother, Tom. He runs several venues on the West End. Although he's always had his eye on the theater on the island, and I think at some point if he can make it work, he'd like to bring that back to life as well. He has a five-year-old daughter named Aria. We all are wrapped around her little finger. As well we should be."

There was no mention of a mother. "Is he raising her alone?"

"He is. Her mother is Lyla Imogen, but their relationship didn't work out, so he is happy to have primary custody of Aria. We're all happy that he does."

Josie's eyebrows rose. "*The* Lyla Imogen? The pop star?"

"Yes. That one," he said shortly.

Obviously, there was a great deal more to the story, but she didn't push for it. She didn't want to pry into the Sullivans' family business. She was just curious about Malcolm Sullivan.

"And then my sister Fiona is between Tom and Alice. Her husband's name is Lewis. He's a tool."

Josie looked at Malcolm in surprise. "That's not mincing words."

Malcolm's expression darkened. "He really is a piece of work. Fiona's intelligent and beautiful and could do so much with her life, but she's sticking with him, for God knows what reasons."

"I'm sorry to hear that you think things are so bad in their marriage."

"Who knows for sure? It's mostly just whispers and speculation, so I shouldn't say any more. Hopefully, you'll get to meet her soon. I think you'll really like her. And now that I'm thinking about it, she's the best person to look at some of those furnishings and see how salvageable they are. She's decorated two massive homes for herself and Lewis and, from the sounds of it, has done pro bono decorating for their entire circle of friends as well."

Josie felt there was a lot about his sister that he wanted to say but was keeping to himself, no doubt out of loyalty to Fiona. Josie liked that the family cared about one another, but also that Malcolm didn't want to gossip about his sister and her marriage. However, given the little he'd said, Josie was very curious to meet Fiona. She was impressed that the Sullivan siblings' parents had birthed and raised such a diverse and interesting handful of kids.

"Your parents sound like they must've been busy raising all of you."

He laughed, another warm sound that seemed to come straight from the heart. "Busy is right. We all had the tendency to be hell-raisers. And not just the boys. Fiona and Alice managed to get into quite a few scrapes."

He sounded proud of his sisters for being hell-raisers just as much as he and his brothers. She liked the sound of his family more and more.

"I've already told you about my father, Simon. He's a great bloke. One of the best. And my mother, Penny—everyone loves her. Which isn't to say that she doesn't rule us all with quite a heavy hand. She does. And rightly so. It's the only way to keep us in line."

She heard the affection, as well as the respect, in his tone.

He went on, "My mother is also a curator at the Victoria and Albert Museum."

"Wow," she said. The famous V&A was definitely on her list of places to visit when she had time. "What an impressive family."

Then he turned to her. "What about you? Any siblings?"

"No. It was just me and my mom growing up. My father was killed in a car accident when I was a baby, so I never knew him. But my mom was amazing. She still is. She left Coeur d'Alene for sunnier climes in Arizona a few years back. But she's still always there for me whenever I need her."

"I'd very much like to meet her too," he said. "I'd like to tell her that she raised a remarkable woman."

Josie felt herself blushing. Thankfully, just then

they arrived in front of a beautiful little cottage not far from the bookstore and Malcolm's houseboat. "This is Gran's house," he said.

"It's beautiful. Is this where she writes her books?"

"It is, but I'll let her tell you her story herself."

The front door opened before they were halfway up the brick walkway, and an older woman with white hair and a warm smile stood there. Josie knew it was Mathilda Westcott because she looked exactly like her photograph on the jackets of her novels.

"Welcome," Mathilda said. "You must be Josie. Mari told me how delightful you are."

She felt herself blushing again. "That's very kind of her. And it's such a pleasure to meet you, Ms. Westcott. I'm such a fan."

"Mathilda, please." She leaned forward to kiss Josie on both cheeks. "Come in. I hope you're hungry."

"I am."

Malcolm watched, fascinated to see these two bookish women interact. He'd seen his grandmother with her fans, when she was always a little standoffish, but with Josie, she was warm and open. Clearly, she already liked the American bibliotherapist.

"Excellent. None of the women Malcolm has been with over the years ever seemed to eat, did they, darling?"

He could see what his grandmother was doing—

more matchmaking, just as she had with Owen and Mari. And the way she had just said that, it sounded like she thought Josie was dating him rather than simply working for Mari.

"The cottages are going to be great for the retreats that Mari has planned," he said to his grandmother in lieu of responding to her comment. She'd only ever met a couple of his girlfriends, although she had hated them just as much as Alice had. "They are going to need quite a lot of work, though, before they can be put to use. I'm going to take a couple of weeks off work to help get them in shape alongside Josie, so she can put on at least one retreat before she has to go home."

His grandmother looked between the two of them. "You're going to be working together to prepare the cottages?"

He knew better than to take the innocent lilt of her voice at face value. His grandmother was anything but innocent. He'd heard stories about her youth. She had been as much of a hell-raiser as he or any of his siblings.

"We are," Josie said with a smile. "It's wonderful to create a retreat from scratch, and the cottages are going to be beautiful. It will be good to get my hands dirty."

His grandmother looked intrigued as she led them to the dining room overlooking the river, where afternoon tea was already set up. She invited them to sit, and poured them tea. "You don't mind helping with the dirty work?"

"Not at all," Josie replied. "I worked quite a bit on the Victorian my mother and I lived in while I was growing up. It was always fun working on projects together. Except, possibly, for the plumbing." She shot Malcolm a look. "Plumbing has never been my favorite."

He explained to his grandmother, "I've been kicked out of my flat in the city due to burst pipes. I literally just got a text from the building's management saying that it doesn't look like we'll be able to get back into our homes for quite some time."

Josie looked concerned. "If you need me to find another place to stay—"

"Like I said last night, I'm not kicking you off the houseboat. I can find someplace to stay—like Gran's back cottage, right, Gran? I know that technically Owen still lives there, but we all know he spends all his time with Mari above the bookshop."

Again, his grandmother had that calculating look in her eyes. "Actually, I'm having some work done on the cottage for the next couple of weeks, and I'm afraid the back unit is not going to be habitable."

Before he could ask her about the surely fictional work she'd just concocted out of thin air, she continued, "So the two of you have already spent the night together on the houseboat?"

"In separate bedrooms," Josie piped in, just as she had clarified with Mari.

"Oh, of course," Mathilda said, as though her brain hadn't automatically gone somewhere else. Which it clearly had. "Well, then, it sounds perfectly reasonable to me that you stay on the houseboat with Josie for the duration," she said as she served them delicious-looking finger sandwiches.

The truth was, he didn't want to go anywhere else either. Not only because the houseboat was the one place that felt like home to him, but also because he wanted to spend more time with Josie. Who wouldn't? He found himself wondering if she was single. Somehow he thought she had to be, because she hadn't mentioned a boyfriend or fiancé or, God forbid, husband. But if she was single, that didn't really make sense either. Who wouldn't snap her up? She was beautiful, brilliant, fun. She was the full package. He realized he was staring at her and turned to catch his grandmother noticing that he had been staring at her. She shot him a look, one that he suspected Josie would have been embarrassed to see had she not been eating her smoked salmon sandwich with her eyes closed and her expression one of total rapture.

"This is so delicious. Thank you so much, Mathilda."

"It's my pleasure."

"And I hope it won't make you uncomfortable when I tell you how much I love your books. A couple of years ago, they helped me through... well, something really hard. And the truth is that reading and rereading your books was instrumental in my getting over it. So from the bottom of my heart, thank you for what you do."

His grandmother reached out and put a hand over Josie's. "That's the loveliest thing you could possibly have said to me. When I'm struggling to come up with the next chapter, the next paragraph, even the next sentence, it's knowing that my books have made a difference in someone's life that gets me over that hump. I'm glad I could help, Josie, however I did."

Josie was beaming as Mathilda added, "But I also think you're selling yourself short, because something tells me that you're an incredibly resilient woman and that you would have navigated your rough patch even without my books."

"Thank you," Josie said softly.

"Now, let's finish up these sandwiches so that we can move on to the scones and then dessert."

"Is this where you write?" Josie asked after they'd each eaten several small tea sandwiches—cucumber and cream cheese, and ham and English mustard. Gran was really putting on the dog. "If you don't mind my asking."

Malcolm laughed. "Gran *loves* to talk about her writing process. She's bored me enough with it over the years," he teased.

"You've always been the mouthy one in the family, haven't you?" his grandmother teased back. "Yes. I sit in front of the window with the sun streaming in and glinting off the water. I love watching all the activity outside, from the wildlife to the boaters and the kayakers and the paddleboarders and the people walking by."

"It's lovely that you can just look at the world around you and be inspired."

"As a bonus, writing mysteries has given me license to kill off anybody who's ever annoyed me over the years," his grandmother said with a smile.

Josie laughed. "I always wondered that about mystery writers—if every villain is actually someone from their real life."

"Not always," Mathilda said, "but more often than you think."

"That's why I'm always careful not to get on your bad side, Gran," Malcolm told her.

"Not that careful," she said with a wink. "But I wouldn't love you nearly as much if you weren't such a pain in the rear." She turned back to Josie. "But enough about me. I want to hear more about you.

Where are you from in the States? And what prompted you to decide to create reading retreats?"

"I was born and raised in Coeur d'Alene, Idaho. Strange as it may seem, that was where Malcolm did his year abroad," she reminded his grandmother.

"That's right. So you two knew each other?"

Josie was first to reply, shaking her head. "No. We met once at the end of the year, but it was just a brief few minutes. We never really met properly until now."

His grandmother looked at him, one eyebrow raised. Josie's response had been too quick, and naturally Gran had noticed. "I see. So have you been to England before?" Gran asked.

"No, and I'm loving everything about it. This trip is like a dream come true."

He could tell that his grandmother liked Josie's energy, how she was positive and enthusiastic and utterly sincere.

"And what was it you did before starting reading retreats, or is that what you've always done?"

"I was a freelance editor. I still work for a couple of my favorite clients, which I squeeze in because I can't bear to let them down. But I've almost completely transitioned over to setting up reading retreats now."

"Well, I for one think it's brilliant. In fact, once I heard about reading retreats, I wondered why they hadn't existed before. I can tell you there have been many, many times in my life when I could have used one. I would have loved some time to get away from the difficulties of real life to sink into books and remember how to be happy. I've always said that, apart from travel, reading books is the best way to learn about the world and, perhaps, about ourselves."

His grandmother had never said much to him, or any of them, about her past. The mystery writer was herself a mystery. A part of him suspected it had to do with his grandfather, who'd passed away a number of years ago, but it was nothing she had ever confirmed.

But as his grandmother and Josie looked at each other, he felt that they shared a connection that went deeper than simply loving books. There seemed to be heartache that bound them together.

He didn't usually think along these lines. He wasn't sure what was prompting it now, but being with Josie seemed to be shifting something inside him somehow, making him more aware of other people and their emotions.

As they moved on to the scones that Gran still baked herself, served with clotted cream and strawberry jam, the two women seemed to grow even closer. They talked about the classic mystery writers—Agatha Christie, whom everyone knew, but Josie also read Ngaio Marsh, Dorothy L. Sayers, and Margery Allingham. Malcolm had vaguely heard those names, but

Josie and Gran had read all of their books and could discuss how Lord Peter Wimsey solved a crime compared to Inspector Alleyn. He should have been bored to tears and excusing himself to check email, but surprisingly, he enjoyed the debate. He left the two women talking to fetch the macaroons and ginger cake that Gran had made for dessert.

When they'd emptied the teapot, Josie excused herself to use the bathroom, and after directing her where to find it, Mathilda wasted no time in turning to Malcolm. "She's delightful. You'd be a fool to let her go."

"Gran, I agree she is delightful. But she's not *with* me. So there's no keeping her or letting her go."

His grandmother rolled her eyes. "I'm not a fool. There's obviously a connection between you two. She could be *with* you, if you would only use that pretty face of yours and the charm you too often keep hidden to woo her."

He'd never spoken with anyone in his family about his aversion to finding love for himself. He thought it was great for his parents and his siblings. He hoped they all found love. He wanted them all to be happy and fulfilled. But for him, love had never seemed to be in the cards. As more than one lover had told him, he was married to his work.

"She's not the kind of woman I would want to

mess about."

His grandmother nodded. "I agree. She deserves more than that. She deserves more than any of those other women that you flit around town with." She narrowed her glance. "Don't think I don't see pictures of you in the papers with those whip-thin models who look beautiful on your arm but don't challenge you, don't fill your heart with joy. You can do better, Malcolm. You deserve someone wonderful. Like Josie."

He wasn't sure that his grandma was right. He wasn't sure that he deserved a woman like Josie. What if he let her down again? "I hate to see you get your hopes up, Gran."

"I can't help but wish happiness for each of my grandchildren. I knew the first time I met Mari that she and Owen were perfect together. I have that exact feeling about you and Josie."

Her words settled in deeper than he wanted her to know. He should have been disagreeing instinctively with what she was saying. Everything within him should have been rejecting it. And yet, somehow he found himself wondering. Wondering if his grandmother was right. If maybe, just maybe, Josie was the one for him.

Finally, something inside of him did rebel. Not about whether Josie would be the perfect girlfriend.

But at the thought of ever letting someone in far enough to fall in love, far enough to risk losing her.

Gran leaned in and lowered her voice. "You wouldn't want Tom to swoop in and woo her before you do. You know your brother can be extremely charming when he sets his mind to it."

"Tom?" He shook his head. "Tom would be a terrible partner for Josie. He's still too messed up from his marriage, and he has Aria to think of."

A burning feeling ignited in his chest at the thought of Tom and Josie together. While his grandmother simply sipped tea and regarded him over the rim of her teacup, he recognized the burning feeling as jealousy. Like hell Tom was going to be with Josie.

He was still trying to find words to explain to his grandmother why Tom and Josie would be a terrible match when Josie returned.

"Thank you so much for afternoon tea, Mathilda. It was delicious, and I'm so glad that I got to spend time with you."

Mathilda rose, and so did he.

"It was a pleasure to meet you, Josie, and to be able to talk about some of my favorite books with another bibliophile. I hope we see a lot more of each other."

Josie pinkened with pleasure, and after refusing their offers to help her tidy up, Mathilda sent them on their way.

As they walked back to his boat, he said, "Just as I expected, she loved you."

"Really? I'm still so starstruck. I was trying not to be an embarrassing fangirl the whole time, but I'm not sure I succeeded."

"Even if you had acted like a slobbering fan, which you didn't, she still would have loved you. You talk books like a sensible woman. She appreciates that." Changing the subject, he said, "How do you feel about going over our notes and working out a game plan on the cottages? Or are you too tired? Because right around now is when the jet lag should be kicking in big time."

"I think that tea has woken me up," she said with a smile. "I'm not sure I'll be able to sleep for a few hours at least. Plus, I don't want to let Mari down. The sooner we get the place cleaned up, the sooner I can run my reading retreat."

"I agree. I've already got some people in mind who owe me a few favors. Hopefully, they'll be able to do the work at a cut rate for her."

"It's really nice of you to help her," Josie said.

"Don't paint me as any hero. This is the first truly nice thing I've done in a while, and I haven't even done anything yet besides value some china."

"Are you sure you're not selling yourself short? Because your grandmother clearly adores you, and while we're at it, the two of you should think about taking your act on the road."

He didn't think he was selling himself short. He had a fairly clear view of who he'd become, in particular during these past years when he'd had time only for work and very little else, including his family. But it was nice of Josie to try to see the positives in him, just as she did in everything. Especially when he couldn't get his grandmother's words out of his head.

She's delightful. You'd be a fool to let her go.

He couldn't help wondering—was his grandmother right?

CHAPTER EIGHT

Josie could hardly believe it. She'd had afternoon tea with Mathilda Westcott!

It was the craziest thing. This whole trip so far had been mind-boggling. Surely now it would settle down into something that more closely resembled her normal life, wouldn't it? But then there she and Malcolm were, all cozy on *River Star*, a fire crackling away in the mini woodstove in the corner, music playing on the portable speaker, and the two of them wedged in close on the built-in benches on two sides of the small dining table. Papers and plans were spread out around them as they worked out who to call and what steps to take.

Cleaning, painting, decorating, and furnishing. Maybe a group could go shopping for supplies while another painted and yet another cleaned ahead of them. That would be the fastest route.

Fiona and Alice had both agreed to come by in the morning and head over to the cottages with them to take a look at the garden and the furnishings.

It was so sweet listening to him talk to his sisters. He obviously cared about them both very much, and in the same way that he and his grandmother had teased each other, he and his sisters teased each other, too, but always with a smile and laughter and a foundation of unconditional love and respect. She felt that between all of the Sullivans. It was the same relationship she had with her mother. The same relationship that she'd envisioned for herself and the family she had once planned to have.

Throughout the evening, even though his attention should have been elsewhere as he spoke on the phone, she couldn't help but feel that he was looking at her differently than he had before. A little longer. A little deeper. Sometimes she even thought she saw his gaze lower to her lips, as though he was thinking about kissing her.

Just the thought of it made her own lips tingle. That first time had been her first kiss, and she remembered it vividly. Remembered how it had felt. And now she couldn't seem to stop wondering what would it be like to kiss him again. As an adult instead of an awkward teenage girl.

Not that she didn't feel awkward around him, because the truth was she often did. Especially when he was looking at her this way. She dropped her gaze to their notes and pretended to be busily looking at them, even though the words were swimming before her eyes.

You could kiss him, said the voice inside her head.

The thought startled her. Well, it was true that she didn't need to wait around for him to kiss her. This was the twenty-first century after all, and she was just as empowered as he was to make the first move, but it was still a surprising bend for her mind to take. Wouldn't she be setting herself up for heartache if she kissed him?

How could she have forgotten her vow? No men. *No men* meant *No. Men.* How difficult was that for her heart—and her body—to understand? It was safer this way. It was easier just to go about her life knowing that she wasn't risking any further emotional entanglements with a guy.

Just one kiss. What could that possibly hurt?

She was still fighting an internal battle with herself when he scooted up out of the seat. "I'm going to put another log on to keep us warm."

She knew another way they could stay warm, her brain now running off before she could stop it. Her cheeks flushed, as though he could hear what she was thinking. "That's a good idea."

He was still up feeding the fire when a song from high school came on that she hadn't heard in a very long time—Pink's "Get the Party Started." As the killer beat snuck right into her very being, her feet began to tap.

"I can't believe you have this on your playlist," she said.

He'd connected his phone to the wireless speaker, and they'd been listening to his playlist throughout the evening.

"Of course I do," he said with a smile that was so inherently sexy it warmed her all over. "This is a classic."

She laughed. "I'm not sure many people would agree with you on that one. Although the truth is, every time I hear this song, I can't stop myself from dancing."

He shot her a look tinged with a hint of challenge. "So what's stopping you tonight?"

She'd never been able to resist a challenge. And her hips were swaying beneath the table.

What the heck. They were just friends, right? And with any friend, she would have jumped up and danced without caring what she looked like or whether she seemed foolish. She just would have had fun.

She scooted out off the bench and let her body move to the music. Of course she had to sing along too. Who wouldn't? The next thing she knew, they were both dancing in the middle of the tiny living room of his houseboat. He cranked up the music, and they laughed as they shimmied around each other, bumping hips every once in a while, no different than she would have with a girlfriend.

At least, that's what she told herself.

She grabbed a whisk and pretended it was a mic. He did the same with a slotted spoon. They sang to each other as they danced. She couldn't remember the last time she'd had so much fun.

She was out of breath when the song ended, and a new one started to play. From fast and rocking to slow and crooning. "Fallin" by Alicia Keys.

"Oh, I love this one too," she said, closing her eyes and swaying in place.

Then, suddenly, she was in Malcolm's arms. And hers were going around his neck, his around her hips, and they were moving together, slow dancing. A song about falling, keeping on falling for the same man.

Was that what she was doing? Falling for Malcolm all over again?

She heard him whisper her name into her hair, felt his arms tighten around her, and she drew back so that she could look into his eyes. And then they were kissing, his mouth on hers, hers on his. Both of them moving at the same time, their kiss as perfectly in sync as their dance. He tasted like the Baileys and cream they'd been sipping, the hint of chocolate from a box of truffles he'd had in the kitchen still on his tongue. But that wasn't why he tasted so delicious. No, that was all Malcolm Sullivan himself.

She thought his kiss had been mind-blowing as a teenager. But the way she felt now? Well, she could never remember feeling this way before. Not with anyone. The way he was taking his time to taste. To tempt. To tease. And then to take. Take everything that she couldn't help but want to give him. Her body melted into his. Her hands threaded up into his hair as she tried to get even closer.

So close. She wanted to be so close to him.

Somewhere in the back of her head, that little voice that had been egging her on before was cheering. But there was another voice. A voice that was getting louder and louder.

Just exactly what do you think you're doing? Just exactly how does this kiss fit into your no-men vow?

And yet, even that voice couldn't stop her from wanting more, from kissing him back just as deeply as he was kissing her. She heard someone moan softly, and realized it was herself.

And then his phone rang. Loud and jarring and breaking the moment into pieces. Shattering the sensual haze that had taken her over.

She pulled back. "You should answer that." Her words came out all breathy, almost as though she was panting to try to get them out. "It might be important."

She pushed out of his arms, stumbled back into the galley. The *River Star* had never felt so small. He was everywhere, filling the space. She could feel his heat, smell his skin. It was too much.

"Josie—" His voice was low, thrumming with a desire that she also felt.

She didn't want to hear what he had to say. She didn't even know her own mind right now, so getting into a conversation about the kiss they'd just shared was a bad idea. "I think the jet lag has really kicked in. I should go to bed. Good night."

She dashed out of the room before he could persuade her to stay. Before she could give in to the urge to throw herself back into his arms, to put her mouth against his, and kiss and kiss and kiss him until she couldn't remember all the reasons why she shouldn't.

But even as she brushed her teeth and changed into her pajamas in record time, then slipped beneath the covers to block out the sound of his voice, she could still hear him whispering her name. *Josie.*

The sounds of him moving around in the kitchen and living room reminded her that he was so close, that all it would take was for her to change her mind, and she could experience more sensual pleasure than she'd ever known. That little voice inside her head was calling to her again, asking, *Why? Why can't you just have a fling with Malcolm? Why does sleeping with him have to mean forever?*

She'd never thought like that in her life. Never so much as considered a one-night stand or, as the case would be with Malcolm, a two-week stand. She'd always believed she needed to be in a relationship before becoming intimate. She'd always believed that deep feelings were important before she could feel something physical. But she'd had all of those things with her ex—at least, she'd believed she had them, and look how that had turned out. She'd been a fool to believe that emotions and great sex had to go hand in hand. Especially when the truth was that the sex hadn't been that great. She'd just told herself that was as good as it got. But in the back of her mind, hadn't she known all along that there was more out there?

Were it not for the fact that jet lag really was finally taking its toll on her after a very long and busy day, who knew what she might've done, what that little voice inside her head might have persuaded her to do? But for tonight, sleeping alone in Malcolm's bed was the only thing left on the menu.

Hopefully, everything else would be much more clear tomorrow.

★ ★ ★

That kiss had felt so right. Malcolm was certain it would have led to more—much, much more—if his phone hadn't rung. Work, of course. How he wished he'd turned it off, but he couldn't have known that one minute he and Josie would be talking about paint colors, and the next they'd be in each other's arms, kissing passionately.

He wanted her. Wanted her so badly he had a feeling a cold shower was in his near future. But would that have been the right move? She wasn't the kind of girl you messed around with. Josie deserved far more than a few hot nights in his bed. And he wasn't up for more.

At least he never had been before…

His grandmother's words echoed in his head, suggesting Josie was the woman he'd been waiting for. But he wasn't certain that was true, and the last thing he wanted was to mess Josie's emotions about. Again.

So if he wasn't going to do that, he needed to keep his hands and his mouth off her for the next two weeks. He already knew the self-control it would take was going to come close to breaking even his strong resolve. Especially when they were working and living in such close quarters.

All the while as he cleaned up the kitchen and got ready for bed, he could sense her presence just a few feet away. He couldn't stop envisioning her in his bed, wondering if she was wearing pajamas or if she had slipped in wearing nothing at all tonight because the houseboat was so warm from the fire in the woodstove.

Each thought made him want her more, made his need ratchet up higher and higher. Already, it was taking every ounce of self-control to leave her be. To get into his small guest bed. To sleep so that he'd be fresh for tomorrow, when they'd meet with his sisters and get to work helping Mari prepare the space for the reading retreat.

But even after a cold shower, every time he tried to sleep, he could taste Josie again, feel her again.

He wanted her again. More than he could ever remember wanting anyone before.

CHAPTER NINE

Josie was up before Malcolm, the time change still not settled within her system. She was glad for the time alone to sit with a cup of coffee and try to calm herself. She needed to remember why she was here. Not to get tangled up with a handsome Brit, but to set up a reading retreat for Mari. A special place where people from all over the world could come to enjoy some time with wonderful books. She could hear Malcolm moving around in the guest room, when there was a knock on the houseboat door. She opened it to find two women who had to be his sisters standing on the deck.

"Hi, you must be Fiona and Alice," she said with a smile. "I'm Josie. Come on inside."

"It's wonderful to meet you at last," Fiona said. She was absolutely beautiful and dressed in casual clothes that looked as though they cost a fortune. Her jewelry was what Josie thought of as understated but expensive, and her watch looked very similar to one that Princess Diana had worn. "Mari's been talking about you a lot. She's so excited about her first reading retreat."

As they stepped inside, Alice sniffed the air. "Mmm, coffee. Don't suppose you've got any to spare?" Alice might look a bit like Fiona, but her style was completely different. It was obvious she worked with her hands, and if Josie hadn't known she was a gardener, she'd have guessed. Her hands were free of jewelry, and she had a pair of gardening gloves stuffed in her pocket.

"Of course." As Josie poured coffee for them and refilled her own mug while she was at it, Alice presented her with a bag of still-warm croissants.

"I stopped by the Elderflower Café on the way here. I can never resist their fresh croissants."

Josie suddenly realized she was ravenous. "There's butter and jam in the fridge," she said, going to get them and putting them on the table. It was funny how comfortable she already felt with Malcolm's sisters, and they hadn't even really spoken with one another yet. It just felt so natural to get settled around the table with them, munch on the croissants, and drink coffee. Well, she and Alice were munching on the croissants, at any rate. Fiona said she wasn't hungry and just sipped coffee.

"It's so fantastic to meet you," Alice said, clearly a bundle of energy. Even dressed in a long-sleeved Kew Gardens T-shirt and baggy jeans and work boots, she was beautiful. "When Mari told us that she was going to turn the cottages into a reading retreat, I thought that sounded like the coolest thing."

"I agree," Fiona said, her words far more measured. But she also had a lovely smile, and if she was less effervescent than her sister, she was no less beautiful for it. Although Josie couldn't help but notice a hint of sadness behind her smile. Or maybe she was just imagining it because of what Malcolm had told her.

"I'm really excited about it," Josie said. "And once we get these cottages sorted out, I know that Elderflower Island will be the perfect place for people to come and lose themselves in books."

"It's been a long time since I've been able to do that," Fiona said in her soft voice. "Honestly, I can't hardly remember the last book I was able to read all the way through."

"Fiona entertains a lot," Alice explained. "She and her husband, Lewis, lead very active social lives."

There was an edge to Alice's words, but no malice. Okay, maybe a little when she was talking about Fiona's husband, but it was obvious that she loved her older sister very much.

"I still think you should come to one of my gatherings sometime," Fiona said to Alice. "I'd love for you to meet some new people, instead of always talking to your plants."

Alice laughed. "I love talking to my plants. They're more interesting than some people. But thanks for the offer."

"I'm putting together the party for Mari's book launch in a few days. I hope you'll be able to attend," Fiona said to Josie.

"I wouldn't miss it. I had a chance to see the book when we first met a couple of days ago. It's a beautiful story that both children and adults are going to love."

"I can't believe she showed it to you first!" Alice said. "I've been dying to see it live and in the flesh. If I had time today after looking at the garden, I'd go by and see it, but I'm afraid I'm going to have to dash off pretty quickly. In fact, I really need to get over there now." She turned toward the bedrooms and hollered, "Malcolm? Aren't you beautiful enough yet?"

He stepped out, looking so good in a T-shirt and jeans that Josie's breath actually left her. She was beyond glad that his sisters were present when she first had to face him, as she felt all the awkwardness of the kiss between them, as well as the way she'd bolted.

However, Malcolm showed no sign of even remembering their passion last night.

He said, "Good morning," in a way that took in all three women, then he turned to Alice. "Look what the cat dragged in," he teased. "And, Fiona, good to see you too."

The siblings all smiled at one another.

"I just need to mainline a cup of coffee, and then I'm ready to go." He smelled the air. "Someone brought croissants. Tell me there's one left."

Alice shook her head, then laughed. "Of course I made sure there was one for you. Do you think I want to deal with you being Mr. Cranky Pants all morning?" She turned to Josie. "Be warned. When he doesn't eat, he's not pleasant to be around."

Josie enjoyed watching the three of them together. Fiona got up and poured a cup of coffee for Malcolm, then handed him a croissant on a plate. She was obviously very nurturing, and Josie hoped that what Malcolm had said about her husband's being a jerk was just brotherly overprotectiveness. It didn't seem fair that someone as nice as Fiona should have anything less than perfect love.

A few minutes later, they headed off to the cottages. Alice walked with her, while Fiona and Malcolm walked some distance behind them.

"Thank you so much for helping with this project," Josie said to Alice.

"No, thank *you*. I've been dying to get my hands on the manor house gardens for years. I'm hoping that if I do a great job with them, the council might consider letting me get my hands on the walled garden."

"I hope that happens for you. Malcolm says you

work at Kew Gardens nearby. I haven't had a chance to go yet, but of course I've read about it and seen pictures. That must be an amazing place to work."

"It's a dream job. I'm so lucky to be able to work in one of the greatest gardens in the world." She gave Josie a little smile. "Of course I want more, though."

Josie laughed. "Sounds reasonable to me."

Alice looked dreamy as she said, "I just always loved the manor house grounds, even as a little kid. I would run around, and could *see* how they used to be, even before I had any training. I've actually been collecting old documents and books that talk about the gardens here, even if it's just a passing reference or a single picture. When Mari said that the owner was allowing her to lease the cottages for reading retreats, I was hoping she would ask me to help. And now that all of you have taken me on board, I'm just bursting with ideas."

As they were walking, she pulled some colorful drawings out of her bag. "Here is what the gardens originally looked like," she said, pointing to what looked to be a photocopy from a book. "Wouldn't it be fun to use the original garden design as a jumping-off point and incorporate areas that are inspired by books?"

"I love that," Josie said. Gardens and reading and stories just seemed to go together.

"I was hoping you would. Here." She pointed to one of the drawings. "We could create a seating area that merges into the secret garden. And then over in this section—" She pointed to another drawing. "—we could have a mystical area straight out of *Alice in Wonderland*, with oversized chairs and bright fabrics. Because when you get lost in a story, it's always a bit like slipping down a rabbit hole into a new world."

"Yes," Josie agreed. "That's exactly how I feel."

When Josie almost stumbled over a large rock, Alice said, "Sorry, I should have waited until we got there to show you this. We can go over it once we're there. I'm just so excited about the possibilities."

"Oh, no, I'm glad you're excited, and there's no need to wait. I actually perfected walking while reading a long time ago. And I almost never trip." They laughed together at that.

For the next few minutes, as they walked and talked, Alice showed her other ideas that she had for the gardens, all of them brilliant.

"I don't know that I have the authority to tell you to go ahead and do everything on your plan," Josie said, "but I want you to know you have two thumbs-up from me. It's going to be absolutely incredible. And I really am thrilled that you're involved with this project."

Alice gave her a hug. "Me too. I feel like we're

friends already." Alice glanced back at her brother and then, lowering her voice, said to Josie, "I hope it's been okay staying with Malcolm. I understand he can't get into his flat in the city for a while, so you're stuck with him on the houseboat. But if it's uncomfortable in any way, you know we can find you somewhere else to stay."

Josie tried not to betray any reaction to the idea of sharing *River Star* with Malcolm—or not. If Josie blushed or giggled or got too serious, Alice might guess that something was up. She tried her darnedest to keep her response in the same tone as the rest of their conversation as she said, "Oh, it's great having him right there. It's made it easy for us to go over all the details for this big cleanup at the cottages."

Alice looked a little more closely at her. "You know, the one thing that's a little strange about it is that Malcolm has been glued to his office for as long as I can remember. It's surprising that he is suddenly willing to take an extended vacation to do grunt work on Elderflower Island."

"I'm not exactly sure what his motivations are," Josie said carefully, "but it sounds like he already had a vacation planned, and this is how he wants to spend it. Mari is definitely lucky to have him on board."

"She is," Alice agreed, "but I still have to wonder about his huge change of heart. Honestly, this morning it's like he's a different person. He's not normally so smiley and easygoing. Usually, you can't tear him away from his phone or computer." Alice gave her another little smile and nudged her arm as they walked. "I'm starting to think maybe he has a crush on you."

Josie couldn't help but give an awkward little laugh. Which felt like it gave the whole game away. "I doubt it. I don't think I'm his type. He probably dates models and starlets in London."

Alice rolled her eyes. "I hate all his girlfriends. They do tend to be models, and honestly, I know there are lots of women who model and are interesting and intelligent and kind. But he doesn't pick those ones. It's like he chooses someone who will look good on his arm and never challenge him. I don't know why he thinks he has to live out some cliché of the-billionaire-and-the-supermodel."

That nearly stopped Josie in her tracks. *"Billionaire?"*

"Oh yeah," Alice confirmed. "He's insanely rich. He's always trying to get me to take his money to start my own garden center. And he's offered to buy the old music hall on the island for Tom as a silent partner, and he's offered to help Mari financially with the bookshop. But none of us feel right about taking his money. I know I don't. He earned what he's earned on his own. And I, for one, want the satisfaction of doing the same for myself." She grinned. "We'll all happily take his free labor, though."

Still at little winded by this billionaire bombshell, Josie nodded and tried to gather herself together. "There is a great deal of satisfaction in building something from our dreams and turning them into reality. But at the same time, it's also nice to let people lend a hand, especially if they're well meaning. Malcolm has mentioned your love of gardening to me several times already, and I get the feeling he'd love to be a silent investor if you would consider it."

Alice grew quiet for a moment, the longest period of silence since Josie had met her.

"I suppose you're right. I could still have the pleasure of creating something magical while sharing that pleasure with somebody I really care about and who cares about me," she said. "I'll think about it."

By this time, they'd reached the cottages. Josie focused on their future beauty while Alice only had eyes for the grounds. "These gardens. I still can't believe I get to bring them back to life. I'll take some measurements and more notes before I dash off in half an hour to get to work."

"Do whatever you need to," Josie said. "And anything you need, let me know, and I'll try to make it happen."

As Alice walked away, her spiral notebook already

filling up with her notes, Josie joined Malcolm and Fiona. "Sorry, I didn't mean to ignore you," Josie said to Fiona.

"Don't worry about it at all. I'm sure Alice was talking your ear off about the gardens."

"Her ideas are brilliant," Josie confirmed. "I told her I wasn't sure I had complete authority over things and that she should also check with you and Mari, but she has two thumbs-up from me for everything. She's planning to use the historical garden plan as the springboard and then create several special spaces that connect to gardens in popular books. It's a brilliant idea and one that I haven't seen anybody do before."

"She's very good at what she does," Fiona confirmed. "I've recommended her to a couple of friends who needed gardens designed, and they've been extremely pleased." She gave a small smile. "One of them has a hundred-acre estate in Scotland and tried to hire Alice to be her full-time gardener. But even though she kept escalating the salary, Alice wasn't interested."

"I had no idea she's been turning down offers like that," Malcolm said.

"She has her heart set on her own garden center somewhere nearby," Fiona said.

"We really need to make that happen," Malcolm said, more to himself than to the two of them.

Josie hoped the conversation she'd had with his sister had given her another perspective on letting him help her make her dreams come true.

"She's shared her vision with me," Fiona said, "and I think what she'd most like to do is to revitalize the walled garden at the old manor house and create a nursery with plants for sale. Perhaps even a restaurant onsite. But getting permission is difficult, of course, and then there's the financial investment."

"Oh, it would be incredible," Josie said, gazing across at the manor house.

"If anybody can do it," Malcolm said, "it's Alice. At twenty-five, she's the youngest head gardener at Kew." He was so proud of his little sister, it was adorable.

Josie didn't want to be drawn to this softer side of Malcolm, but she couldn't help it. Time and time again over the last few days, he'd proved to be devoted to his family. He was close to his grandmother, wanted to help his siblings, obviously respected his parents. Now he was giving up his vacation to help create a reading retreat. Not the usual holiday plans for a billionaire.

Did that mean she should exclude him from her no-man-ever edict?

"I can't wait to get inside these cottages," Fiona said. "I studied historical furniture and textiles at university. I had thought to go into restoration at one time, but life had other plans."

"You could still do that," Malcolm said. "Lewis doesn't need you around to take care of everything for him all the time. He can hire assistants for that."

"No, I want to take care of him. He's my husband. But it's really nice to take a few hours occasionally to do something like this too."

Josie had the key Mari had given her, and she unlocked the first of the cottages. "Here it is. Prepare yourself. It needs a lot of work. But I thought there might be some chairs and tables and perhaps even some embroidered wall hangings that might be salvageable."

Fiona didn't seem to be listening. She was already exclaiming over a chair.

"This is Georgian. It's an absolute crime that it's sitting here neglected." She ran her hand over the curved back the way she might lovingly stroke a favorite pet. Then she peered closer at the needlework on the seat. "And if I'm not mistaken, this embroidery on the seat cover and back is more than a hundred years old." She tipped the chair to study the underside. She glanced up, her eyes shining with excitement. "It could even be original. That would make it more than two hundred years old. I can't believe this furniture has just been moldering away all these years."

Josie glanced around. "It feels as though someone, sometime in the past, left in a hurry, and nobody's been in until now." She recalled the story of the family who'd lived here and the widow and her son who'd left, never to return. The cottages would be so much better once they'd given them some TLC and elbow grease.

Over the next hour, Fiona took copious notes on the furnishings and the handful of other embroidered pieces. When they had gone through all the rooms, she said, "I have a friend who sells secondhand curtains and rugs that have come out of grand homes. They're gorgeous and a fraction of the price of buying new. And of course I'm happy to do whatever work might be necessary to get everything fitted in the space. It will just depend on how much time I can carve out—" Her phone rang, cutting her off. "Excuse me, I should get this. It's Lewis."

To Josie's ear, she sounded a little nervous as she quickly took the call.

"Hello, darling."

From Josie's end, it sounded like Fiona's husband was barking orders at her. There was no sweet greeting such as Fiona had given him, and the call was over before his wife could say more than, "Yes," and "Certainly, I'll take care of it immediately." Fiona hung up and tucked her phone away in her bag. "I'm afraid I have to run. Lewis needs me to set up a cocktail party for a group of Norwegian businessmen in town for the night. If I leave now, I should just have enough time to get everything in order for it."

"Can't he have someone else do that, Fiona?" Malcolm asked. "Especially since he threw it at you at the last minute?"

"Oh no, I'm happy to do it," Fiona said. She gave him and Josie a kiss on each cheek, and then she was off, her expensive perfume the only thing lingering behind.

Alice had waved through the window earlier as she'd headed to work, so it was just Josie and Malcolm again.

"God, her husband infuriates me," Malcolm said. "All of us. I don't know what she ever saw in him. The way he treats her…"

"She seems fairly happy, doesn't she?"

"No. When we were kids, you should have seen her laugh. She was the wildest one of all of us. But as soon as she met Lewis, she let him turn her into a perfect society robot. Instead of rebelling, she gave in to his every whim. And the problem is, I've heard things about him. Bad things. Whispers in the business community."

"You mentioned that yesterday."

"What I didn't mention is that I'm sure he has a mistress. At least one."

"That's horrible," she managed. Her heart was

hammering. It was all hitting too close to home.

"The woman he's cheating with should be ashamed of herself. She's just as disgusting as he is," Malcolm said.

Josie felt her cheeks flame. "Maybe that woman doesn't know he's married."

Malcolm scoffed at that. "How on earth could anyone not know that the guy they're seeing is married?"

Josie voice was barely above a whisper as she said, "I didn't."

Malcolm gawked at her, clearly stunned by what she'd said. "You were with a married man?"

Her mouth had gone completely dry. This was why she hadn't wanted to say anything to him about it. She hadn't wanted him to judge her.

"I didn't know," she said in a hoarse voice. "I swear I didn't know. I thought I was in love with a good man. He'd even started talking about marriage." How her chest burned to even repeat those lying words. "And then one day, a woman showed up at my door, carrying their baby. She was his wife. So, yes, I think it's possible that Lewis's mistress doesn't know he's married." She felt cold all over, just remembering. "If I could undo every moment I spent with him, believe me, I would. I never intended to hurt anyone. And I'll never stop hating him for all the lies he told me. Every single word was a lie."

Malcolm was silent for a long moment, and she knew that he was disgusted by her now.

"It wasn't your fault, Josie. It was his fault. All of it." His voice rumbled in his chest.

"I should have known. You're right. I should've seen the signs." The words of self-blame came from her throat before she could stop them. She couldn't forgive herself. Not yet.

"No. You've made me see how judgmental I was being to a woman I know nothing about. How could you have known a man you trusted was lying to you? If he's anything like Lewis, he's a master of deception. Probably thrived on the lies. Maybe he got extra kicks knowing that you believed every single lie he told you. That's what guys like that are all about. Who they can fool. Who they can cheat."

"Then why was I ever even drawn to him? Because now I can look back and see what you're seeing. What he was really like. Shouldn't I have been able to cut through his lies?"

"Never underestimate the charm of a snake. Some of the most charming people I've ever met have had the blackest souls," Malcolm said.

"*You're* charming," Josie said.

He laughed suddenly. "I was like a bear with porcupine quills stuck in his paws when I picked you up at the airport. You call that charming?"

"Okay, so maybe you weren't then, but you *can* be really charming. But I don't get the sense that your soul is black."

"In high school, my soul was pretty damn black. But that wasn't the man my parents raised. And it's not the man I want to look at in the mirror." He reached out and took her hand in his. "I'm sorry you were treated so poorly by your scumbag ex. But you have to know it's no reflection on you."

"It's nice of you to say that."

"I'm not just saying it, Josie. I've spent two days with you, and what I know to be true after those two days is that you don't have a mean, bad bone in your body."

She didn't know what to say. Didn't know what to do when it seemed that at any moment he might kiss her again. And she wanted it.

Then he said, "Let's see what absolutely has to be done to make the entrance look welcoming."

He walked away to stand outside the smallest cottage. She was still trying to get her thoughts straight when all of a sudden, she heard a *crack*. One of the very heavy roof tiles made of slate was falling straight toward Malcolm's head.

"Malcolm, watch out!" Moving fast, she tackled him, pushing him out of the way. Both of them tumbled into the dirt just beyond the stone steps of the cottage. The slate shattered, the chips of stone clipping the very edges of her pants and his.

"Are you okay?" she asked. "I didn't mean to knock you over like that."

"Thank you." He put his hands on either side of her face. "That was quick thinking," he said, his low voice rumbling all the way through her, his hard, muscled body warm and strong beneath her as she still lay atop him. "If you hadn't acted so quickly, it could have gone a lot worse. Did it hit you?"

She shook her head, unable to move away from him, loving the feel of his hands on her skin. Her gaze dropped to his mouth. And then shifted back up to his eyes, which she swore were smoldering now.

"I'm all right," she said.

They got up, and he said, "Right, first thing we'll do is get the roof looked at and make sure nobody gets hit by a falling slate." He glanced around. "Some of this rock wall is crumbling, and the stone steps could be made safer. I can do that. In fact, I'd enjoy it."

* * *

Looking down at her, even while he mouthed inanities, Malcolm wanted to tear Josie's ex apart with his bare hands. Teach him a lesson and make him pay for what he'd done to her, for the way he'd hurt her. But more than anything else, right now all he wanted was to kiss her again.

He couldn't stop himself from leaning forward, giving her lots of time to pull away, but she didn't. Instead, her eyes widened, and her lips parted in clear invitation. He leaned in slowly, breathing in her vanilla scent, watching her eyes flutter closed, and then his lips were on hers.

This warmth was more than simple lust. He pulled her hard against his body and deepened the kiss, hearing a little moan of pleasure in her throat as she threw her arms around him and kissed him back with everything she had. It was a long time before they pulled apart, and he felt shaken by the deep emotion he felt.

"Last night, I tried to convince myself kissing you wasn't this good. But it is. So damn good I don't ever want to stop."

"I don't want to stop either," she said, her voice sounding no steadier than his. "But I need you to know I'm not ready for a relationship. Not ready for anything that could be even remotely serious. Not after what happened with my ex."

"I'm not looking for a relationship either."

What she just said should have been music to his ears. But all he could think was, *Why not? Why not fall deeper, just this once?* Because she was special. What was he waiting for? Why was he continuing to hold back?

At the same time, he couldn't break his promise to

her. "I vowed I wouldn't hurt you again," he reminded her.

She stared into his eyes for several long moments. Her curves pressed against his, her body warm and soft. Her lips were so kissable, he almost gave in and took them with his. But he needed to wait for what she was going to say. For the decision that he could tell she was trying to make.

"I've never done anything like this before. But I believe you. I believe you won't hurt me again. And I want this. I want you. Eyes wide open. These two weeks only."

He was so tempted, even though a part of him was saying this wasn't right. That Josie deserved more than two weeks together in bed. More than being friends with benefits.

But in the end, he wanted her too much to say anything other than, "So we'll just be friends? Really, really good friends?"

She nodded. "No messy emotions." She suddenly looked shy as she said, "Just great—"

"—sex," he finished for her.

"Yes," she said, barely above a whisper. "Just great sex."

He couldn't hold back a smile, even as he shoved his concerns away. He'd be an absolute fool to turn Josie down.

CHAPTER TEN

Josie tried not to let nerves get the best of her as they walked from the manor house cottages back to Malcolm's houseboat. But there was no way to stop the fluttering in her belly or her worries that she somehow wouldn't measure up. After all, she hadn't been with very many men. And she suspected that Malcolm had far more experience than she did. On top of that, what would he think of her body? She was no supermodel. Just a totally normal woman, with unexceptional curves and an average percentage of body fat. What if, once she was naked, he didn't like what he saw?

Oh, if only this walk weren't so long. The longest fifteen minutes of her whole life. Long enough for her to think maybe the best idea would be to call the whole thing off. To say she was just kidding. To say it was better if they focused on the project at hand and didn't tangle things up with friendly sex.

"I swear," he said, "I can hear every single one of your thoughts."

His comment startled her, made her laugh. "That

obvious, huh?"

He stopped on the path, not caring that other walkers and bikers had to go around them. "Whatever you're worried about, don't be. Whatever we do together, it's going to be great. And if you don't like it, don't want to keep doing it, you just tell me, and we'll stop."

She swallowed hard, nodding. "I appreciate that. I know you'd never make me do anything I don't want to do. It's just…" It was embarrassing to talk about her lack of experience. But if she was about to take off her clothes and roll around with him, she should be able to say this, shouldn't she? "I haven't… I haven't been with very many people."

He kissed her then. Just pulled her close and kissed the breath out of her. Kissed all the thoughts out of her too. Maybe that was his goal—and if it was, it worked like a charm. "I'm glad, Josie. The truth is, I haven't either."

She looked at him in surprise.

"I'm not saying that I haven't earned my reputation as a bit of a playboy," he told her. "But it's far less earned than people think. One-night stands got old pretty quick when I was younger. And I like to think I have some standards."

Hearing that did help put her mind at ease a little. Maybe the playing field wouldn't be that uneven.

Oh, who was she kidding? It was still totally uneven. Because he was Malcolm Sullivan. And she was just normal.

"I'm not a supermodel," she blurted. Then, realizing what she had said and how it sounded, she felt compelled to add, "I mean, of course I'm not. You can see that. You don't need me to tell you that. But I just don't want you to—"

"You're beautiful, Josie. The most beautiful woman I've ever kissed."

That made her laugh again. "That's really nice of you to say, but you don't have to lie."

But he didn't laugh. He only looked more serious. "I'm not lying. You're beautiful on the outside. And you're beautiful on the inside. Let me tell you, it's quite a combination. Every time you smile, you make my head spin. I haven't been able to think about anything but you since I picked you up from the airport."

She blinked at him, wanting to believe him, but finding it so hard to do.

"I don't know what to say—what to think."

"Then don't. Just come back to the boat with me and let me love you."

He kissed the gasp from her lips. She knew how he meant the word *love*. In a purely physical sense. That he would be making love to her body. And yet, just hearing him say it did something to her. Made her heart flip inside her chest. Made her feel a little breathless.

Most of all, despite wanting to keep her heart closed off, she longed for an even deeper love. For a love that went straight to the heart and stayed there. The kind of love that would last forever. A love that she had written off after the heartache she'd been through.

In time, they finally pulled apart.

They all but ran back to *River Star*. Her doubts had been, at least for the moment, overwhelmed by desire—stronger than she'd ever felt for anyone. She was glad to see that his hands were shaking just a little bit as he unlocked the door to let them in.

Once they were inside, there was no time for her worries to come back, because he was pressing her back against the door, covering her mouth with his again. Oh God, the way he kissed. Even though his lips were on hers only, it felt like they were roaming every part of her.

And then they did—over her face, her cheekbones, her closed eyelids, her chin, then down to her neck, where she found herself arching to give him better access. Of its own volition, one of her legs moved to wrap around his hips, to pull him closer. He lifted his lips from her skin.

"Too many clothes. I need you naked. I need to see

you. Feel you. Taste you."

She couldn't say anything, couldn't think anything, except, "Yes. Please."

In the back of her mind, she realized she was begging. Already begging him for all the pleasure that he could give her.

But it didn't feel wrong. It didn't feel like giving up her power. No, on the contrary, it felt like he was showing her just how powerful she was. She held power over him that he could want her this badly. This much.

He slowly dropped his hands from her hips and moved back just enough that he could reach for the top button of her jeans. He held his hands there for a few beats and looked her in the eyes. "Promise you'll tell me if any of this isn't okay with you. Promise you'll ask me to stop if you want me to stop."

She couldn't speak, could only nod. But she knew she wouldn't ask him to stop. Because she was going to love every single second of this, even if she'd never done anything like this before and even if, deep inside, she was still a little scared.

She held her breath, not letting it go until he'd popped that button free. And then the zipper came down, and he was still looking her in the eyes as he pushed the denim from her hips. Let it fall at her feet. She kicked off her shoes and stepped out of the pants.

He finally lowered his gaze, letting it roam to her hips and her bare legs.

Of course she hadn't packed any of her fancy lingerie. Heck, she'd burned it all after she'd learned the truth about her ex, not wanting it to remind her how foolish she'd been when she bought it, hoping to tempt and entice him. Now she was just in plain black panties.

Malcolm didn't say anything, but from the way his breathing sped up, it didn't look like he was disappointed.

He reached for the hem of her shirt next, slowly pulling it up over her abdomen, the tips of his fingers lightly tracing her skin, sending shivers all through her. He lightly grazed the outer curves of her breasts through the fabric of her bra, the same plain black fabric as her underwear. And then he pulled the shirt over her head, her arms going up so that he could get it all the way off.

And then she was standing before him, wearing very, very little.

"You're even more beautiful than I thought. Absolutely perfect."

He lowered his mouth to hers, threading his hands into her hair and kissing her so passionately she could hardly believe that any of this was actually happening. She'd never thought to be the object of anyone's desire. But what Malcolm seemed to be feeling for her, how could it not be real? When her ex had told her how much he loved her, that she was his everything, he'd never kissed her like this. Like he never wanted to let her go. Like she was all of his dreams come true. This was better than any kiss she'd ever read about in any book or seen in a movie.

Again, he kissed his way from her lips, over her cheeks, down into the hollow beneath her chin and over her collarbones. This time, he didn't stop there, because there were no clothes in his way anymore. Well, almost.

As he rained kisses over her shoulder, he gently slid one bra strap aside. She inhaled a shaky breath as she felt the fabric fall, and then he did the same to the other side, not yet touching her breasts, not until those straps were falling, and the cups were falling away, too, her slightly labored breathing raising her breasts higher and higher in the fabric that remained to cover her. And then it was gone, the clasp in the back undone before she even realized it, her bare flesh springing free into his hands. His thumbs moved gently over her, over the swell of aroused skin and then the tender peaks.

She was aching for more, for more of his touch, aching for him to do exactly what he did—he lowered his mouth to her, pressing fervent kisses along the upper swells of her breasts, one at a time, but never,

never going to the part of her that ached the most. Until at last, he laved that aroused skin, drawing moans from her lips. Moans that she couldn't possibly contain. That seemed to drive him on. Drive him further. Again and again, he went from one breast to the other, loving them with his tongue, his lips, even the faint edge of his teeth.

He drove her crazier and crazier. Made it so she couldn't control the flexing of her hips into his. A silent plea for more. He must've understood, because the next thing she knew, he was dropping to his knees, running kisses down over her rib cage, her belly button, her hip bones. And then he was sliding his thumbs into the sides of her panties and pulling those down over her thighs. There was no room anymore for embarrassment or fear. There was only a desperate need. Need for him. To take her. To claim her. A need for her to give herself to him wholly in this moment, the future be damned.

He pressed his lips to her sex, and a moan escaped her throat. She tilted her head back against the door. They'd never even made it farther inside. He lifted one of her legs, rested it over his shoulders, opening her to him, and she loved every second of it. Loved the way he played over her, in her, with his fingers, his mouth.

She couldn't catch her breath. Barely knew how she was able to remain standing. Knew she would have collapsed if he hadn't been holding her up. Everything was rising higher. Higher. So high that she could hardly believe how sweet it was. How sinfully, wonderfully sweet his touch was. His intimate kisses.

And then she was leaping. Flying. Soaring. Higher than she ever had before. His name on her lips. Her body shuddering as he held her. As he took her even higher. Not stopping until he'd wrung every last ounce of pleasure from her.

And, *oh*, what pleasure it was.

★ ★ ★

Malcolm had never felt like this before. The only thing that mattered was Josie's pleasure. Of course, he always wanted his partners to feel good, but the truth was, there had always been a selfish component to it. He had always wanted something for himself too. But tonight, it honestly didn't matter to him if all he did was make her come over and over and over again. With no release for himself. Simply giving her pleasure was the greatest pleasure he'd ever known, he realized. Just that alone, just hearing her cries, feeling her body growing warm and damp and then breaking apart beneath his tongue and hands—hell, it was so damn good he'd never experienced anything like it. Never realized that sex could be more than it had previously been for him. Slowly, he kissed his way back up her body.

Every inch of her was sweet. Perfect. He lingered over her curves, and by the time he was standing, he was desperate to start all over again.

Her lips tilted up in a slightly shy smile as she looked into his eyes. "That was... amazing."

He loved the complete honesty with which she told him her feelings. Whether she was nervous. Whether she was shy. Whether she was loving the way he'd made her feel.

"That was the most amazing thing I've ever felt." Then her eyes clouded. "But you haven't even—"

He kissed her before she could finish the sentence. Kissed her to say without words just how much she pleased him. Just how much he adored giving her pleasure. "I want to take you to my bed," he said as he drew back. "I want to make you come apart again and again. That's all I want."

This time, she was the one pressing her lips to his, kissing him sweetly, but with a new confidence, it seemed. And even more desire than before. "That sounds incredible," she said softly. "But I'd love more than that. I want all of you, Malcolm. For the next two weeks, or for however long we're both having fun, I don't want you to feel you have to hold anything back. Whatever you want to give me, I want it. All of it."

He groaned, her words inflaming him further. He

lifted her in his arms and strode back to the main bedroom, where she had been sleeping without him for the past two nights. He laid her on the bed, allowing himself to take his fill of staring. Just staring and loving every part of her.

"I could gaze at you for hours." He saw her cheeks flush, watched other parts of her flush, too, but she didn't cover herself up.

"I want to take *your* clothes off now. I want to stare at you too." She sat up on the bed and opened her legs, pulling him into the V of her thighs. She put her hands flat on his chest. His heart was racing, and he knew she could feel it. Knew she could feel how she was affecting every part of him.

"My heart," she said. "It's racing that fast too."

"Good," he said. "I'd hate to be the only one who feels this way. Who wants this much."

Slowly, she slid her hands beneath his T-shirt. His abdominal muscles flexed and pulsed beneath her exploring hands. "You have so many muscles. You're so hard all over."

"*Hard* is the right word for it," he teased, loving it when she laughed softly. And then she was pulling his shirt up over his head. He liked the way her eyes widened when she saw his bare chest.

"Do you live in a gym? I thought you were working all the time."

He shrugged, enjoying her frank enjoyment of his body. "I do work out some, run and do weights, and get out on the river when I can. But I admit I got good genes from my parents. We tend to build muscle pretty quickly, we Sullivans."

Somewhere along the way, though, it seemed that she had stopped listening, because she was pressing her lips to his skin, first to his pecs, which instinctively flexed beneath her lips, and at the same time, running her hands over his abdomen again and then around his lower back, sliding her fingers beneath the denim of his jeans over his hips.

He never wanted her to stop kissing him. Touching him. In the same way that he worshiped every inch of her, he felt that she was doing the same with him. That she was enjoying the journey to pleasure as much as she would enjoy the eventual explosion when they came together. She was still kissing his chest, his neck, and then his lips. Then she moved her hands to the fastening of his jeans. Her fingertips trembled slightly as she undid it and then pulled down the zipper. And frankly, he wasn't feeling much steadier than she was.

Every second with Josie was glorious. The sexiest, hottest evening he'd ever known.

She pushed the denim down off his hips, and his boxers went with them. His damn boots were still on, and he gave a growl as he kissed her and then turned to yank them off. As soon as he was completely free of his clothes and shoes, he leaned over her on the bed.

She laughed, and the breathy sound reverberated through the small shiplap room. He'd brought women here before, when he was younger and lived on board, but making love with a woman in his bed on *River Star* had never felt so joyful.

For a moment, he dreamed about just locking them in and making love to her over and over until they ran out of food.

But that wasn't realistic, especially as Mari was counting on both of them. So tonight, he'd live out that fantasy as much as he could. Tonight, he'd love her in every way that she wanted, just in case she woke up in the morning and changed her mind. He had to get his fill of her. Even though a voice in the back of his head told him that would never happen, he had to at least try.

He rolled over so that she was straddling him, so beautiful, luminous as the setting sun poured in through the window. "My river goddess. That's what you are."

He didn't know where those words came from. He just knew they were true. That she felt like the one thing that had been missing all these years. That having her here, on *River Star*, made the houseboat feel like a true home.

She laughed, another wonderfully warm sound. "I love that," she said with a smile. *"River goddess."*

She leaned down to kiss him, her breasts against his chest, all of her teasing him with a promise of even more pleasure. She began to run kisses down his chest again and then lower, low enough that he was soon groaning as she tasted him with her tongue, with sweet little kisses that drove him crazy. But when she took him into her mouth he knew he wouldn't be able to handle another second.

A little rougher than he intended, he lifted her back up over him. "Condom." The word was raw, barely intelligible. "In the top drawer."

Please God, let there be at least one left. He hadn't had sex on his boat in so long. But thankfully, his wish was granted, because there was a partial box there.

"You had me worried," she said. "All I could think was, what if there wasn't one in here?"

"Thank God there is," he said, taking it from her and shoving it on. "I need you. Now. I can't wait."

And neither could she, it seemed, because she was moving her hips so that she could take him in, her wet center clasping around him, welcoming him home.

Sweet Lord. It felt so good.

She stopped him after only the first couple of inches. "It's been so long," she said, her breath coming in pants.

"Take it as slow as you want," he urged her. "I'm not going anywhere."

And then he reached up, one hand in her hair, the other still on her hips, and he kissed her again. Long and slow and hot. And her body responded, opening up even more for him. Taking even more of him in. Taking him in so deep, so true, that it was all he could do just to whisper her name against her lips.

"Josie."

But she was lost to him. Lost to pleasure. Just as he was. As she moved, rocking into him again and again, he moved his other hand down to her hips and rocked with her. Both of them completely ensnared by ecstasy. Ecstasy that grew bigger and stronger with every thrust. With every gasp of pleasure. Until he couldn't wait anymore. And all he could do was give her everything that he was. At the exact moment that he erupted inside her, her orgasm came with more shuddering breaths as she shattered over him, her body drinking him in even deeper, tighter, hotter.

This was everything he'd ever wanted.

She was everything he'd ever wanted.

CHAPTER ELEVEN

Josie woke to the sound of Malcolm's heartbeat beneath her ear, the feel of his hard body beneath hers, and moonlight spilling in through the bedroom window. As she stirred, she felt his large hand caress her back. "I didn't mean to fall asleep. What time is it?" Just then, her stomach grumbled.

He laughed softly. "Obviously time to feed you." He put a finger beneath her chin and tilted her face up to his, kissing her softly. "And then... It's time for more."

She shivered at the sensual intent of his words. Every part of her was already aching for more, even though he'd already given her more pleasure than she'd ever known was possible.

"You better get out of bed quick, before I forget about feeding you altogether. How about we wrap up in the rugs and take a couple of glasses of wine up to the roof deck?" he suggested. "I'll cook tonight."

The last thing she wanted to do was leave a bed that he was in, but she also knew that they really did need to eat. Not only because they'd had an incredibly busy day and had another one on tap for tomorrow, but because they needed to keep up their strength for more lovemaking.

She dragged herself away from him, trying not to blush as she walked naked from the bedroom into the living room, with Malcolm just steps behind. She grabbed a blanket and wrapped it around her body, but he wasn't nearly as modest, remaining completely nude as he followed her.

Her laptop was sitting on the table in the galley, and she told him she'd check email while he cooked.

While they were working to clean up the cottages, she was squeezing in email conversations and video calls with the people who'd signed up for the retreat, already suggesting titles they might want to read and making lists of books to stock for when they got to Elderflower Island.

"You work nearly as hard as I do," Malcolm said as he got to work. "And I'm a workaholic, as I believe you've pointed out."

"I love what I do, and once this retreat is organized, I won't have to work so many hours."

After she read an email from a woman reeling from a recent divorce, Josie offered sympathy and made some notes on titles that might help with the woman's bitterness, which was apparent in her email. Josie put

The Dance of Anger by Harriet Lerner on her list.

When she'd replied to the three emails that she needed to, she shut her laptop.

Malcolm uncorked a bottle of wine and poured two glasses. "You take these up, and I'll be there shortly."

It felt so naughty and decadent to be completely naked beneath the blanket, but holding the wine, she headed up the stairs to the rooftop deck.

It was late enough that no one was out. All the boaters had gone, and even the neighboring houseboats were dark. Whatever happened up on this deck tonight, no one would see them. She shivered again at the thought, amazed at who she had become in such a short period of time. She hardly recognized herself. She'd never been a woman who threw caution to the wind and decided to have a fling. She certainly wasn't a woman who planned to have sex on the roof.

Because, obviously, that was in the cards. And she loved that it was.

She loved that Malcolm was so different from her, that he would even think of something like this. And she was entranced by his lovemaking. Her entire body tingled just from her thoughts about it, from remembering the way his hands, his mouth had moved over her. Oh yes, it had been incredible. And he was promising her more. So much more. She couldn't wait. And thankfully, it didn't seem she would have to, because she heard his footsteps.

He was coming up with another of the blankets wrapped around his shoulders, carrying a large tray of what looked like meats, cheeses, and French bread.

"When did you get that? I've been with you all day."

"I called in a delivery, figuring we might be too tired and too busy to go to the market."

She looked at him. Surely he hadn't thought…?

Obviously reading her mind, he laughed. "No, I didn't predict we'd be busy in this way. I just thought we might be busy with the cottages."

Phew. She wouldn't want him to have seen her as a sure thing. Although, would it really have been a bad thing if he had? After all, it wasn't like she hadn't had more pleasure than she could ever have imagined.

He took a seat on the chaise longue with the thick cushions that she'd sat on by herself the previous night. "Come sit with me," he said.

She picked up the wineglasses and walked over from the railing, where she'd been standing looking out into the night. The moon wasn't full, giving just enough light for her to be able to make her way to him. But that was just as well, because she might've been nervous about being naked with him here had there been a fuller moon.

When she got close enough, he opened up his blanket and spread his legs. "Sit between my legs," he suggested.

Oh, it was already even naughtier. That hadn't taken long.

She did as he suggested, moving the blanket around to the front so that they were skin to skin. She settled against him, loving the heat of his body against hers, the hardness of his muscles against her softer skin.

"You feel so good," he said in a low voice, pressing a kiss to the side of her neck.

That might've been the beginning of more lovemaking had her stomach not growled right at that moment. They both laughed.

"Okay, I get it. Food first," he said.

He loaded a freshly cut slice of French bread with cheese and prosciutto, feeding it to her. Food had never tasted better. It had never been fresher. And she'd never felt more alive, head to toe, inside and out.

When she'd finished it, she gave in to the urge to lick his fingers clean. Not just stopping at that, but sucking them inside her mouth, laving his fingertips with her tongue. She turned her face to the side so that he could steal a kiss, one she very much wanted to give him. And then she fed him. He seemed ravenous, wolfing the food down. Or maybe it was simply that he wanted to get the eating over and done with so that they could move on to other pursuits.

They ate and drank like that until the platter was nearly empty and their glasses were too. And then he was running his hands over her, from her collarbones down over the sides of her breasts and her waist and down to her hips and down her thighs, then he ran them in the opposite direction, warming her skin at the same time that goose bumps rose across every inch that he touched.

"Do you like this? When I touch you like this?" he asked.

"I love it." Her words seemed to incite him to touch her even more intimately, his hands cupping and caressing her breasts. Learning every inch of her, what made her squirm with pleasure, what made her gasp, what made her moan, and then he was moving one hand farther down, down over her stomach, into the aching flesh between her legs.

She closed her eyes, her head going back against his shoulder, her cheek against his. As he touched her, finding her wet and hot, all for him, her legs fell open naturally to give him better access to her. To her pleasure. Soon, she couldn't stop her hips from moving up against his hand. Wanting. Demanding. Needing more. And he gave it to her. Everything she needed. Everything she desired.

He moved inside of her first with one finger and then two, bringing her so much pleasure. So much that, before she was even aware she was that close to the peak, she cried out, her body trembling against his as he took her over the edge and then beyond. And beyond some more, to even farther reaches of bliss. But it wasn't enough. Nothing would be enough until he was inside of her again. Thankfully, he felt the same way, because she heard the tearing of a condom wrapper, and she shifted her languid body just enough that he could put on protection.

She was about to turn to face him when he whispered in her ear, "No, like this. Just like this."

He put his hands on her hips and shifted them, shifting her, lifting her so that she was over him and able to take him inside. Oh, this was wicked. Beautifully, perfectly wicked with both of them covered by the blankets as she rode him, her back to his front, his hands on her hips, moving her, directing her for both their pleasure. The greatest pleasure anyone had ever known. Surely, there was nothing better than this.

She gazed up at the midnight sky above, inky black with a few stars twinkling as if just for them. With his heart beating against her back and her name on his lips, they both came apart at the same moment. One body, it seemed. One heartbeat. He turned her face as she was about to cry out and captured her cry with his kiss. A deep, passionate kiss that only bonded them further.

In that moment, he was everything.

Everything she'd ever wanted.

CHAPTER TWELVE

Malcolm woke the next morning to find Josie standing beside the bed, holding a mug of coffee. "We need to go soon, or we're going to be late to meet Mari at the bookshop to brief her on our progress."

He took the mug and put it on the side table, and then he took her hands in his and pulled her onto the bed. "Not so fast." Then gave her a proper good-morning kiss, the way she should have woken up in the first place. He thought he might've convinced her when sixty seconds later, she was kissing him back just as passionately.

But then she withdrew, pushing back up to standing. "Seriously, we really should get going in a few minutes."

He sat up in bed, the covers falling to reveal his bare chest and pool around his hips. "Is everything okay? You're not regretting last night, are you?"

She shook her head, her color going slightly pink. As if their kiss hadn't been enough of a reminder. "No, of course I'm not regretting any of it. It's just that I want to make sure that nobody finds out about… this."

It shouldn't have grated so much to have their lovemaking reduced to *this*. After all, that was the way he'd looked at it his entire life. As something fun, something pleasurable. But not particularly world-changing, when all was said and done.

"Okay," he said, the word coming out grumpier than he intended.

Of course she picked up on it. "You don't want anyone to know, do you?" She looked confused. "I mean, wouldn't it just get more complicated if your family and friends though that we were an actual couple?"

"Right." But it didn't feel at all right. "It's fine." But it didn't feel fine at all.

What felt fine was having Josie in his arms. What felt fine was laughing with her. What felt fine was working together to clean up the manor house cottages so she could run her reading retreat. Hiding the fact that they were together, even if just for a little while, felt anything but fine.

Obviously sensing that he was better left to himself at the moment, she said, "I'll just finish getting my things together while you hop in the shower and get dressed."

He was ready fifteen minutes later, and they headed off on foot to the bookshop. He kept wanting to grab her hand. Kept wanting to hold it. Kept wanting to stop and kiss her on the path, the way he had yesterday. They hadn't been worried about anyone seeing them then, had they?

He was being a grumpy git again. And she was right. It would just get messy if his family found out. Messes were bad, he knew that. He was all about efficiency. About right action. It was just that *he'd* always been the one wanting to keep things on the down-low. Josie had surprised him by being the first to say what was obvious, that was all. What they'd agreed on already.

He actively worked to shake off his mood.

They were soon walking through the door of the bookshop. Mari smiled and greeted them, but she definitely looked less calm than usual.

"I take it you've had a very busy couple of days," he said after they hugged their hellos.

She nodded. "It's been a madhouse in here. It's fantastic, of course, because I can always use more business. But I had no idea a bookstore could ever be this busy."

Malcolm could feel the stress she was trying to hide. He had so much experience with business owners who expanded. Had she taken on more than she could handle? He loved and admired Mari for her go-getter attitude and entrepreneurial zeal, but he knew better than anyone how taking on too much too soon could cause stress.

"I'm really pleased for you," Josie said. "If I get a chance while I'm here to break away from the cottages, I can always come help out in the store."

But Mari shook her head. "Thank you, but you're already going above and beyond by cleaning them up. If you get any spare time, it should definitely be working on the retreat master plan. That's what you came here to do, after all."

Malcolm watched as Josie flushed at Mari's words. He knew what she was thinking. That she had come here to work on the reading retreat, not to sleep with him. But she had nothing to feel bad about. They'd put in a full day's work. And they were going to get the cottages ready in time. A little downtime in the sack wouldn't hurt anyone.

"I could work on the master plan here in the shop so you'd have help if you needed it. I think I'd do a better job anyway, surrounded by books and readers."

Instead of surrounded by him?

"We have our schedule to go over, if you have a few minutes," he said, hoping to pull Josie out of her guilty conscience.

"That'd be great," Mari said. "Can I get either of you a cup of tea?"

"No, thanks, I just had coffee," Josie said.

"Me too. I'm fine," he said.

They went to sit down, and Josie picked the absolute farthest seat from him. Which didn't make any sense, given that they'd made the plan together, and they should present it together. He got up and moved beside her, making her flush even more. It was one thing to keep their affair on the down-low. It was another to act as though they didn't even like each other.

She took the schedule they'd put together out of her bag and laid it on the table. For the next several minutes, they walked Mari through the plans.

Painters and cleaners. Plus, an electrician and a plumber he'd insisted on hiring to ensure the old wiring and plumbing could handle the demands of the retreat. He was not going to put Josie or the guests at risk of a fire. "Josie and I are going to take the morning to clear out some of the junk that's accumulated in the buildings over the years."

"But don't worry," Josie added. "We're not going to get rid of anything that's potentially valuable."

Mari looked at them, her eyes shiny. "I don't know how to thank both of you enough. I honestly couldn't have done any of this without you. Even now, I feel terribly guilty that I can't lend a hand, but I've got the book launch party this evening." She put a hand to her stomach. "I'm as nervous as if I'd written the book myself."

"Your father would be very proud of you," Malcolm assured her, knowing it was true.

"Is there anything we can do to help get ready for tonight?" Josie asked.

Once more, he sensed that Mari was feeling overwhelmed. She obviously hadn't anticipated that good publicity and having his grandmother appear at the bookshop, plus the launch of her father's book, would flood the shop with customers. It was a good problem to have, but he could see she was struggling to stay on top of everything.

"No. Owen's been helping me, and I think we have everything under control, but I am sorry I'm not with you at the cottages."

"Don't feel guilty at all," Josie insisted. "This is a really fun project. And we both just want to make it a beautiful space for you and all the people who are going to come to read and get away from it all for a little while on Elderflower Island."

He could have hugged Josie in that moment. She'd said exactly the right thing. Already, Mari looked calmer.

Mari smiled at them both and then looked back at Josie. "Elderflower Island is already doing wonders for you. You have that same bright-eyed expression that I know I did when I arrived here. The island is just so magical, isn't it?"

Josie looked for a moment like a deer caught in the headlights. As though Mari were intimating that more than just being on the island had put the glow in Josie's cheeks. Finally, she snapped out of it and said, "Oh yes, it really is magical here. I've loved every single second I've been here so far."

He knew he shouldn't tease her, knew he'd agreed to keep everything secret, but the devil inside of him couldn't resist. "We've enjoyed the rooftop deck on my boat a couple of nights. It was particularly nice out last night, wasn't it, Josie?"

She almost shot him a glare, then caught herself at the last second. "It was really nice up there."

"Is living on a houseboat as romantic as it seems?" Mari asked Josie.

This time, she didn't answer with words. All she did was nod. Clearly, she felt that actually using words might betray her.

Just then, the door chimes sounded. Malcolm's brother Tom and his young daughter, Aria, walked in.

"Mari, do you have the book for me?"

Mari got up, a huge smile on her face as she went to hug the little girl. "Of course I do. You're getting the very first copy. I saved it just for you."

She gave Aria a copy of her father's book. Aria hugged it to her and then ran to the children's section and its smaller-sized chairs. She settled herself and opened the book as though she was unwrapping the most precious gift. Tom watched his daughter with affection, then seeing she was settled and happily reading, he walked over to say hello.

"You must be Josie. I've heard a lot about you already, from practically everyone."

Malcolm noted his brother wore his most charming smile. The one that made women's panties fall down around their ankles.

Josie stood to shake his hand. "It's lovely to meet you. I think you and Aria are the last of the family, apart from your parents, that I have yet to meet."

"How are you liking the island so far?" Tom asked.

"Oh, it's absolutely beautiful. I'm having a wonderful time."

"I'm glad to hear it. I was worried that Malc might not be showing you a good time. He's always glued to his phone, or about to head into a meeting. Whereas I know all the great places for nightlife. I'd be happy to show you around the city if you can spare an evening."

Malcolm narrowed his eyes. His brother was out-and-out flirting with Josie. All but asking her on a date. "We're busy," he growled. "The cottages need a lot of work. That's why we're here right now—to go over everything with Mari before we head over there and get back to work."

Tom's eyebrows went up. "Okay, but…" He

turned back to Josie. "If you need to get away from Mr. Cranky Pants here, just let me know. I'll give you my number."

Mr. Cranky Pants? It was obvious Tom spent a lot of time with a five-year-old. Malcolm nearly stopped him from giving Josie his number. Heck, right at that moment, he was stopping himself from slugging his brother.

Aria ran over, the book under her arm. "Hi, I'm Aria," she said to Josie. "Who are you?"

Josie knelt down. "I'm Josie, Mari's friend from the United States. You're so lucky to have the first copy of her father's book."

"I know. Do you want to come over to my special rug with me, and I can read it to you?"

Josie smiled. "I'd love that." She shot another smile at Tom as they walked away, her hand in Aria's.

Obviously, as if Tom's charm wasn't enough, he was wooing her with his daughter. *Damn him.*

Tom shot him a slightly evil grin. "So that's the lie of the land, is it?"

Malcolm didn't pretend not to understand. "She's off-limits to you, Tom."

Tom's eyebrows went up. "But not to you?"

Malcolm would have answered that definitively had he not agreed just an hour ago to keep things with Josie completely secret. "It's complicated."

"Doesn't seem that complicated from where I'm standing. You like her. She likes you. You date. And then if things start to get serious, you see where it goes from there."

Malcolm frowned. Tom was making things sound easier than they were. "You know better than anyone how messed up relationships can be."

"True," Tom agreed. "Relationships can be a mess. But only if you pick the wrong person."

What had come over Tom? He almost sounded like he was becoming a romantic. Just then, Aria's and Josie's laughter sounded throughout the bookstore.

"She's beautiful, she seems fun, and Mari says she's brilliant at what she does," Tom said. "That's quite a combination."

Malcolm couldn't keep from snarling, "Back off."

"I'm just saying I'm not going to be the only one who notices how great she is." Tom shrugged. "Not that she'd necessarily go for a guy like you. You're not exactly the most cheerful person in the world."

Malcolm knew he shouldn't rise to the bait. He should just shrug off what his brother said. But he was jabbing him in all the places that he knew would get a rise out of him. "If it was between the two of us," Malcolm said, "I'd make damn sure she chose me."

Tom's eyebrows went up again. "Is that a challenge?"

Malcolm refused to be drawn in any farther. "We've got to go. The painters are waiting." But before he left, he had to say one more thing. "Josie's heart isn't for us to battle over. Whatever choices she makes in her life, they're hers, not ours."

He headed over to where Aria was reading the last page of the book to Josie.

"That's the best story I've ever read," Aria said.

"I agree," Josie said.

They were adorable together and instantly made him think how great she'd be with a child of her own. But with his brother's challenging words still ringing in his ears, he was gruffer than he intended to be when he said, "We should head out. The painters are going to be there in a few minutes."

Josie smiled at Aria. "I hope we'll get to read together again someday soon."

"Daddy," Aria called across the bookstore, "can Josie come over and read with me sometime soon?"

Tom smiled at her. "Of course, honey. Josie can spend as much time at our house as she'd like."

At that, Malcolm all but yanked her up off the carpet she and Aria had been sitting on.

She shot him a confused look, clearly wondering what the problem was.

"Bye, sweetie," Malcolm said to Aria, giving her a kiss on the cheek before he dragged Josie out of the bookshop, barely giving her time to wave and call a good-bye to Mari.

"Are the painters waiting to be let in? Is that why we're suddenly in such a crazy rush?"

He knew better than to tell her that Tom had been acting interested in her. What if she preferred his brother over him? And why wouldn't she, when he hadn't exactly been all sunshine and rainbows? Tom had a lot of charm. Even Malcolm could see that.

"We were losing track of time in the bookstore." Again, he was a gruff jerk. Not exactly winning her over, was he?

Though she was still frowning slightly at him, she let his lame explanation go. "Your niece is so sweet," she said. "And your brother seems like an amazing father."

"Aria is great," he agreed. But he wasn't in any mood to say nice things about Tom.

Fortunately, by the time they got to the cottages, the painting contractor Malcolm knew was just pulling up in his van. Malcolm went to speak with him while Josie unlocked all the buildings.

Within minutes, all systems were go. The decorator Fiona had recommended showed up, alongside his sister, who was there to explain what needed to be done with the remnants she had begun to collect. The hours flew by as they answered questions from Fiona, the decorator, and the painters, and continued to clear out the cottages ahead of them. Alice came by during her lunch break, bringing them sandwiches, which they wolfed down before getting right back to work.

The painters would begin the next day, painting the ceilings and trim white. Then Mari, Josie, Fiona, and the professional decorator would decide on wall colors. Meanwhile, there were curtains and soft furnishings to arrange. Mari had been disappointed when she realized there wasn't time to prepare bedrooms, but she'd asked Malcolm and Josie to work out a plan and schedule for when they could be ready. She was definitely feeling optimistic that there would be future retreats.

Malcolm couldn't help noticing how good Josie looked, how he'd catch the faintest whiff of vanilla and know she was near. He couldn't get the feel of her, the taste of her out of his mind.

When she ran upstairs to grab a tape measure she'd left up there, he found an excuse to follow her. She turned an inquiring gaze on him when he shut the bedroom door. Okay, so there was no bed. It was an empty room with boxes of old dishes and junk that needed to be cleared out, but he still found himself in a bedroom with the door shut, alone with Josie. She must have interpreted the expression in his eyes correctly, for he saw the way her breath huffed in, causing her beautiful breasts to rise and her lips to part. He felt as though she were pulling him toward her.

"Malcolm," she said. It was as far as she got before he was pulling her into his arms. She wrapped her arms around him, opening her lips, letting him taste her, tease her.

"I haven't been able to stop thinking about kissing you," he said. "It's been driving me crazy." She tasted so damn good. Hot and sweet, and when she made little moans deep in her throat, his desire ratcheted up to a burning need.

"The bedrooms are quite a shambles," he heard Fiona say just before she threw the door open.

He barely had time to pull away from Josie and walk to the window, pretending to be studying the windowsill while he tried to get his body under control.

"Oh," Fiona said, surprise packed into the single syllable. "I didn't realize you two were up here."

"Just grabbing the tape measure," Josie said in a tone that was probably supposed to sound breezy, but to him sounded guilty. He'd bet his first million that she was blushing.

"Hope we didn't interrupt anything," his sister said as soon as Josie's feet could be heard pounding down the stairs.

"Not at all," he said, hoping his casual tone sounded more believable, but suspecting it didn't. Not to a woman who'd known him her whole life. "I was just making sure there was no dry rot in the windowsill." It was the lamest excuse he'd ever come up with, but why else would he be staring at the window?

"And is there?" Fiona was grinning. He knew it without even turning.

"No."

"Good. Then maybe you can move aside so we can measure the windows for curtains."

After lunch, he found the house so overrun with people that he told Josie he needed to see her outside. She followed him, and he grabbed her hand and led her into the gardens. A hedge so wildly overgrown that it was practically a forest gave him the shelter and privacy he needed. "I don't believe we finished what we started upstairs," he said, pulling Josie back into his arms.

She felt exactly right there, as though she fit, and his entire body exploded with need. How did she do this to him? They couldn't spend too long making out like teenagers, or they'd be missed, but still, he couldn't seem to let her go.

Until a voice trilled far too close for comfort. "Malcolm? Josie?"

Alice. Of course, if it wasn't one sister nearly walking in on him and Josie, it had to be the other.

Josie gave a tiny giggle and pulled away, straightening her hair and shirt. He could have told her she was wasting her time. Her lips were wet and swollen from his kisses, her eyes heavy-lidded with desire. He was certain he looked similarly blissed out.

"Just checking the property boundary," Malcolm called, pleased to have thought up something that sounded half believable.

"Why? Are you planning to buy the place?" Alice laughed, but the idea took root.

Just for a fleeting moment, he imagined buying the cottages so Josie could have retreats whenever she wanted to. He could picture her here, maybe living on the houseboat, or even more heart-poundingly, he imagined the two of them buying a place somewhere together. Somehow he knew that she wouldn't fall in love with his flat in central London. Josie would want a real home, with bedrooms for children and gardens to play in. The image was fleeting, but it warmed him, all the way through to his heart.

They emerged from the brush, and Alice sent him a sharp look that promised massive teasing and intrusive questions later. Hopefully, he would think of something that would satisfy her and still be relatively truthful.

He didn't even know himself what was going on with him and Josie.

CHAPTER THIRTEEN

The day had been a whirlwind from the moment she'd woken. Josie hadn't had so much as a moment to breathe. But that wasn't what had her feeling like she was spinning slightly out of control. It was Malcolm's kisses, kisses he'd given her all day long. Kisses he'd stolen while pulling her into hallways and closets and bedrooms and behind garden walls. Every time, he'd kissed her until her head had spun and she'd been breathless. Several times, they'd almost been caught by his sisters.

Still, they couldn't seem to stop.

She should insist that they hold off until they were back on his boat. But how could she possibly resist him? And how could she pretend she didn't want him as much as he wanted her? It was bad enough that her lips were swollen from his kisses, her cheeks flushed pretty much every minute throughout the day.

But it was the heart that she'd vowed to keep hidden and protected that was proving to be the real shocker. Because with each kiss that he gave her, every time he pulled her close, another little piece of the wall around her heart fell. Every time she heard his laughter with his sisters or one of the workers, another piece fell. And to cap it all off, the day had been warm, and when he'd been helping to patch a broken wall outside, he'd taken off his shirt. She'd barely been able to keep from drooling. She could still hardly believe that she'd had her hands and her mouth all over his gorgeous skin, all those muscles that rippled in the sunlight with a slight sheen of sweat.

It was almost impossible to think straight about the work that she was trying to get through. There had been several times when someone had asked her a question—a question that she should've had a ready answer to—and she had to ask them to repeat it. Because she'd been unable to tear her brain, her body, her heart away from Malcolm. It was foolish, the most foolish path she could possibly walk down. She knew better. Again and again, she reminded herself that she was in the UK for two weeks only. Two weeks that would be wonderful. Breathtakingly wonderful. But that was it. There was no future in what they were doing. She would not just be foolish, but downright crazy to harbor any hope there could be more.

The sun was just beginning to set as everyone left, and Josie locked up the cottages for the night. Malcolm had put his shirt back on, but it didn't really help. She was almost shaky with need for him.

"How did everything go today?" he asked as they headed back to the boat.

"Good." She should give him a bigger answer than that, but her brain wasn't working right at the moment.

He gave her a hungry look. "I feel the exact same way," he said in a low voice that rumbled through every one of her aroused cells. "I can only think of making love to you."

She should have denied that's what she felt. She should have been able to act like she could focus on anything but him. But she wasn't a liar. And she couldn't have got the words out anyway. Instead, she swallowed hard, and when he reached for her hand and picked up the pace as they all but ran back to his boat, she was almost giddy. Giddy with relief and knowing she wouldn't have to wait much longer. That soon they could give in to the need that had only ratcheted up higher and higher throughout the day.

They barely made it inside before they were tearing at each other's clothes. Until they were naked on the couch. She was under him, and he was levered above her. She wrapped her legs around his waist, holding him around his broad shoulders, his mouth lowering to hers, their bodies nearly connected again.

And then he cursed.

"Protection, dammit." He jumped off her, dashing into the stern and returning triumphant. "It's the last one. We need to get reinforcements."

Again, relief bubbled out of her, this time on laughter. "We'll make good use of this one first."

"We damn well will," he agreed as he leaped back onto the sofa with her.

She welcomed him, welcomed him in a way she'd never welcomed any man into her bed, inside of her body. It was as though the whole day had been foreplay. Crazy, desperate foreplay.

She took all of him in, drinking in his kisses, the almost rough caresses of his hands over her skin, her breasts, her stomach, her hips, between her legs. She arched into him, eager for his touch. For everything that he could possibly give her. And she gave him back just as much. Held nothing back, despite all her reminders earlier in the day that she needed to safeguard herself. Or her heart, at the very least.

But when she was with him, and when he was kissing her like this, touching her like this, driving her absolutely wild, making her want more than she'd ever wanted anything or anyone in her life, she forgot about keeping safe, about holding back. And then they came together, both of them wild on the couch, pillows flying off in their haste to have each other, to love each other.

For those moments, everything in the world was right. Everything was perfect. And pleasure had never been more exquisite.

"Wow," he said when they were still clinging to each other, their skin slick with a faint layer of sweat from the exertion of devouring each other.

She smiled into his neck. "That felt really, really good."

He laughed, pressing a kiss to the top of her forehead. "Now, that's an understatement if I've ever heard one."

She laughed as well. "Okay, it might have been the best thing I've ever felt," she admitted.

He grinned down at her. "That's more like it." Then he lowered his mouth to hers, adding, "And I completely agree." He stroked one hand over her bare hip. "Actually, I planned to take you out in the dinghy tonight. Up the river past Hampton Court Palace, to see it lit up in the evening. Not just to tear your clothes off like this."

"Well, I'm not complaining about the clothes, obviously, since I was tearing yours off too. But if there's still time for the boat ride, I'd love that."

With some reluctance, he got up off the couch and pulled her with him. "I need to get the dinghy ready."

"And I'll make something to bring aboard for dinner."

They kissed again, and then they put their clothes back on, and each of them went to do their part.

She felt like she was floating. Flying again. It was like the sweetest treat she'd ever tasted. Like she'd somehow found nirvana with him. With the last person on earth that she would have thought to find it with.

In as stern an inner voice as she could muster, she reminded herself, *This is just temporary. By all means, drink in every moment of the joy of being with him and the pleasure, but don't ever kid yourself that it's forever. Because it's not. He's not looking for anything permanent, and neither are you. You both have your reasons.*

Her reasons, however, made more sense than his. At least to her. She had been betrayed, lied to—of course she wasn't about to go trusting a guy to promise her forever anytime soon. But for Malcolm, she wasn't exactly sure why he seemed to hold himself back from relationships. After all, he had such a close relationship with his own family. It sounded like his parents had a wonderful marriage. So what had happened in his past that could have turned him against the idea of falling in love? Was it simply that he was a workaholic who always put the deal first? But he was giving his time freely to her and Mari, helping to clean and restore the cottages.

Was what had happened with his father when he

was a teenager somehow a part of it? Something inside her felt it must be, but she couldn't quite figure out how the two things would have played off each other.

She would have loved to have asked him. But while having hot sex with him seemed it would make the question okay, since they'd put up the boundaries around it, there was a part of her that thought it wouldn't be a good idea to ask him to explain to her why he was so shut down about love. Maybe he'd think she was desperate, asking him to love her. And asking him why he wouldn't. No, she wouldn't give him that impression. Because that wasn't what she was asking for. Even if the little voice inside her head seemed to think it wouldn't be a terrible idea at all to be loved by Malcolm Sullivan.

It was another beautiful night. Yet again, Josie wanted to pinch herself, hardly able to believe that she was out on the Thames, floating under the twinkling stars, headed toward Hampton Court Palace. And all of that, with Malcolm at the helm.

He'd called his smaller boat a *dinghy*, but she was certain this was no dinghy. The boat was twenty feet long by her estimation, made of a gorgeous, highly polished wood, with leather seats. It was an antique boat, and she could see that he took pride in it.

"You rebuilt this yourself, didn't you?"

He nodded. "It was completely trashed in a junkyard, but I could see its potential. I could see what it once was and what it could be again."

"You said I was the one with the bright outlook," she noted. "But you do too. Whenever you see something that most people would write off, like a broken-down boat or a cottage that's been neglected for years, you use your imagination and your hands and your skill, and you bring it back to life."

He wasn't someone who ate up praise. It was more like he never seemed to think he deserved it. Which he proved yet again when he said only, "I enjoy doing it."

"Have you ever thought of doing it more?" The question fell from her lips before she could stop it. "Of transitioning from the work that you currently do to working with your hands?"

"If I gave up my career to rebuild old boats and cottages, everyone would think I was crazy. I don't like to boast, but what I do is quite lucrative."

"Just because you're good at one thing doesn't mean you have to do it forever, does it? I mean, look at me. I think I was a pretty good freelance editor. I still am, with a couple of clients who I still work with from time to time. But just because I'm good at that didn't mean it was wrong for me to transition into setting up reading retreats. I think people can be good at a lot of things. And I also think that we're not just here necessarily to live one specific life. I mean, we are only here for a limited time, but while we are, we should experience as much as we can. I'm not sure money is the only reason to do something. Is it?"

Belatedly, she realized she was almost lecturing him. "I'm not trying to tell you what to do. It's just that all the books I've read over the years filled me with a longing to experience more and see more of the world. It's partly why the reading retreats made sense. Because it meant I could go and see things and do things and experience some of the things that I read about. Some of the places. Smell the smells in the marketplaces in Morocco. Haggle over a gold leather jacket at a flea market in Paris. See the northern lights in Norway. When you read about places and experiences, that's one way to experience them, but there's nothing like going there in person."

She'd never been to England before, but every book from *The Secret Garden* and those by Jane Austen to modern romances set in Cornwall had had her longing to come here. And now that she had arrived, this country felt like a second home—that's how familiar it was.

He didn't reply for a few long moments. She started to worry that she'd offended him.

But then he finally said, "You're right. We shouldn't be locked into anything in life. After all, I've been saying the same thing about Fiona. That she should try another life on for size. Leave her unhappy marriage and see what else is out there waiting for her. Owen did that, when he left the law and went to work for my grandmother. Alice wants to do that. Tom too."

They motored slowly up the river, but he didn't seem to be seeing it. He seemed to be chewing things over in his head. "I do really like working with my hands. I'm not going to deny, though, that there is a thrill in what I do now, taking a product I believe in and expanding its horizons."

"And that's great, if you love what you do. I'm not trying to convince you to do anything else."

"But I'm not sure I love it anymore," he admitted. "In fact…" He frowned. "I don't. That high I used to get from closing a big deal, it's barely a blip now. Barely even ends up on the radar screen. It's just more of the same old thing. But today, working on the broken wall, fixing it so it looks good and is safe again, that felt good. Really good."

When his frown didn't lighten, she felt she should apologize for upsetting him. "I didn't mean to make everything so serious."

"I'm glad you did," he said. "I've spent enough of my life making pointless small talk." He held out his hand, and she intertwined her fingers with his. "That deal I've been chasing for years seems like the one I really have to complete, and then maybe I'll take some time, think things through. Genevieve, my second-in-command, and I may need a quick trip to New Zealand to sort some things out."

She sensed he was talking to himself, so she didn't comment, but wow, did she feel a clutch of alarm when he mentioned New Zealand. Maybe they had only two weeks together, but she wanted every single one of those days. If he suddenly jetted off to the other side of the world, she'd be brokenhearted, and that scared her, because she had to admit she was developing feelings for Malcolm Sullivan. Feelings that wouldn't just disappear when their two weeks were up.

"I'm glad you're here," he said softly. "Not just here in England, but with me. I like being with you, Josie."

His words made her feel all fluttery inside. "I like being with you too."

Holding hands, they glided up the river, past a number of locks, which she enjoyed helping him with, and then finally they reached Hampton Court Palace.

"I know I keep saying this," she said, "but I feel like my breath has just been taken away."

The brick castle that had once been the home of Henry VIII was absolutely stunning from the river at night. They could see through the back garden to the lights, and to the lit-up trees.

"I've always loved living in Coeur d'Alene," she said. "And even though I've done a lot of traveling over the years, there's nowhere else I ever thought I could move to that would feel like home. But here, all I can think is how hard it's going to be to leave at the end of the two weeks. Everything is so beautiful. So awe-inspiring. I could explore forever in England. Maybe it's because I've read so many English novels, but this feels like a second home."

"And hopefully," he said, "the company isn't too bad either."

She leaned forward to kiss him softly. "The company is great."

He lowered the anchor so that they were able to float in place, then put his arms around her so that they could take in the beautiful night sky, the stars twinkling, and the moon shining above.

He kissed her again, and she realized that if she didn't pull away, they'd never eat dinner. "I think it's time to eat," she said on a laugh.

He helped her set out a mini feast of cold roast chicken, French bread and cheese, and sausage and fruit. Again, the galley had magically produced all the makings of a delicious meal, though she knew it wasn't magic but Malcolm's delivery service that had brought the food.

Clearly, there were some benefits to being a billionaire. Not that she would ever want that kind of stress or pressure for herself. Because even though he said he had once really liked his job—and she was glad that he had—she could imagine how stressful it must've been. How stressful it still was.

She sent a silent wish out into the night that he would find true happiness and pursue it. That he wouldn't let anything hold him back. It was what she wanted for all of her friends. Especially for Malcolm, who felt like so much more than a friend after only this short time they'd spent together.

When they were finished and had packed up the remaining food, she yawned. "I think I'm about to turn into a pumpkin."

"You stayed awake a lot longer tonight," he noted. "But between jet lag and hard work, it's no wonder you're exhausted."

He pulled up the anchor, then turned the boat around so that they could head home.

Funny, *River Star* truly did feel like home already. Just as she truly felt like his river goddess, at least for now. "I think my jet lag might be waning." Then she smiled at him. "Thank you for the date."

"This is the best date I've had in... ever," he said once they were back at the riverboat, and she was helping him tie up the dinghy.

"Me too."

They smiled at each other in the moonlight, and then with one more kiss, he stepped out of the dinghy and offered her his hand. It felt so natural to take it and walk into his arms, and then to walk up the stairs and into the houseboat. It was so easy, too easy, to imagine this being her life. To imagine actually being a local on Elderflower Island. And to imagine being in a relationship with Malcolm.

One that lasted not just two weeks, but forever.

CHAPTER FOURTEEN

Malcolm could get used to this. To waking up with Josie in his arms after a night full of the sweetest lovemaking imaginable. It'd been hard to let her sleep at all. But he knew she wasn't just here for him. She was here to work with Mari to get the reading retreats up and running. And he needed to catch a few hours of sleep as well so that he could continue to help out in any way he could.

Yet again, they woke too late to do anything more than give each other a lingering kiss, gulp down some coffee and a quick bowl of cereal, throw themselves in the shower, and head out. The painters and the decorator were already there, waiting for them.

"Sorry we're late," Josie said, dashing over with the keys to unlock the doors.

A part of him wanted to lay claim to Josie in front of everyone, to make sure all of them knew that he was the reason they were late, because she hadn't wanted to get out of his bed. But he knew she wouldn't appreciate that, so instead he headed over to finish work on the rock wall.

A couple of hours later, he was able to give her the good news. "The rock wall and the stone pathway are completely repaired. No one coming to the retreat will trip on tilted or fallen stones."

She launched herself into his arms, giving him a huge hug. For a moment, it looked like she was about to kiss him, but then she realized at the last moment that wasn't their agreement.

He wanted to tell her to forget about their agreement. That he didn't care who knew they were together. Hell, that he wanted everyone to know. But it wasn't just him in this relationship. Because that's how it felt—a proper relationship. More real, in spite of their agreement that it was just a casual fling, than any relationship he'd ever had. And what she wanted mattered as much, if not more, than what he wanted. So he wouldn't dare do anything without discussing it with her first.

It was the mark of not just a real relationship, but an actual partnership, he found himself thinking. He could see it all so clearly in his mind. The two of them working together to set up reading retreats all over the world. Exploring all those places that she had talked about and more, while they both enjoyed the work. Working with his hands, building and rebuilding. Josie making the spaces cozy and welcoming and filled with books and private gardens that would delight people. It was crazy to have such a clear vision of the future with a woman, especially with one who'd made it plain she wouldn't be staying.

Reluctant to let her out of his arms, he finally let her go. He needed to spend more time with her and had an idea.

"Will you be okay to take off for a few hours with me? I'd like to take you somewhere."

Josie looked surprised and then uncertain. "But there's so much I have to do here. I wouldn't feel right about just blowing off the afternoon."

"Oh no, this would come under the category of work," he told her. "When I was renovating the houseboat, I found an outdoor marketplace in East London that sells the tiles I used in the kitchen and bathroom, and some of the rugs and even some of the paintings on the walls. I thought it would be good for us to go there today and see if there's anything you might be able to use. Fiona's doing a wonderful job with the soft furnishings, but we might find some paintings and furniture that would fill in the extra spaces."

Her face lit up. "That's a great idea. As long as we're back in a few hours so I can continue working, I'd love that. But Fiona might—"

"I already told Fiona our plan, and we have her

blessing, plus a list of things she wants us to look for specifically."

What he didn't tell her as they headed out, catching the Tube to make their way from West to East London, was that there were also several antique booksellers in the market. He had a feeling she was going to want every book she saw. Fortunately, it would be simple to ship as many as she wanted to acquire to the cottages.

He forgot that it was Josie's first time on the Tube until they went into the station.

"Wow, the London Underground," she marveled. "I've always wondered what it would be like to travel on the Tube."

He was glad that he was there for her first ride. She loved everything about the Richmond Station, and he couldn't wait to take her to some of the older, more ornate stations. She even seemed to think that being in this crowded carriage with dozens of other people was romantic.

"It's just as I imagined," she said in a soft voice. Everyone else was reading or looking at their phones, and she spoke softly enough that it would be difficult to listen in.

Strangely, he found himself enjoying the ride too. "The key is to avoid rush hour," he said. "It's not nearly as fun then." And yet, how much of his life had he spent on Tube trains during rush hour? Barely able to find space to stand, let alone sit and read a paper. Not that he spent much time reading the paper either, even if there had been space, because he'd always been so busy dealing with another call or email or another fire that needed to be put out. He could have afforded a chauffeur-driven Lamborghini, but he preferred to pop out and use the Tube.

He hadn't stopped thinking about their conversation on the dinghy last night. He'd always thought that he was an adventurer. And because he had spent so much time on planes in exotic locales, he figured that counted.

But did it really? Did it count when all he saw was the inside of a boardroom or another airport? He hadn't ever been free to explore. No, that wasn't true either. If he really had wanted to explore, he could have made time. He could have told his assistant to hold his calls, to deal with his email until he could get back to deal with it himself. He could have blocked off time. Delegated more. He'd had choices. But he'd chosen work. Genevieve Duvall was a brilliant woman, ready to take on more responsibility, but he still felt he needed to be involved in every deal.

Being with Josie made him see that maybe he had other choices. She'd grown up with a single mother, and he had a feeling that money had been tight. And yet, it sounded like they had done so much together. They'd made choices to enrich their lives, rather than getting locked into a job that demanded every hour.

"Penny for your thoughts," she said.

"Just miles away," he said.

"I can see that," she said with a smile, then she reached for his hand.

He liked that she wasn't shy about showing her affection to him in the Tube, because the likelihood of either of them knowing anyone was quite low. And yet, it didn't feel like enough to him. He still wanted more. He found himself wanting to declare that she was his, and not just to the people on this train, but to everyone. To his family. To hers. And to her as well.

He leaned over and kissed her gently. That was when he heard someone say his name.

"Malcolm."

Josie drew back, her eyes big.

One of the guys from his firm was just getting on the Tube at St. James's Park.

Edward Willoughby was on their finance team. Young and entitled, Edward had attended all the right schools, knew important people. His grandfather was a lord. He was perfectly competent at his job, but more than happy to coast on his connections rather than putting in real work wherever possible. He was also addicted to gossip.

"Edward," Malcolm said, nodding and doing his best to signal to the man to leave them alone.

He turned back to Josie, trying to be as dismissive as he could.

But Edward wasn't so quick to be dismissed. "Is this the famous Katrina I've heard so much about?" he asked in an accent so posh it sounded like he was putting it on. He looked at Josie, clearly confused that she wasn't six feet tall and whippet-thin.

Before Malcolm could even try to explain, Josie spoke up. "No, I'm Josie. A friend from the States." She smiled at the man, but it didn't completely reach her eyes the way her smiles normally did.

Edward offered a hand. "Edward Willoughby. Make sure Malcolm shows you around London properly." He raised an eyebrow, clearly having caught them kissing and no doubt wondering what Malcolm was playing at taking a date on the Tube instead of in a chauffeured car. "Aren't you supposed to be on holiday somewhere exotic this week?" he asked Malcolm.

It was pretty obvious Malcolm hadn't been in the office, and he had cleared his schedule to go on holiday, so it wasn't an outrageous question. But he'd be speaking to Edward later about reading the room. Or the train carriage.

Malcolm shook his head. "I had some family matters to attend to this week and next," he told Ed, even though it was none of his business. Malcolm had never warmed to the man. He reeked of everything that Malcolm found distasteful about the financial world over the years. A sense of self-importance. An arrogance that he and he alone knew everything and that anyone who disagreed with him was automatically wrong. And worst of all, that he was untouchable and didn't have to abide by the same rules as mere mortals.

"Well, this is my stop," Edward said when they reached Blackfriars. "Nice to meet you, Josie."

Willoughby got off the train, and Josie looked at Malcolm. "I'm not wrong in thinking that your kissing me is going to be all over the office by tonight, am I?"

He wasn't going to lie to her. "No. If I had known that someone might see us…"

But that in itself was a lie, the idea that he would have not kissed her. He leaned in close and whispered in her ear, "I don't think I would have been able to keep from kissing you, even then." He felt her give a slight shiver as his breath wafted over her earlobe. And he was glad when she didn't pull away.

He wasn't nearly as glad, however, when she said, "Well, I don't know how much of a scandal it could possibly be, given that I'll be gone in a little over ten days. Just another woman to pass in and out of your life, that's all I'm claiming."

That wasn't what he wanted anyone to think. And

even hearing her say aloud that she was leaving made his chest clench tightly. Previously, whenever he was with a woman, and they talked about the future, *that* was when his chest would clench, at the idea of being "stuck" with her for much longer. But it was the exact opposite with Josie.

He was the one who didn't want to let go. She was the one who reminded him that he would have to do exactly that.

* * *

Josie tried really hard to take being spotted by Malcolm's associate in her stride. What did it matter if someone from his world had seen them together? Sure, there was that obvious look of surprise when the man realized she wasn't a supermodel. And she got the clear sense that he thought she was punching way above her weight. She was, so she couldn't argue with that. But she'd assumed that Malcolm would be more upset about it. And at first, it seemed that he had been. Until he whispered in her ear that he would have kissed her all over again even knowing they would be spotted. She couldn't quite add that up. Couldn't quite make sense of the way it sometimes felt like this was more than a fling to him. That when he looked at her, when he touched her, when he kissed her, she meant something to him.

Something big, something special, something real. Something lasting.

In any case, she refused to let being spotted spoil her day. Her time here was so precious, and she already felt like she was counting down the minutes. It was so great that Malcolm had thought to bring her out to East London, an area she had heard so much about and had longed to explore.

After they got off the Tube, they stopped first for incredible falafel from a street vendor. They were so delicious and yet another wonderful thing about being in such a cosmopolitan city. She had heard London referred to as one of the ultimate melting pots, and she was witnessing it. People from all cultures and countries, all coming together to enjoy this incredible city.

And then, hand in hand, their appetites sated, they headed toward Old Spitalfields Market. There was yet more food at the street market, but also fantastic vendors who sold everything under the sun, from clothes to handmade purses to wooden carvings to exquisite tiles.

"This is perfect," she exclaimed for what felt like the hundredth time as they sourced lamps and side tables and even cushions for the retreat.

Mari had made it explicitly clear to her in the past couple of days that she fully trusted Josie to set up the cottages according to her vision. Of course, Josie was sensitive to the fact that Mari's funds were limited. But whenever the price of something seemed too high, Malcolm was able to negotiate it down to a more reasonable amount, or he claimed he'd give it to Mari as a gift. First for her birthday and then as an early Christmas gift.

And then, when he needed to come up with another occasion, he decided the item would be a sort of business-warming gift to commemorate the launch of her reading retreats. He was generous, almost to a fault.

Josie sensed that he wanted the time that he had put into his work and the money he'd earned doing so to mean something. To matter. To be more than about what he could buy for himself, but how he could help the people he cared for. So while she knew Mari would probably have discouraged him from buying half of everything they chose, Josie understood why it meant a lot to him to be able to do so.

From there, they wandered around the area, and Josie's attention seemed to dart everywhere, from the people on the streets, to the pubs that had been standing for hundreds of years, to the trendy boutiques. And then Malcolm was pausing with an expectant smile on his lips as she gazed into a huge and well stocked vintage bookstore.

"Did you steer me here?" All this time, she'd

thought they'd just been wandering, but when Malcolm nodded, she knew he'd brought her here, knowing how much she'd love this bookstore.

He looked gratified to see her joy. "I was hoping you'd be pleased."

"I'm beyond pleased." She caught his face in her hands and drew him down for a kiss. "Thank you. You're so thoughtful."

His skin flushed lightly at both her kiss and her words, and she was glad that she could make him happy too. He deserved nothing but the best. All the joy in the world.

Her stomach twisted at the thought that he'd find that joy with someone else one day. That when he decided he was ready to fall in love, some other woman would come along, and they would have a life together. A life without her.

The thought was like a sharp pain in the center of her chest.

She silently reminded herself yet again that she wasn't going to waste time lamenting a future that would never be, but would instead fully appreciate what she had now. This beautiful moment with Malcolm.

And, of course, all of these incredible antique books. And, oh, what a treasure trove it was. Everything from Dickens to Harry Potter. Old Penguin paperback books and leather-bound and beautifully silk-bound editions of famous novels packed the shelves.

"I was thinking that having some of these in each cottage, just sitting on the shelves, might inspire some impromptu reading," he said.

She nodded, almost overwhelmed. "I was planning to ask Mari to order some titles, but I didn't want to ask for too much. I'd love to have as many options as possible for the retreat participants. Sometimes I don't know what's right for a person until I meet them."

"You knew pretty quickly to give me *Walden*."

She smiled. "That was easy."

"I've been reading it. It's definitely making me realize there's more to life than making money."

So many of the titles were on her various lists, and there were books she wanted to add to her library of resources. A bookseller came up to them, clearly spotting a serious buying couple. When she explained what she wanted, he pointed out a full set of Anthony Trollope novels. He had a section of prewar female novelists, some of whom she'd never heard of, and she immediately wanted to read every one.

Malcolm seemed to enjoy her excitement over the books almost as much as the bookseller, who was clearly a fellow bibliophile. She didn't want just one copy of some of the books she knew well—she wanted several.

After a while, she came to her senses, as though snapping out of a dream. "Oh my gosh. What am I thinking? This will cost a fortune. Mari can't afford so many books right at the start, before we even know if the retreats will be successful."

"These will be my gift to Mari. Although I'm going to need a forklift to get them to the cottages." He chuckled at her delighted expression.

A few quiet words with the bookseller got him a bulk discount and the business card of a delivery company. While Josie was still poring through the books, he made a quick call, then told her, "They'll ship everything to the cottages by tomorrow afternoon. The painters should be done by the end of today, and we've got the bookshelves coming in tomorrow."

"You really do take care of everyone and everything, don't you?" She put her arms around him, needing to kiss him again. "You're a wonderful man, Malcolm Sullivan."

When it looked like Malcolm was going to argue with her, she put a finger over his lips. "I won't hear any arguments on the matter. What's happened in the past is in the past. For both of us. Right now, today, I'm having the most wonderful time with you. I don't want to think about the past, and I don't want to think about the future. Just right now with you. That's all that matters."

He smiled into her eyes. "So wise. And so beautiful."

He kissed her again, and she momentarily forgot that they were in the middle of the crowded market hall. Were it not for the books that she was clutching to her chest between them, the kiss would surely have deepened. But the time was ticking away, and not only was there still a lot of work to be done at the cottages this afternoon, but there was Mari's big book launch tonight. They couldn't miss that.

All their purchases made, they headed back toward the Tube. Everybody else on board was used to this and it was no big deal for them to be traveling beneath the streets of London through these marvelous stations that were each so unique. But for her, it was yet one more thing to add to her memory bank. She'd never forget coming here. And never regret a second of it, even as her heart broke into a million pieces when she had to leave Elderflower Island and Malcolm.

Fortunately, they made it to Richmond and to the cottages without any issues on the train line, as Malcolm had warned her there might be.

They both got to work. He pitched in with the painter to finish up the sitting room on the last cottage, while she got dusty cleaning out the last of the cupboards. They were close to being able to decorate the common areas, just as he'd said. She couldn't wait to see it all come together even more than it already had. This reading retreat was going to be absolutely beautiful.

And the work that Alice had done in the garden while they were gone was incredible as well. She'd done more than just cut back overgrown shrubs and clear away the brush. She'd also planted flowers, bushes, and even a little tree in the corner.

Josie could see it all come to life, and she made herself a promise that, no matter what, she'd come back to Elderflower Island one day and see it when it was full of happy readers and when the garden was lush and blooming. And if Malcolm happened to be married with children, she would be happy for him. Even if on the inside, she would wish that he was with her. That she had been strong enough to let go of her fears of being hurt again so that she could actually give her heart to him.

That stopped her short.

The thought that she might truly regret holding back. Not telling him how she felt. Not even fully admitting it to herself. That maybe staying safe and keeping as many walls around her heart as she could wasn't the best plan, when she had convinced herself so thoroughly that it was the only plan that made sense.

"Are you ready to head out to get changed for the book signing?" Malcolm said, surprising her.

She almost bonked her head on the shelf she was cleaning, catching herself at the last moment.

"Yes," she said. "I'm ready." But she didn't feel ready. Because it finally occurred to her she was going to meet his whole family. And if they were just friends, that really wouldn't have been a big deal. But now that there was this part of her that was suddenly longing to be so much more than just friends with benefits, she was constantly going to be wondering, *What if?* What if their relationship was real? What if his family became hers? But no, she thought with a firm inward shake of her head. That was crazy thinking, given the boundaries they'd both set out and especially when it had been only a matter of days.

As it was just the two of them alone in the cottage, he drew her to him and kissed her until she forgot her spiraling thoughts, her worries, even her fear of letting him get too close. Every time he kissed her, she forgot everything except how much she wanted him. And how much he was coming to mean to her.

And when he drew back and looked into her eyes, she couldn't help but wonder if he was feeling all the same things.

CHAPTER FIFTEEN

Josie was glad she'd packed one nice dress. She hadn't been sure where she'd wear it, but she'd found over the years that it never hurt to bring along some black velvet. The skirt fell to the knee, but with a pair of black tights and ankle boots with small heels, along with sparkly earrings and a necklace and some makeup, she felt like she'd cleaned up pretty well. Then she caught sight of Malcolm as she walked out into the lounge area of the boat.

He took her breath away. He was wearing a suit. It wasn't the first time she'd seen him in one, but this one was slightly darker than he would wear to the office. Closer to black tie.

"You're beautiful," he said as he came toward her, a hungry gleam in his eyes.

"I was going to say the same to you," she replied.

He kissed her before she could say anything more—kissed all the lipstick right off her lips. And it was well worth needing to reapply it later just to have someone want her this much. It was a heady, delicious feeling. One she found herself craving.

"I don't want to disappoint Mari," he said in a low voice, "or we wouldn't be going any farther than this tonight."

She loved it when he talked to her like that, without the need to hold back how much he wanted her. Which was how it would be tonight. They would pretend that they were nothing more than friends. Two people staying together for a short while on his boat and working together to get the reading retreat up and running. Her chest squeezed. But for all that she was tempted just to let that caution go, she knew better. That caution, that self-protection, had held her firmly together these past two years after betrayal had cut so deep.

It wasn't that she thought Malcolm would lie to her. No, she already knew him better than that. He was an honest man. It was more that he might not realize he was lying to himself. That he might think she was the most beautiful woman he'd ever seen right now, in this moment, and then he'd wake up and realize she wasn't.

Of course, as there had been for so much of her life, there was a part of her that simply felt she couldn't be enough for him. That average Josie Hartwell somehow wouldn't measure up in the end. So that was why she had to keep those walls up—the ones she'd managed to keep standing—when every kiss, every touch, had knocked down so many more.

"We had better go," she agreed. "I want to make sure Mari knows she has my support on all fronts. I really am excited for her, getting a chance to have a book launch for her father's book."

"We are all pleased for her, my brother most of all," he said as they headed into the evening.

It was cooler tonight, and she was glad she'd packed her fitted leather jacket, which slipped over the velvet dress so perfectly. She felt more worldly tonight than the girl who had lived the bulk of her life in Idaho. As they headed along the pathway past other couples and families, she felt like she belonged here. In London, on Elderflower Island, she didn't stick out as the small-town girl.

From a distance, almost before they could see the bookstore lights, they could hear voices. Laughter. Music. Excitement bubbled up in her. Josie loved book launches. Heck, she loved anything to do with books. Few things were better than when a new one came out, and people got to discover all the wonders between the pages. She was a regular at the bookstore in Coeur d'Alene, to the point where the owner often joked that she might as well pay Josie a salary. She loved the smell of a brand-new book that had never been opened as much as she loved the smell of an older one that had shared its story with other readers. It was always a thrill to have an author inscribe a note to her, even if it was something as simple as *enjoy*.

"It's great what she's done with the bookshop," Malcolm said. "She's really brought it back to life. Even during her father's heyday, it was never like this. She's got so many fresh ideas, and we all are so happy to see yet one more venture on Elderflower Island succeed. With the bakery, the boathouse, the teahouse, all the little shops, the island feels more alive. And the reading retreats will be one more business that infuses life into the community."

"It really is amazing, that this one small island has so much life and so many wonderful little businesses," she agreed. "In some ways, it doesn't feel all that different from Coeur d'Alene." She laughed before he could respond, adding, "I know that sounds crazy."

But he was nodding. "It's not crazy. I see what you're saying. Elderflower Island, while still in London, somehow manages to have that small-town feel. I think that's what I've always loved about it. There's a real sense of community here, where everyone is looking out for each other."

They arrived at the bookstore and joined the throngs of people waiting to get inside.

A man and woman who looked to be in their mid to late sixties turned as Josie and Malcolm arrived. The woman smiled at them. "Malcolm, honey, isn't this wonderful?"

Josie knew in an instant that this was his mother. And the handsome man next to her was his father.

As soon as Malcolm had finished greeting his parents with a kiss on each cheek, he said, "Mum, Dad, I'd like you to meet Josie Hartwell. She is—"

"—here to create the reading retreats for Mari!" His mother hugged her. "I've heard so much about you already—from all of my children. It's the most wonderful thing, what you're doing."

Josie felt pleased by his mother's enthusiasm, if not slightly overwhelmed by her joyful greeting. "I'm really happy to be here, Mrs. Sullivan."

"Oh, no. Call me Penny."

"I'm Simon," Malcolm's father said, shaking her hand, which somehow managed to be almost as warm as Penny's hug.

"The family resemblance is uncanny." It truly was amazing how much Malcolm looked like his father. They could practically be twins, if not for the decades separating them.

"Even as a child, they looked so much like each other," his mother agreed.

Malcolm and his father both smiled.

She could see he was very comfortable with his parents, just as she was with her mother. She found herself really glad that he had them in his life. That he had his whole family. He worked so hard and expected so much from himself, it was nice to know that he would always be surrounded by love, even when she was gone.

Love. The word lingered in her head, but she pushed it away. Now wasn't the time to wonder about what could or couldn't be. Now was the time to enjoy getting to know Malcolm's family. And to celebrate Mari and her new book.

"We were surprised to hear that you are helping to clean up the cottages," Simon said to Malcolm.

"Well, some travel plans fell through," Malcolm explained, "and when Mari and Owen needed help, it made sense to volunteer, along with Fiona and Alice. You've all done it for me."

"I remember what a good time we had working on renovating your houseboat," his father said. "Let me know if you need any additional help with the cottages."

It was obvious to Josie that Malcolm's father wanted to spend time working with his son again. And obviously the joy of working with their hands ran in the family.

"We could probably use you," Malcolm said.

His father's face lit up. "Fantastic."

Josie added, "There are so many little details, every

extra pair of hands really helps. Alice and Fiona have already done so much."

"I'd quite like to take a look too, if that wouldn't mean too many cooks in the kitchen." Penny seemed a little hesitant, which was crazy, given that Malcolm had said she had curated collections at the Victoria and Albert Museum.

"I'd love it if you would," Josie said. "Malcolm told me a little about what you do for a living, and I'm so impressed. I'm sure you will have great ideas for ways to really make the cottages shine for the guests who come to the reading retreats."

Josie found herself telling Penny about the wonderful day she'd had and how Malcolm had taken her to East London to look at small furnishings and how much fun they'd had choosing vintage books to stock in the cottages.

Penny smiled fondly at her son. "I can see you're definitely in good hands."

Josie's face flushed, surely bright red, at his mother talking about Josie being in Malcolm's hands. That was exactly where she had been, again and again, over the last few days. She ducked her head, trying to hide her blush. It didn't help when he surreptitiously put his hand on the small of her back as they moved forward in line. It could've been the action of a friend, but she knew how much more they were. Or at least, how much more it felt like they were.

"I'd love to hear more about the reading retreats. How you set them up and how your guests enjoy their time," Penny said. The Sullivans were perfectly happy to wait in line along with everyone else.

"Honestly, it's pretty simple. The biggest thing is to really understand each person as an individual and what kind of books they need to read. Sometimes reading the right book is like getting advice from a trusted friend. They can give a fresh perspective on a problem."

"Interesting how you use the word *need*," Simon said. "How do you ascertain that?"

"I meet with each guest, either over a video call or email, whichever they're most comfortable with, and we talk about their favorite books and a little bit about what's going on in their lives, if they're comfortable sharing. Then I pull together reading lists for them. I try to add fun titles as well as thought-provoking ones. Inspirational stories and biographies can really help too. And I like to throw in more visually oriented books as well, like what you might see on coffee tables, because that can be a wonderful break for people, give them time to digest what they've been reading."

"Fascinating," Penny said. "You must really get to know your retreat participants."

Josie nodded. "That's exactly right. It can be a lot of

work sometimes, particularly as the list of reading retreats I've set up has grown, but I really love that one-on-one time with people who love books. And even people who don't, but decide that they want to give a reading retreat a try."

"I was wondering about that," Simon said. "If anybody ever signs up for a reading retreat who isn't a big reader."

"It happens more often than you might think," Josie said with a smile. "There have been a few instances of a married couple coming, where one of them is a big reader, and the other isn't, but they want to take a vacation together. I always tell people the point isn't for it to feel like you're in school again and you have to be reading from nine to three with no breaks, or you have to check off a certain number of pages. It's much more that you should feel there's nothing else you have to do. That if you want to sit on a chair beneath an apple tree and read for a while and then doze for a while and then pick up where you left off when you wake up forty-five minutes later, that's absolutely perfect. And if something you read inspires you to write or run or sing, then that's perfect too."

"You do put in a lot of hours," Malcolm said, "emailing and speaking to clients, but I have to say, you're always smiling when you're working."

She nodded. "I've been really lucky that I've always

loved my work. I was a freelance editor before," she explained to his parents, "and to be able to transition into a new career where I help people take the time to read books and also get to find them those books—it's truly the best job in the world."

"Apart from mine," a voice said.

Josie turned to see Mathilda Westcott standing beside them.

"Oh, hello!" She was so pleased when Mathilda embraced her with a kiss on each cheek.

"Oh good," Mathilda said, "you've met my daughter and son-in-law. Isn't Josie absolutely delightful?" she said to Simon and Penny. "Owen's been telling me how brilliantly she and Malcolm are getting on with the cottages," she said with a bland smile.

It seemed as though all of them shot surreptitious glances between her and Malcolm before nodding. If Josie wasn't mistaken, they were matchmaking. And it was very flattering that they seemed to think the idea of her and Malcolm pairing up wasn't a bad one. But again, she was surprised that they would think she was his type. Although, given the fireworks in bed, she was his type in one way, if not the supermodel they were used to seeing with him.

At last, they made it inside. The bookshop was filled with people, and Mari came by to say hello, looking excited but a little nervous too.

"It's going to go beautifully," Josie said after giving her a hug. "Remember, I've already read *Mars at the Beach* and read it again with Aria, who loved the book." She scanned the room. "Look at this crowd."

Mari swallowed hard. "I have never spoken in front of so many people before."

"Just speak from the heart, as you always do. You're going to be great," Josie promised her new friend.

Malcolm looked at the stacks of books near the register, Owen standing proudly beside them. "Do you think you have enough books?"

Mari shook her head. "I was sure we had way too many, but now I don't know."

"Well, the publisher will be extremely pleased if you sell out, I'm sure," Penny said. "I'm hoping to buy a few to give as gifts to parents of young children." Then she gave Mari a hug. "I'm so proud of you, my dear."

Malcolm knew a number of people there, but even Josie recognized a few. All the Sullivans, of course, and the man from the bakery with his partner. She recognized a few faces that she must have passed on the island.

A photographer from a local paper was even present.

"Come and meet my mother and brother," Mari

said, pulling Josie toward a woman who was an older version of Mari, and an attractive man who looked almost as proud as Owen did.

"You must be very proud," Josie said to Mari's mom, who nodded.

"It wasn't easy when my baby moved to the other side of the world, but seeing her so happy makes it all worthwhile." Then she looked sad. "Her father was a complicated man who made some mistakes, but I'm pleased that he left all the evidence Mari could have wanted that he loved her very much."

"I had a wonderful stepfather," Mari said to her mom. "And you, so I always knew I was loved."

Josie loved the way Mari reassured her mother, who obviously had some difficult feelings about her first husband.

Then Alice and Fiona arrived and called Josie back to where they were standing with Malcolm and their parents. "Isn't this exciting?" Alice said, almost jumping up and down. "Imagine owning a bookstore and publishing books."

"And running reading retreats," Fiona added. "I hope she's not taken on too much."

Then Owen went up to the microphone. "Hello and good evening, everyone. Thank you for coming tonight. Normally, Mari would be the emcee at our author events, but because she is the star attraction tonight, I am going to take over." The look he gave her was adoring. Hers to him was just the same.

"All of us were very lucky when Mari decided to travel here from Santa Monica, California. The Elderflower Island Bookshop was her father's, and many of us here knew and loved him. Charlie was a wonderful man who we all miss every day. Thankfully, he passed the store on to Mari, hoping that she would fall in love with it and this island and all the people on it, just as he had. And thankfully again, she did. I won't say too much more. I'll let her tell you the rest, but I just want to take a moment to say how grateful I am that you decided to stay, Mari, and how much I love you."

Oh my gosh, it's practically like being at a wedding and listening to the groom toast his bride. Josie was practically welling up, and they were at a book signing.

It looked as though Mari was tearing up as well as she walked up to Owen and kissed him. And then she was standing behind the microphone, and he moved off to the side, proud as could be. "Thank you so much for that, Owen. I'm the lucky one." And then she laughed. "Okay, enough of the mushy stuff. That's not why you all are here."

Everyone laughed.

"Many of you know my story, and I've told it enough times that I don't want to bore anyone, but suffice it to say that after losing touch with my father for most of my adult life, finding out that he had bequeathed me this bookstore after he passed away was one of the most momentous experiences of my life. Coming to Elderflower Island changed me and my future forever, in all the best ways. I'm not going to deny that my background in accounting has been helpful when dealing with purchase orders and store finances," she said to more laughter, "but the opportunity to spend my days surrounded by books and the wonderful inhabitants of Elderflower Island is a gift that I don't ever take for granted. Every single day, I'm so grateful that I get to be here and do this."

She paused as though to collect her thoughts before she picked up a copy of *Mars at the Beach* and held it to her chest. "Of all the unexpected twists and turns that my life has taken, however, I never saw this one coming. I had no idea that my father had written books. Or that those books were about the two of us. The little girl in this story is me—Mars was his nickname for me."

Josie looked over at Mari's mother, who was with Mari's brother, Carson. They both looked so proud. And Mari's mother definitely looked emotional as well.

"When I found my father's stories and his beautiful illustrations, I fell in love with them and wanted to share them with the world. Thanks to Owen Sullivan and Mathilda Westcott, it did happen. I need to thank my mother and stepfather for supporting my dream to come here and my brother, Carson, for believing in me. Always. Finally, I'd like to thank my publisher and agent, who were also instrumental in bringing my father's dream to life. I truly believe that although he isn't here with us today, he's looking down on us, and he's as thrilled as I am to launch the stories of a little girl and her father into the world." Her words sounded choked as she finished her sentence, and she cleared her throat. "And now I would like to read the beginning of Mars at the Beach to you."

Although Josie had read the book already, Mari's delightful reading made it even more entrancing. As she always did with a great book, she got lost in it. She didn't realize that her hand had slipped into Malcolm's until the reading was over, and everyone applauded.

She realized she had only one hand free. She turned to look at him, and in that moment, their eyes caught, and it was all she could do not to lean in just enough to close the gap between them with a kiss.

But no, she couldn't do that. Their temporary fling was a secret. And so she made herself pull her hand away. And tried to ignore that pain in her chest from the loss of his touch.

CHAPTER SIXTEEN

Malcolm had loved it when Josie slipped her hand into his during the reading. He didn't think she was even aware of it at the time, which was confirmed at the end of the reading when she looked surprised to find her hand in his. And it felt right. What felt wrong, however, was her pulling it away. And then taking a step away from him. He was frustrated. Frustrated by her reticence to be with him—despite the fact that when they had set the boundaries for their relationship, he had told her he wasn't interested in anything serious either.

"Marvelous, wasn't it?" He turned to Fiona behind him. She'd come with Alice rather than her husband. Naturally. "Lewis couldn't make it?" But he already knew. The douchebag was too "busy."

"I'm afraid he had dinner with clients tonight."

Malcolm's stomach twisted at his suspicion that *dinner with clients* was anything but.

Josie jumped into the awkward silence with natural tact. "I had already read the book," Josie said, "but I think it's one of those you can read again and again, and it just gets better every time. It's a children's book, but it works on so many levels. I just hope that if Mari sells out tonight, she can bring in more copies in time for the reading retreat. This would be a wonderful story to read to children whose parents are no longer together. It'd even help the parents themselves who are grieving the end of a marriage."

"What a wonderful idea," Fiona said. "I'd planned on buying a dozen to give to all my friends with children. But it doesn't look like she's going to have nearly enough."

Malcolm heard the wistful note in his sister's tone. He knew she wanted children, but he also knew that wouldn't happen with Lewis. He'd never wish anyone's marriage to end, but surely Fiona would be happier with someone else. However, that was a decision only she could make.

They heard a little girl's laughter and turned to see Aria holding a copy of the book with a big smile on her face. "Aunt Mari is the greatest!"

Tom ran a loving hand over her hair. "She certainly is." He turned his smile to Josie. "It's nice to see you again. Aria hasn't stopped talking about you since yesterday."

"Josie!" The little girl threw her arms around Josie's lower half. "Do you want to read the book again? In my special spot?"

Josie's smile was so wide it stretched from ear to ear. "There's nothing I'd like more." Hand in hand, the two of them walked off.

"It's like she's one of the family already," Tom drawled.

Fiona had a speculating look in her eye as she turned to Malcolm. "Do you have anything you'd like to share with us?"

He loved his siblings dearly, but sometimes they got on his last nerve. "The cottage cleanup is going well."

Fiona rolled her eyes, giving them a hint of the person she used to be before Lewis demanded she act so posh all the time. "I don't know. When I saw you two together there the other day, I couldn't help but think that you fancied her, and she looked the same with you."

"I'm not allowed to ask her out, so that should tell you something," Tom said to Fiona.

Malcolm was pretty sure there was steam coming out of his ears. "My personal life is none of your business."

This time, both of his siblings rolled their eyes. "Well," Fiona said, "I would hate to see you in denial about the nicest woman any of us has ever seen you with."

"I told him the same thing," Tom said. "I'm afraid he's going to be too thickheaded to listen, though."

Penny and Simon walked up. "Why do the three of you have your heads together?" Penny asked. "Or is it a secret from parents?"

Fiona smiled. "Oh, nothing much—we're just thinking Malcolm and Josie would make an excellent couple."

Penny nodded, smiling. "Your father and I were saying the same thing."

"Now, Penny," Simon said, "we agreed we weren't going to meddle in his business."

"I'm just looking out for his welfare," she said before turning back to Malcolm. "In all seriousness, she is lovely. And we are not trying to be matchmakers. We simply notice how she makes you smile more than we've seen you smile in a long time."

"Hear, hear," Mathilda said, materializing as if out of thin air to join the group. "This is your chance," she said bluntly to Malcolm. "Don't blow it."

Normally, Malcolm would've brushed them off. But the difference this time was, first, they actually all agreed that they liked a woman he was with, and second, he really liked her too. "I'm not sure what you all want me to say," he said, "but all I can tell you is that you're right. Josie is very smart, very talented, and a lot of fun to be with."

From the look on everyone's faces, he might as well have announced their engagement.

"I knew it!" his mother said, throwing her arms around him.

"No, don't misunderstand me," he said once she let him go. "We're just friends."

"Just friends, my arse," his grandmother said.

Fortunately, right then, Josie and Aria returned to the group. "We read the book again, and we each made up voices for the characters this time," Aria said.

Josie smiled down at Aria. "You're such a good reader."

Aria beamed with pride.

Mathilda said, "Aria's an exceptional reader. Her teacher said she's one of the best in the class. We always read together when she comes to me for the afternoon, don't we, darling?"

Josie looked very happy. "I was like you, Aria. I loved to read from when I first learned my letters, and now books are my friends and my work."

"I want to have a bookstore just like Mari when I grow up," Aria announced.

Malcolm had a feeling his precocious niece might end up in the book trade. It clearly ran in the family.

"I know you're very busy with the cottages," his mother said to Josie, "but we would be delighted if you could join us for Sunday roast this weekend. Everyone in the family who's available comes, and you would be a wonderful addition."

Josie flushed with pleasure at the invitation. "I'd love to, thank you."

At this rate, his mother was going to propose to Josie for him. Malcolm said, "We should probably get going. We have a really early start tomorrow."

She nodded, looking regretful. "He's right. We do have a lot to do. It was so wonderful to spend time with you all tonight, and I'm really looking forward to Sunday," she said. "I'm just going to say good-bye to Mari, and then I will meet you by the door, Malcolm."

He couldn't take his eyes off her as she went to give Mari a hug.

Mari had finished signing books, and there were only a few left. Malcolm was so happy for the woman he suspected would soon be his sister-in-law. And the fact that Mari and Josie got on so well made him just as happy. If Josie ever did decide to move to the UK, she'd have a ready-made best friend.

"Man, you've got it bad," Tom said under his breath beside him.

He couldn't honestly disagree. He did have it bad for Josie.

Strangely, the worse he had it for her, the better he felt.

CHAPTER SEVENTEEN

As soon as they were out of the bookshop, Malcolm took her hand. They both agreed that they were thrilled to see *Mars at the Beach* already looking like a success. Josie told him that she'd asked Mari to keep a few copies for the reading retreat guests.

Suddenly, he blurted, "I'm going to miss you when you're gone."

She squeezed his hand. "I'm going to miss you too."

It was as close as either of them had come to talking about having feelings for each other.

Malcolm was more tempted than he had ever been to add that he didn't want her to leave. Or that even if she did, what if they tried having a real relationship and continuing it long distance? But the same part of him that had always held back kept the words inside.

Though he couldn't get the words out, he needed her to know how much she meant to him. That he would more than miss her. That he would long for her.

They didn't say anything else as they walked beneath the moon down the towpath to his boat. Once they were inside, just like nearly every time before, they fell into each other's arms.

His mouth was on hers and hers on his. But this kiss was different. This kiss was about more than just hot sex or the thrill of finally getting to be with someone he'd fantasized about for so long. This kiss was about expressing something that he'd always kept way deep down inside. Emotions that he'd never let run free. In the light of day, he knew he might regret it, but tonight he couldn't hold back.

He whispered her name between kisses. And every time he spoke those five sweet letters, she melted even more against him. He ran kisses over her face and then back to her lips, slowly undressing her, needing to strip her bare long before they made it to the bedroom. This dress was one of the easier outfits, as it just unzipped at the back and then slid off to pool around her feet. Yet again, she took his breath away, whether with clothes or without.

"So beautiful," he said in a low voice, following up his words with the stroke of his hands over the bare skin of her arms before threading his fingers with hers and pulling her close to kiss her again. He tasted her mouth, the fullness of her lower lip, their tongues tangling, their breath coming faster now. He lifted her, still in her bra and tights and heeled boots, in his arms and carried her astern to the bed.

He was pleased he'd remembered to stock up on protection earlier in the day.

It seemed she wanted his clothes gone just as much as he did hers, because before he could divest her of the rest of her garments, she was sliding his jacket off his shoulders and unbuttoning his shirt, running her hands over his pecs as soon as the fabric was pulled away.

"Every time we make love," she said softly, "part of me feels like I'm dreaming."

"For me too," he said. "Being with you feels like all my dreams are coming true. Even the dreams I never let myself have." He stared into her eyes. "Especially those." It was the most he'd ever admitted to anyone about how tightly he kept his heart locked up.

And then her hands were in his hair, and she was pulling his mouth down to hers, kissing him so sweetly, and yet so simply, that he forgot everything but her. But how much he wanted her. Everything but how much he needed her. How grateful he was to have these precious days and nights with her. She'd made him look at everything differently. As though he was seeing life through a new lens.

Soon, they were both naked, and he was leaning over her on the bed. "You... Us." He didn't have the words for it, but he needed her to know anyway. "This is special."

She looked into his eyes, her legs and arms wrapped around him, their hearts beating against each other. "So special," she agreed.

He slipped on a condom in record time, and then he was moving into her, and her eyes were closing, her neck and back arching as she gasped in pleasure. He wanted to remember her forever like this, in his arms, lost in pleasure, her warmth wrapped all around him. He couldn't look away, couldn't seem to get close enough or hold her tightly enough.

He found her mouth with a kiss so full of the emotion he was barely holding inside that it was almost rough. But she didn't seem to mind, kissing him back just as passionately, moving with him just as urgently, not only taking everything he had to give, but giving it back tenfold.

They were both desperate for each other as they flew together to the peak and then tumbled over in each other's arms. And throughout, they never stopped kissing, even long after release.

Holding her in his arms, he could kiss her forever.

★ ★ ★

Josie had never known it was possible to feel so good. Not only while making love with Malcolm, but afterward too, when she was in his arms and they were softly kissing as though neither wanted their time together to end. He was so tender and deliciously passionate too. She was spoiled now for all future lovers.

Even the thought made her chest clench. She couldn't imagine being with anyone else. No, no one would ever make her feel so good, so beautiful, or as happy as Malcolm Sullivan did. It was a good thing that she had already written off men, because after him, a relationship with anyone else would seem so boring.

There was a part of her, growing bigger by the second, that longed to ask, what if they changed the rules? What if they moved the boundaries? What if there weren't any anymore? What if they actually did this for real?

She wrapped her arms tightly around him. No, that wasn't in the cards. He'd been clear. And yet, it was harder and harder not to wish for things to be just that little bit different.

At last, the grumbling of their stomachs drew them apart.

"I swear, if we both weren't so hungry all the time, I'd never let you out of this bed."

She smiled up at him, knowing that to have had this time with him was such a blessing. She wouldn't waste it lamenting what could never be. "What do you say we whip up something together tonight?"

"I'd say that's exactly what we just did," he said

with an eyebrow raised.

She laughed. "Something to eat, I mean."

The other eyebrow went up. "That can be arranged," he teased.

She lifted his hand from where he was starting to stroke her curves and kissed his fingers. "Yes, but later. After we've had some sustenance for round two."

His eyes gleamed. "I hope you're planning on many more rounds than that before the night is through."

A shiver of anticipation ran through her. "Of course I am," she confirmed.

And then she slid out of the bed, held out a hand, and together they walked into the kitchen to make a feast that would see them through so that their stomachs wouldn't interrupt their lovemaking again.

CHAPTER EIGHTEEN

Josie and Malcolm both woke early and spent an hour on their laptops with their various projects. Malcolm was surprised at how much reading Thoreau's *Walden* was helping him see he needed to simplify his work life. What was the point of all he'd achieved if he simply stayed on the hamster wheel of deal after deal? Twice in the last week, where he would have jumped in to handle an issue that had come up, he'd delegated it to Genevieve Duvall. Maybe she hadn't handled things exactly the way he would have, but she'd been successful both times.

Turned out he wasn't as indispensable as he'd thought, which was quite a revelation. Still, he was glad he hadn't left the country. They were having a tricky time with House in a Box, the New Zealand company that Malcolm knew in his gut was going to be big. If only the founder could just do what Malcolm was learning to do and let go of control. Until he did, he could never expand globally.

While he worked on that, Josie talked to a man

who was coming to the retreat suffering from burnout. Malcolm had a pretty strong feeling that *Walden* would be on the exhausted exec's reading list. For a moment, he imagined what it would be like to take a holiday from work, not to go to an exotic location or throw himself down a mountain on skis or over water on a speedboat, but simply to sit in a beautiful, historic cottage garden and read. He already knew that Josie didn't allow phones or laptops at the retreats. He'd struggle to be disconnected from business even for a few hours a day, and that made him understand how much he needed to change.

They managed a quick breakfast, fast and satisfying sex, and then showers, and still made it to the cottages by nine.

Malcolm was fitting bookshelves, and Josie was cataloging all the books that had been delivered. He could see her eyeing the bookshelves and knew that the second he finished, she'd be filling them with books. In truth, he was excited, too, to see the reading retreat taking shape.

There was a knock on the door, and Mari came in. She walked around and then gave first Josie, then Malcolm a hug. "I can't believe how good this looks already. You two are an amazing team."

Even though it was just the two of them working this morning, Josie hastened to remind Mari that a team of people, including Sullivan family members, had helped get the cottages turned around quickly.

Then Mari cried, "You'll never believe what's happened!"

She seemed happy and not upset, so Malcolm was fairly sure it was good news.

"Tell us," Josie said.

Mari was grinning from ear to ear as she said, "We're sold out for the whole year." She laughed. "I know neither of you have any idea what I'm talking about. Sorry, I just logged in this morning and couldn't believe my eyes." She laughed again. "The reading retreats. For the rest of the year. They're *already booked.*"

Josie's mouth fell open. "Really? How can that be? We're not even ready for the first one."

"I know," Mari said. "I honestly wasn't expecting anyone to sign up yet. I mean, we haven't even done any promotion. But I mentioned them in a couple of interviews I've done recently, and I decided I might as well put up the website that you got going just in case there were any inquiries. An internet influencer picked up the news and ran with it. But I didn't think the entire calendar would fill up so fast."

Josie had pulled out her phone. "I have to see. Maybe there's a mistake." She quickly logged into the backend of the website. And then stared at what she saw, stunned. "I just never thought—I mean, I hoped the retreats would be a huge success here, but selling out this quickly? That's amazing."

She and Mari looked at each other as the reality of it all sank in. "We *really* need to finish setting up the bedrooms," Josie said as Mari nodded.

Was Malcolm the only one who saw this as not unqualified good news? One of the things he admired about Mari was how much of a go-getter she was, but he'd seen so many small-business owners take on more than they could handle, and he was worried Mari had done just that.

Gently, he said, "How are you going to manage the bookshop, the publishing schedule for your father's books, and a full year of reading retreats?"

"I—Well, of course I—" Mari blinked and looked as if lightning had struck. "I can't."

This might be the first time she'd admitted it.

She shook her head. "I can't do it alone."

Then, to both his surprise and Josie's, she grabbed Josie's hands. "Don't leave. Stay, Josie. Stay here on Elderflower Island. I know you have other retreats that you work with, and we could find a way to make sure that you can work with everyone, but... what if these became your primary ones? What if these were your home base?"

Josie looked even more shocked now. "But they're

not mine. They're yours. These are the retreats for your store."

"Yes, a store that is booming so quickly now that I can barely keep up with it. Plus, I'm publishing my father's books. It's all so much more work than I anticipated, even though I love every minute of what I do. The truth is that if you don't stay to take over the reading retreats, I'm going to have to hire someone else to do it. That just doesn't seem right. It should be you. And you're uniquely qualified to do this, so hopefully we wouldn't have an issue with getting you a work permit in the UK."

"But I—" Josie barely got two words out when Mari looked at Malcolm.

"This is a great idea, isn't it, Malcolm?" Before he could reply, she said, "Convince her!"

And now the two of them were looking at him. How had this become *his* decision? The truth was that the idea of Josie staying, about Elderflower Island being her new home, did feel right. It meant he wouldn't have to say good-bye. And that was all he could think, after the time they'd spent together—he wasn't ready to say good-bye.

He smiled down at the woman who'd become such a vital part of his life in such a short time. "Stay, Josie." It wasn't eloquent, but it was exactly what he was feeling. He turned and took her hand in his. "How does the idea sound to you?"

She seemed speechless for a moment, looking deeply into his eyes as if she were trying to read his mind. Trying to see if he truly meant she should stay.

"Well, since my mother's moved away from Coeur d'Alene, it's not the same without her, even though I have great friends. And I do absolutely love it here. It has felt like home from the first moment I arrived. Mari, you and your bookshop are amazing. And Malcolm, your family has been so friendly and welcoming." She paused as though she was trying to corral her thoughts. "Can I think about it? Can I have a little time to digest all of this?"

"Of course," Mari said. "I didn't mean to just spring this request on you, for you to uproot your entire life and change everything. It's just—it would be so amazing if you were here full time. Elderflower Island just doesn't feel like it would be the same without you now. I know you've only been here a week, but I really feel like you belong here. Like you're a local already. Doesn't she, Malcolm?"

He nodded, smiling. "It's true. You really do fit in here."

She smiled at both of them. "Wow. Of everything I thought might happen today, I never saw *this* coming."

Mari's phone rang, and after a glance she said, "It's my book editor. I really need to take this. I swear I don't mean to pressure you, but whenever you make your decision, let me know." She gave Josie a hug and dashed off.

Josie sat on an antique painted bench that Fiona had brought over for the garden. "I am floored by this. Move here? Sure, there's been a part of me the entire time I've been here that was dreaming of it. But actually making it a reality? I don't know what to think."

He sat beside her, knowing that he should give her time and space to process. But he couldn't keep the words from spilling out. "Stay, and we won't end at two weeks."

Her head whipped around so she could face him. "What? What did you just say?"

He took both of her hands in his and drew her closer on the bench. "Let's try. Let's try to make this be real. A real relationship, not just a two-week fling. If you're going to live here, then don't you think we're worth a shot?"

She looked at him as though she couldn't believe what he was saying. "What have you done with Malcolm Sullivan? When we first decided to have the fling, you made it totally clear that you had no interest in a real, permanent relationship."

"I know, and I meant it then. But things have changed."

"What has changed?"

A part of him had assumed that when he told her he wanted to have a real relationship, she would jump at it. Instead, she was questioning him. Almost as though she was questioning his sanity.

"Being with you, that's what has changed things. Every moment we spend together… I love it. I love being with you." He'd never said those words to anyone else. Because he'd never felt what he felt for Josie. He'd never loved being with anyone the way he loved being with her.

"I love being with you too," she said softly. "But I don't want either of us to make a hasty decision just because my career and living plans might be changing."

"Why not? Why not take the risk?"

She stared at him, and he knew that she was mulling over the question, thinking about her answer. "Because I've been hurt before. Badly. I swore I wasn't going to get involved with anyone again. That even our fling wasn't going to move into any kind of emotional territory where I would end up hurt."

"Did that work?" He studied her face, realizing that her answer mattered. Deeply mattered. "Were you able to keep things with me from becoming emotional?"

She shook her head. "No. I haven't been able to do that."

He couldn't hold back his smile. "Then jump with me, Josie. I know you've been hurt. I don't want to hurt you, not the way he hurt you. I care about you. More than I've ever cared for anyone, apart from my family."

He released her hands to cradle her face. "Be mine. For real."

Then he kissed her. Kissed her with all the emotion he felt, kissed her with all the passion she inspired, kissed her because it was what he wanted to do all day long and all night.

When he finally let them draw back for air, he had to know. "So, what do you say?" He couldn't give her even the rudimentary amount of breathing room that Mari was giving her to make her decision. He had to know.

"If I stay…" She licked her lips, still looking a little uncertain. "Yes. I'm willing to try. I'm willing to trust you."

He kissed her again, a kiss of pure joy, a kiss that felt like all of his dreams had come true.

A throat was cleared behind them. "Sorry to interrupt," Alice said, "but I have that huge flat of flowers in the van I was planning to plant this morning before I head off to work. And I need some help bringing it all out."

Josie laughed, her cheeks flushed. "Of course." She

jumped up and gave his sister a hug.

"Good morning." Malcolm kissed his sister on both cheeks as well.

Alice had one hand, clad in a gardening glove, on her hip. "So, I assume you two are out in the open now?" she asked. "Or am I supposed to pretend I didn't see that?"

Malcolm was the first to reply. "You don't have to pretend anything. We're together. In a proper relationship." He felt proud saying the words. They felt right. Telling Alice felt right.

Alice's eyebrows went up. "That's great news. Everyone is going to be so thrilled!"

Josie looked surprised to hear that. "Why?"

Alice laughed. "Are you joking? All of us think you're the best thing that's ever happened to Malcolm. Everyone from Gran to Aria have been wishing and hoping and praying that the two of you would get together." Then something occurred to her. "Can I spill the beans? Or should I let you two do it?"

Malcolm turned to Josie. "Got any preference?"

She looked a little steamrolled, but said, "Whatever works for you works for me."

"See?" Alice said. "That's one of the reasons why we all adore you. You're so easygoing. And also fabulous and brilliant. I don't know what we're going to do when you leave. I suppose you're going to have a long-distance relationship? Malcolm, you could always open an office in New York."

"Prying much?" Malcolm said, then led the way to the van. Alice opened it up so that they could each grab a flat of flowers.

"Actually," Josie told Alice, "I might not be leaving."

He was 99.9 percent sure she would stay. After all, he knew firsthand how much she loved everything about Elderflower Island so far. She got along great with his family. And he knew the idea of being completely in charge of the reading retreats appealed to her.

"Why? Are you getting another job here after you finish setting up the retreat and the cottages?"

"Mari came by this morning and said the retreats are completely booked out for the rest of the year. She's asked me to take them over."

"You could do more than that even," Malcolm said. "Remember how you said it would be fun to have reading retreats on houseboats? What if that's what we did? What if we renovated a bunch of houseboats and turned each of them into a floating reading retreat?"

He didn't know where the idea had come from, only that he knew it would work.

"Oh my gosh," Alice said. "That would be amazing. And I could help set up all of the plants on the decks, and some flower boxes by the windows, and any land around the dock of wherever the houseboats are, if you needed it."

Josie held up her hands. "That sounds amazing, but right now I just need to focus on one thing at a time. I've got to get these cottages ready faster than ever, and then decide whether it's feasible for me to stay."

"Sorry, I don't mean to pressure you," Alice said.

But Malcolm didn't apologize. He wanted her to stay. And that meant she needed to take this job.

CHAPTER NINETEEN

The rest of the day passed in a blur. Josie had never worked so hard or so quickly on so many different fronts—the garden, the furnishings, and filling the bookcases Malcolm had put together with books and more books. The people who had signed up for the retreats were already emailing to ask questions about how it all worked and to give her their information on the kind of books that they loved, which meant that she didn't have a moment to breathe until the sun had fallen and only she and Malcolm were left on the property.

They hadn't had a chance to talk again since this morning, not even to eat alone together. His parents had dropped by with lunch and raved about how much they'd done. Penny took on the task of stocking the kitchen with snacks for the retreat guests. She pulled on rubber gloves and washed the mismatched china they'd found in the cupboards, and talked about stocking the brand-new fridge with juice, water, and soft drinks.

Simon helped Malcolm put together the remaining bookcases, and Josie could see how happy it made the two Sullivan men to work together, chatting easily as they did so. Fiona had brought by some pillows and throw blankets for the couches and the outside furniture, reminding Josie that even in summer, it could get cool outside. Fiona was a lifesaver in so many ways. But she hadn't been able to stay, saying that she was working on yet another event for her husband and his clients.

When Josie went into the kitchen, she found Penny happily drying dishes and placing them inside the kitchen cupboards. Malcolm's mother smiled at her. "We're so pleased to hear the news. Simon and I both think you and Malcolm are wonderful together."

Josie blushed, feeling like she'd received the greatest compliment. Alice hadn't wasted any time telling the others about her and Malcolm. She wondered if that was why Penny and Simon had dropped by today—to let Josie know they approved.

Even Tom and Aria came by after school. Luckily, Josie had already shelved some children's picture books that contained useful lessons for adults as well. She showed Aria the shelf containing *Winnie-the-Pooh*, *The Little Prince*, and *The Velveteen Rabbit* among others. But the one she reached for was a book that had been a childhood favorite of hers. *Where the Wild Things Are* by

Maurice Sendak was about managing difficult emotions, but it was also about the power of imagination, something she knew Aria had in spades.

While Tom helped the men, she and Aria went outside to a cozy nook Alice and Fiona had created. An old rosebush was blooming, now freed from the weeds that had surrounded it, and the pretty flowers Alice had planted that morning added splashes of color and fragrance. They curled up together on an old wooden bench that was comfortable thanks to Fiona's cushions. A sundial caught the sun in one corner of the garden, and butterflies and birds seemed to love the garden as much as Josie did.

As they read together, Josie was filled with happiness.

After everyone had left for the day except Malcolm, she went back out and sat in another part of the garden. Alice had said this was an old kitchen garden, and she smelled thyme and rosemary and lavender.

She loved it here. Even more than that, she was falling in love with the people, with everybody she'd met and worked with. And especially Malcolm. She couldn't deny what was in her heart, and being scared to risk again no longer felt like reason enough to keep her distance.

The truth was, she could go back to her old life in Coeur d'Alene, and she could continue to live exactly as she had. Or she could risk it all by moving here for an amazing new opportunity, shifting her career yet again to have more of a focus on Elderflower Island reading retreats. Maybe even to pursue what Malcolm had mentioned with the houseboats, something they could work on together.

And she could risk her heart. One more time. She could trust that the man she loved had changed. And that he was ready for more than he had ever let himself have, or had ever gone for in a relationship.

She took a deep breath, letting the idea of saying yes, yes to everything, sink in. Letting herself feel it.

She hadn't heard him approach until he was sitting beside her. He reached out and threaded his fingers through hers.

"Nice spot you've created here," he said.

"All of us," she corrected him. "We've created it together." She turned to him, knowing she'd made her decision. "I'm going to stay."

She'd never seen his smile so big. "Thank God."

She leaned in and kissed him. A soft, sweet kiss. One that was full of trust. Trust that she hadn't thought she was willing to give. Until now.

"I should let Mari know," she said a few moments later.

"She's going to be absolutely thrilled," he said.

"It's exciting." She took another deep breath. "I'm

nervous, but I think I'm ready for this change."

"And I'll be beside you every step of the way," he said. "We all will. Let's go tell Mari in person."

They kissed again, and then they locked up and headed off toward the bookstore.

Though it was after closing hours, the light was still on, and Mari was behind the computer near the register. When they knocked, she let them in immediately.

"Are you here to give me your decision?" she asked as soon as they were inside.

Josie smiled. "Yes. I'm going to stay."

Mari threw her arms around Josie. "This is the best news ever!"

Owen appeared from the back of the store. "I take it your answer is yes?" he said to Josie.

"It is."

He joined in the celebrations, saying, "I'm very pleased to hear that. You two, you're going to be an unstoppable team."

Josie was so thrilled to have met Mari. And to be part of a team with her.

"We have to open a bottle of bubbly!" Mari announced.

Owen was already headed up the stairs. "That's exactly what I'm going to get now."

He was back shortly with four glasses and a bottle

of champagne.

"My agent sent me the champagne as a gift after *Mars at the Beach* was published," Mari said, "and this feels like the right time to drink it."

Mari popped the cork and then filled four flutes, handing them out. "To our amazing new adventure together," she said. "And to Josie moving to England."

They clinked glasses and drank.

Then Malcolm held up his glass again. "There's something else we have to celebrate," he said. He looked at Josie as if to get her permission, and she nodded. "We wanted to let you know that Josie and I are together."

She knew he'd specifically asked Alice not to tell Mari and Owen, as he and Josie wanted to tell them.

Mari's eyes got big. "Like *together* together?"

Owen didn't say anything, simply looked between the two of them as if waiting for confirmation.

"Yes," Josie said with a smile. "Together. A proper couple," she said, echoing the way Malcolm had put it just a short while ago.

They all clinked again and drank.

"Your head must be spinning," Owen noted.

She couldn't help but wonder at Owen's slight reticence. Why he didn't seem completely overjoyed by the news that she was dating Malcolm. Was he worried that something would happen between them that would interfere with her business relationship with Mari? That was a valid concern, actually. Still, she was intent on pushing those worries away. She'd made her decision to risk, well, everything. And now that she'd decided, she was going to stand by it. No matter what.

* * *

While Josie and Mari remained in the bookshop to have a meeting about the upcoming retreat, Malcolm and Owen went upstairs to the flat above the shop and sat in the comfortable armchairs by the window.

"A proper relationship, is it?" Owen said. "I'm as pleased as can be, but you're hard on women."

Malcolm nodded, trying not to be defensive. Of course he understood why his brother would have doubts when Malcolm had been anything but a relationship man before now. "She's different. She's special."

Owen nodded. "I agree with both of those things. The question is—is that enough for you?"

Malcolm's jaw tightened. "Of course."

Owen said nothing for a few long moments. "I hope so. I think she's good for you. Really good. We all think that, as you know. I would just hate to see things turn sour."

"I'm not going to let our relationship affect her working relationship with Mari, if that's what you're concerned about," Malcolm stated.

Owen shook his head. "No, you take business a lot more seriously than that. I'm sure you'll go out of your way to make sure that nothing you do, or don't do, negatively affects either Josie or Mari. And I can't tell you how much Mari appreciates the help that you've given on the cottages. You've been a lifesaver for her. Both of you have." He paused again, for just a moment. "This has happened pretty fast, that's all. I want to make sure you've thought it through."

Malcolm worked to keep his expression and body at ease. "Things were fast with you and Mari too. And it's not like you didn't have any issues or damage going in."

"You're right, it was quick. But I knew it was right, from the start."

"Then you get it," Malcolm said. "It's how I feel as well."

"Good," his brother said, looking relieved. "If you need anything, want to talk anything through, anytime, I'm always here."

"Thanks," Malcolm said, a little gruffly as he was hit with a swell of emotion. He knew his brother wasn't just looking out for what might happen to Josie if he ended up changing his mind about having a "proper relationship." Owen was also concerned about him. They were all close, he and Owen especially, as they were the oldest and so close in age. They'd banded together so many times over the years. And yet, he'd never spoken to his brother, or any of his family, not even his mother, about finding his father in the black pit of emotional despair all those years ago.

A part of him considered bringing it up now. But that was water under the bridge. Long-past history. And he was completely over it. Getting together with Josie was just more proof that he'd healed from the trauma of finding his father, the man who'd always seemed like a rock, shaking and crying, drinking whiskey straight from the bottle. That had shattered something in the teenage Malcolm, some sense that he could trust another human being fully.

The two women came back, and Owen poured them all refills. The celebrations continued with takeout Chinese. It was another hour before Josie and Malcolm headed back to the houseboat. He wanted to prove to her, prove to Owen, prove to all of them, that he was making the right decision. And that he wasn't going to let anyone down. Yet again, he found he didn't have the words.

But he could always show Josie how he felt with his lips and his body and pleasure.

CHAPTER TWENTY

As they walked hand in hand back to the houseboat, everything felt different somehow. They weren't just playing around anymore. This was real. No longer a temporary fling, but something that might last forever. Even thinking the word stopped Malcolm in his tracks, and though he tried to cover it, Josie noticed.

"Everything okay?"

He resumed his normal stride. "Yes, everything's great." Her expression seemed a little strained. "What about you?" he asked. "How are you doing? It's been a hell of a day, huh?"

She smiled, and that ray of sunshine never failed to make his heart beat a little faster. "I'm good. Really good. Everything is just so amazing. So many things I didn't see coming have happened. Moving here. Making new friends so quickly. And… you."

His brother's words still lingered in Malcolm's mind as he leaned over to kiss her. "You won't regret taking a chance on Elderflower Island. And the new job. And me." He kissed her again. "Especially me."

She gave him another smile. "I hope so." Her light reticence made him want even more to prove his feelings for her.

They walked past the handful of other houseboats, and he unlocked his door. As he closed it behind them, it felt like they were in their own private, special world. A world made just for the two of them. One where nothing could come between them. A world with no room for any doubts. Any fears.

"Nearly every time we've walked in this door, I've ripped your clothes off and pounced on you," he said. "But I want you for so much more than just sex. You know that, don't you?"

He had never cared whether a woman knew that he was emotionally invested before. This was the first time.

"I do know it." And then she closed the gap between them. "And you don't have to worry—you can always rip my clothes off the moment we're behind closed doors. I love that about you. How you don't hold back your passion."

But he always had, before her. Held his passion in check. On all fronts. It was only now, only because of her, that he was finally letting those passions run free.

"You're special to me, Josie. So damned special."

She laid one hand against his cheek. "You don't need to convince me. Everything you do has convinced me." And then she moved even closer, wrapping her arms around his neck as she pressed herself against him. "Drinking champagne on an empty stomach made me feel a little wild. Do you want to be wild with me, Malcolm Sullivan?"

"Hell yes," he growled, glad for the chance not only to love her, but also for the lovemaking to push away the voices inside his head asking if he really did know what he was doing. "Tell me one of your fantasies." His request was raw, possessive. He didn't want to give her one fantasy, he wanted to give her all of them. More than that, he wanted to be the only one to bring her pleasure ever again.

"When I'm with you," she said in breathy voice, "I have so many fantasies. I don't know which one to pick first."

Her words thrilled him, knowing that she wanted him as much as he wanted her. "We're going to do them all," he promised. "So you can pick any of them, and you don't have to worry. All I want is to give you pleasure. So much damned pleasure."

He drew her closer, lowering his head to the curve of her neck and shoulder. "Tell me," he breathed against her skin.

"Blindfold me." Her cheeks became a beautiful rose color as she betrayed a hint of shyness at her own request. "I want to be nothing but sensation."

He pressed a kiss to her lips, and then he quickly walked back into their bedroom to get a tie. He came back, dangling it between his index and middle finger.

"If at any point you want to change the game, we change it."

She nodded, staring at the tie.

He moved behind her, his heart beating hard inside his chest. Already, it was difficult to breathe normally, and he hadn't even stripped her clothes off or started touching her. That was what she did to him. She made him feel. Feel everything.

Gently, he brought the silk fabric over her eyes and then lowered it into place, tying a firm enough knot at the back of her head that it wouldn't slip, but still making sure it was loose enough not to distract her. He didn't want anything to distract her from all the ways he wanted to make her gasp and moan and cry out his name.

He lowered his hands to her shoulders, then ran them down her arms so that he could thread his fingers through hers. He lifted her hands up over her head. "Hold them there for as long as it's comfortable."

He smiled at the little shiver that ran through her. She was sweet and she was sexy. It was a heady combination. Not moving from behind her, he reached for the hems of her sweater and T-shirt, letting his fingers deliberately brush over the soft skin of her stomach and loving her little shivers beneath his touch. He slowly lifted the fabric up her torso, over her stomach, and then her rib cage, and then her breasts, and then all the way up over her head.

He threw the clothes to the floor, then leaned in and whispered, "You can put your arms down now. But don't do anything else unless I tell you." He liked the little hint of a smile he saw in her profile, the proof that she was enjoying herself. He reached around and undid the snap on her jeans, lowering the zipper next, then pushing the denim down her legs before kneeling to untie and help her slip out of her sneakers. Then he pushed the denim all the way off her legs.

Slowly, he made a circle around her in the very small lounge of his boat. He wanted her to know he was looking, as that would heighten her excitement. He spoke softly. "You're beautiful. The most beautiful woman I've ever seen."

Her smile grew bigger. He still wasn't sure she believed him, but she should. Because he was telling her the complete and unfettered truth. Her beauty was both skin deep and far deeper than that. A light shone from within her, a light that had captivated him even when they were in high school.

He came to a stop in front of her this time, reaching out to let his fingers play over the straps of her bra. He stroked over them and then beneath them, but didn't slide them down. Not yet. Then he ran his hands along the sides of both breasts, along her chest and the inward curve of her waist, and then to her hips, finally sealing them over the fabric there. Again, he stroked over and then between the fabric and her skin, but he didn't take anything off. Not yet.

He stepped just a little bit closer and then lowered his lips toward hers, close enough that he could feel her breath, but not quite close enough for their lips to touch. He could hear how the breath shook in her lungs. And then, finally, he pressed his lips to hers. Her breath rushed out in a gasp. And she tasted so sweet. Always so damned sweet.

He ran kisses from her lips, down her neck, down to the hollow of her throat, where he slipped his tongue out once, twice, until a low moan emerged, and he could feel the vibration against his lips. Then he ran his kisses lower, over the swells of her breasts and then lower still, down the very center of her body. Down to her belly button, where he tasted her again, before running kisses down still farther. He cupped her hips, loving the feel of her curves, knowing he couldn't wait another second to have even more of her. He wasn't just teasing her. He'd been teasing himself too. And he'd hit the end of his restraint.

He slid her underwear down slowly, but he couldn't wait any longer to press his lips to her sex to taste her fully. She moved her hands to his shoulders, holding on, and he could feel her legs trembling as he gently widened her stance. Every part of her was sweet, and he swore he could have stayed like this for hours, learning every inch of her with his lips, his tongue, his hands.

Soon, she was whispering his name and then shuddering beneath his touch. And even then, he didn't stop—not yet. Not until they both had more. He was gentler now, leisurely as he drove her higher, up so high that when she came for him, she was no longer whispering his name, but crying it out.

★ ★ ★

Josie didn't think her body could withstand this much pleasure. But Malcolm was relentless in giving. Giving. Giving. And, oh, it felt so good, but she didn't want it to be a one-way thing. She wanted to give him pleasure too.

As if he could read her mind, he said as he kissed his way up her body, "Do you have any idea how good this makes me feel?"

She licked her lips, shook her head. "But the pleasure's been all mine so far."

"Wrong. It's been both of ours. Every time you cry out my name, it's the best it's ever been for me."

He gave her a kiss, and then he drew back and

moved his hands around to the latch of her bra. And then he made her wait. Wait to have that final layer of fabric stripped from her skin. Wait to be completely bare to him. Wait for another onslaught of pure sensation. Because with her vision temporarily gone, she was a mass of aroused nerve endings. Awaiting his next kiss, the next stroke of his tongue over her skin, the next brush of his fingertips.

"I love seeing, feeling your anticipation as it mounts," he said in a low voice.

She licked her lips again, finding it increasingly harder to breathe. "I like it too."

On a groan, he kissed her again, lingering this time. And then, at last, he freed the clasp at her spine and let the bra fall. She felt him cup her in his hands, felt the awe in his touch, felt the desire in the way he slowly moved the pads of his thumbs over her aroused flesh. She was the one groaning now and arching into him, putty in his hands, letting herself be molded by him, by his desire, and by her own.

"I want to touch you too," she said, and reached for his shirt, trying to pull it up and off.

His laugh was raw and hoarse with need as he helped her, pulling off his sweater and shirt until his torso was bare. With greedy hands and mouth, she touched him, craving him more and more with every second they were together. She simply couldn't get enough of him. She needed him completely naked, just like her. So that she could touch all of him. Love all of him. She moved her hands to his jeans, but he was already one step ahead of her, yanking the zipper down, then shoving them off.

She reached for the warm skin of his hips and then around the front to clasp his hard heat in her hands. Soft like silk and yet hard like steel. She gripped him gently at first and then with a firmer touch as he pushed into her hands, and she ran them up the length of him and then down and then up again. Until the next thing she knew, he was lifting her in his arms. He had barely laid her back on the bed when she heard the tearing of the condom package. She wanted to help, but without sight, she'd only make the process take longer.

And she couldn't wait any longer for him. For the ultimate pleasure of becoming one with him. There were faint bits of light coming in under the blindfold, but not enough that she could see. No, there was only his delicious masculine scent. The sound of his ragged breathing to match hers. And the pleasure of feeling him move over her at last and then fill her. Not slowly this time, but in one hard thrust that she welcomed with a gasp of pleasure.

She wrapped her legs around him and would have wrapped her arms around him, too, except he threaded their fingers together and lifted her hands above her head, holding them on the pillow. Holding her right where he wanted her as he moved over her, into her, harder, faster.

There were no words, only the sounds of the purest bliss. Unrivaled ecstasy. More sensation than she had ever felt before. Everything was heightened, and she fully gave herself over to it.

This was different. And not just because of the blindfold. Tonight, everything felt bigger, heavier, because this was real now. This was no fling. This wasn't just a passing couple of weeks in her life to experience pleasure. This wasn't just about her body anymore. It was about her heart too. And it was about trusting Malcolm not only with her body, but also with everything she was.

She crested the peak on a cry, but she didn't fall alone. Malcolm was there with her, every heartbeat, every breath, every blissful explosion of pleasure.

CHAPTER TWENTY-ONE

Sunday morning, Josie and Malcolm took a stroll around the island before heading over to the cottages. The local café would be catering breakfast and lunch at the reading retreat, so Josie wanted to make sure everything was on track. Malcolm liked having a meeting with Jacob over coffee and fresh croissants in the bakery. It was so far removed from the life he'd lived for the last decade.

There had been satisfaction in closing the big deals, he wasn't going to deny that. But there was something about creating something beautiful with your bare hands and with the kind of partnership that he and Josie had so naturally together. They often thought of the same thing at the same time, and when one of them did have an idea that the other hadn't thought of, it was always a good one and easy to agree upon.

He loved working on the cottages with her, taking a lunch break with her and whoever else was onsite—usually one of his sisters—under the shade of a cherry tree, sprawled on the lawn, eating a sandwich and an apple. It all felt so simple, in the best way.

The life where he took clients out for two-hundred-dollar lunches felt like someone else's life now. And yet, it had only been a week. Funny how much had changed in that week. Not just what he did during the day, but how he felt about the woman he was with.

Before Josie, his heart could always stay closed and, frankly, a little cold. But with her, everything was warm. He'd never been with anyone like her. Never thought he would find anyone like her. And the truth was, even in high school, she'd been different from everyone else. And he'd never stopped regretting what he'd done or how bad he'd made her feel back then. She'd forgiven him, absolved him of the sin he'd carried around for so long. And yet, in his heart of hearts, he knew that what he'd done could never be completely erased and that it had affected her deeply. He'd spend the rest of his life making it up to her.

The thought stopped him cold. The rest of his life? Was that really what this was?

Malcolm had never been a man who questioned his path. Not until recently, anyway. He made a decision, and he moved forward. In business, he made quick decisions and stuck to them. It was one of the things he was known for, that he never wavered. And that he never operated out of fear. But now he had to wonder if the reason why he never had any fear in business was because he'd just never really cared that much.

This last week, he'd found himself caring more than he had in a very long time. Of course he always cared about his family, but he never got that deep with women. No long-term relationships. That was what made a guy start to think about things like forever. But was he truly cut out for that? Was he truly a man who could stay the course, no matter what?

He was a realist. Just because things were butterflies and rainbows now didn't mean they'd be like that forever. He and Josie were certain to have bumps.

When they left the Elderflower Café, they spent a couple of hours at the cottages. It was mostly small stuff left now to be done. Picking up books from Elderflower Island Books that had been special ordered for particular guests, making sure there were enough seating areas inside and out, and enough plates and cutlery.

They were also setting up tradespeople to help transform the bedrooms so the guests of the next retreat would be able to sleep in the cottages.

To shut out his thoughts, he turned and pulled Josie against him, kissing her hard. Kissing her so that it would block out all the other thoughts.

Then he checked his watch. "Are you ready for Sunday roast?"

She smiled up at him, her cheeks rosy from his kiss.

"I can't wait. Partly because everyone in your family is so great. And partly because I'm starved, and Sunday roast sounds amazing."

He kissed her again. "The way Mum makes it is better than amazing. My aunt in Maine—well, she's an aunt once removed, but close enough—is from Ireland, and she is the chef at her own café. I've often said to Mum that she could do the same. But she loves her job at the V&A enough that cooking was only ever second place."

"Now I really can't wait." She looked down at herself. "I need to change into something cleaner first, though. If we leave now and drop by the houseboat, we should still make it on time, right? I want to make a good impression."

"Yes, we've got plenty of time. But even if we didn't, I don't think it's possible for you to come across badly with my family. At this point, I'm pretty sure they'd trade me in for you."

She laughed. "No, they all adore you. Even the way everyone teases you. You're all so great together. I always wondered what it would be like to have siblings."

His answer was easy. "Great most of the time, a pain in the neck for the rest."

She reached up and put a hand on his cheek. "Has anyone ever told you how sweet you are? Especially when you're being all grumbly." She went on her tippy-toes to press a kiss to his lips.

A burst of sunshine exploded in his chest, the same thing that always happened when she kissed him. But there was also that tightening in this gut, the tightening he was doing his damnedest to ignore.

As expected, forty-five minutes later, when they arrived at his parents' house in St. Margarets, everyone was overjoyed to see Josie again. He almost felt invisible, but frankly, that was a nice change. He felt like all eyes had been on him for many years. While plenty of people assumed he enjoyed the limelight—just because he tended to be in it frequently due to his big business deals—the truth was he enjoyed being in the background. He liked having a chance to watch and to take in everything around him.

For the first time in a long time, it was nice to simply sit quietly beside Fiona and appreciate the joyful chaos in the home they'd grown up in.

"I'm so pleased things are going well for you, Malcolm," she said.

"I never saw this week coming, that's for sure." Part of him was afraid to jinx things by talking about how great it was.

"So what do you think you'll do?" she asked. "Stay on the houseboat and give up the London flat? Do you think you'll chuck in the job while you're at it and focus more on carpentry and renovation projects?"

He knew she was asking partly because she was curious about what he was going to do, but also because there was a part of her that clearly longed for the same thing. He still didn't understand why she wasn't at least working as an interior designer. And why she always had to be at her husband's beck and call.

"It's tempting," he replied. "The thought of going back to suits and an office indoors... It's lost its allure after this week."

She nodded. "Thought as much."

Just then, her phone rang. Not surprisingly, it was her husband. She looked a little anxious. "I'd better get this." She walked off, holding the phone to her ear, probably on the receiving end of another laundry list of tasks he demanded she take care of for him.

Malcolm got up, grabbed a beer, and took one over to his father, who was standing in the garden grilling some vegetables to go with the roast. Everyone else was inside, so it was just the two of them.

His father had always been the most quiet and reserved of anybody in the family. He thought before he spoke, and he was quite measured in his actions. Gratefully, he took the beer from Malcolm. "Cheers."

They clinked and then took long pulls of their drinks.

"How are the cottages coming along? I'd like to help when you get to work on the upstairs bedrooms. Of course, as you know, I have to leave immediately if I get a call."

"Thanks. We're actually ahead of schedule, at least if we keep pushing forward at the rate we've been going. And no worries, I know that when you get a call, it's serious, and you've got to be there for other train drivers and workers dealing with trauma." He was so proud of his father for the work he did helping others cope with PTSD.

He studied his father's face. "I know you probably can't give me the details, but is everything going all right with the man who drove the train that hit that boy?" Malcolm knew the bare bones of the most recent story. The driver had heroically managed to stop the train before the boy on the tracks was killed, but still, the teenager was in the hospital. Hopefully, he'd recover fully, but the driver would never erase that vision and experience from his mind.

"Yes, I think he'll be all right. It'll take time. It always does, but fortunately he has a very supportive wife and extended family." His father was silent for a moment. "I was lucky too. I was lucky to have all of you when I went through my own traumatic event."

Malcolm looked down the neck of his beer. Guilt boiled in his chest because he didn't feel that he'd been there. In fact, he knew he hadn't. He'd not only run, he'd jumped continents to get away from his father's pain.

"Malcolm," his father said, "all these years, I don't think I ever adequately found the words to thank you for being there for me that day."

"It was nothing." Malcolm didn't deserve praise. He hadn't done all he could have, should have.

"It was everything. Who knows how much more I would've drunk, or how far I would've sunk if you hadn't been there to take that bottle away and to tell me that everything was going to be all right? To listen to me? And not only that, but I want to apologize for placing that burden at your feet. A son should never have to save his father the way you saved me."

He went on, "And all these years, there's been a part of me that's worried that what happened to me affected you badly. But seeing you now, with Josie, I'm so happy you're happy. She is a wonderful woman. She's everything you deserve."

Malcolm had grown increasingly uncomfortable with their conversation. When he'd brought over the beer, he hadn't thought his father would immediately bring up the past. About that night. "She is great. And I am lucky." He knew his father was waiting for him to say more, to talk about his feelings about that night back in high school before he'd left the country. But that clenching in his gut was only growing tighter.

He tipped his head back and emptied his bottle. "Can I get you another?"

He could feel his father wanted to say something more. Instead, he simply shook his head. "I'm okay with this one."

"I'll see if Mum needs anything." He could feel his father's gaze on him as he walked away. And when Josie reached out a hand to him as he passed, he squeezed it lightly before continuing on to the kitchen and working like hell to ignore that clenching in his gut.

* * *

Josie was having the best time. The Sullivans were amazing. Although she knew she'd miss her mother terribly upon moving to England for her new job, she felt as though she would still be surrounded by family simply because the Sullivans were so incredibly welcoming to her. She had offered to help Penny in the kitchen, but both Penny and Fiona said that she was a guest and that they had everything covered. Alice had been excited about her further plans for the cottage garden, showing Josie pictures on her phone of additional blooms she wanted to incorporate. Owen and Mari were still flying high from the book launch, and Mari had said repeatedly how excited she was that Josie would be staying to work with her.

Aria had run over to give Josie a hug as soon as she and her father arrived, and Tom was full of his usual flirtatious grins. She didn't take any of it seriously, though. She got the sense that's just how he was. That he lived life with a permanent smile on his face.

Malcolm shared so many similarities with his siblings and his parents, and yet, he was so unique. He was a little more serious, and despite the charm that he was capable of putting on, fairly reserved. Upon meeting his father for the first time, she had been struck by their physical likeness. But she could see now, after spending more time with his family, that Simon shared that same reserve. These men didn't speak just to hear the sound of their own voices. They waited until they had something to say, and then people knew to listen.

It was time for them to take their seats, and she loved the way Malcolm took her hand as they walked over to the very large dining table. It was a beautiful and comfortable home a few blocks inland from the river. The style of this house and the others in the neighborhood was different from what she was used to in the United States—these homes were all two stories, and none were ranch houses, at least, not in this neighborhood.

Penny's kitchen looked a little different, too, along

with furnishings that were decidedly European. But despite the differences, the warmth was the same. Her mother had always made sure that their house felt warm and inviting. The Sullivans' house also felt like a place where you wanted to kick up your feet and laugh with people you cared about and who cared about you.

Malcolm lifted her hands to his lips and kissed her knuckles lightly. Just that one small kiss sent shivers running through her. She knew her face must be coloring and that everyone could see how deeply in his thrall she was, but she didn't mind. This was his family, and she wanted them to know how much he had come to mean to her. And yet, there were a few times over the course of the past hour or so when she'd looked across at him and felt that something was troubling him. But whenever he caught sight of her, he'd smile, and she'd wonder if she was imagining it.

Once they were all seated, Simon Sullivan raised his glass. "I'd like to propose a toast to the pleasure of having Josie Hartwell here with us today. Though we've only known you a week, it feels like we've been friends for much longer. I know everyone at the table is so glad that you came to England and Elderflower Island, and we're so pleased that you have decided to stay on."

They were all about to clink their glasses when Alice piped in with, "And we're really glad that you've decided to stick with Malc too. I thought he was a lost cause there for a while."

Josie put her free hand on his leg and squeezed it. She knew how much Alice and the rest of his family loved him, but they could be hard on him. She wanted to love him in all the ways no one but his family had ever loved him. Wholly and completely, unselfishly and unconditionally.

And she hoped—oh, how she hoped—that he would love her the same way. Silently, she reminded herself yet again that he was the one who had suggested they make things serious, real, proper. That always made her grin—a "proper" relationship. Especially when the things they did when their clothes were off in the dark were anything but proper. Pulling her mind from the delicious gutter, she said, "Thank you. Thank you for being so welcoming and for making England feel like home. I am so excited to start this new adventure."

Mari was also bubbling with excitement. She said, "The first reading retreat starts Wednesday, and it's just the first of many." Now she raised her glass. "I want to thank all of you for helping us get the cottages ready in time. To the Sullivans."

After they'd all sipped, Malcolm's mother spoke up. "If you ever need anything, all you have to do is ask."

It was so touching, Josie thought. Amazingly, the

retreat was only a few days away, and in spite of all the work they'd had to do, the cottages were going to be ready. She could hardly wait to welcome the first guests.

And then, with the toasts out of the way, it was time to eat her first Sunday roast.

When Malcolm offered to serve her, she took some of everything. How could she resist? It all looked so delicious—roast beef, roast potatoes, cauliflower with cheese sauce, grilled vegetables drizzled with gravy, plus big, fluffy Yorkshire puddings.

Around a mouthful of beef, Tom asked, "So, Josie, are you planning to stay on Malcolm's houseboat, or will you—"

"She's staying on my boat."

Josie turned to Malcolm, a bit surprised at his insistence and the fact that he hadn't even let Tom finish his question. They hadn't actually talked about whether or not they'd move in together right away.

"And I take it your flat's out of commission for a while still?" Tom asked, one eyebrow raised.

Malcolm seemed to glare at his brother. "As far as I know, that's the case. But I wasn't planning on returning to it anyway."

Again, this was news to Josie. They'd been so busy with the cottages and then making love once they were back at the boat, plus keeping up with their two businesses, that they hadn't really discussed the logistics of how this would work. Only that they were together now.

She didn't know why it worried her, but it felt like things were moving so quickly. Shouldn't this be what she wanted? For them to fall head over heels for each other and never want to be apart? But the thing was, with Malcolm she wasn't convinced it was quite that easy. After all, he'd been a lone wolf for pretty much his entire life. For him to want to switch that abruptly, well, she wasn't going to say it felt forced. It was more that she wasn't quite sure it rang completely true. She didn't doubt his feelings for her. On the contrary, she knew how much he cared. He told her and showed her constantly. But she also understood that just because you decided something didn't mean that it was simple to just switch to it overnight.

Which was only reinforced when Tom next asked, "And the job? Are you chucking that in too? Not that I don't think you should, because I've wondered how you've managed to stick it out in an office that long."

There seemed to be a bit of a rivalry between the two brothers, maybe because they were so close in age, or maybe because Tom didn't tiptoe around Malcolm quite as much as everyone else did. They were all honest with him, but Tom seemed more likely to go straight to the heart of things. Almost as though he was trying to provoke a response.

"The more I think about it," Malcolm said, "the more I'm starting to wonder if it's time for a career change. Back to working with my hands."

Yet again, this wasn't something they'd discussed. Of course, she knew that he really enjoyed working on the cottages, and she also knew that his work wasn't nearly as fulfilling as it had once been. But the fact that he might not only decide to change his relationship patterns with her but also to switch careers, all in one fell swoop?

Unsettled sensations swirled low in her gut. But maybe this was just her own fears popping up. Maybe this was just being worried that she would be hurt again. But he had promised he wouldn't hurt her. That was one of the first things he had said to her after they'd started to connect. And she believed him. So then, why did her smile feel slightly forced as everybody chimed in on what a pleasure it had been to work on the cottages and what a great job she and Malcolm had done? This time, his hand was the one going to her lap. And under the table, she clasped it, as though she was trying to hold on to the sweet feeling she had whenever it was just the two of them and they weren't thinking about the real world.

When the meal was over, she insisted on helping with the cleanup. And it was lovely drying dishes at the sink with Malcolm and his mother and father. She just wished she could shake off that slight sense of unease. Would her past relationship battles always be with her? Or would she one day be able to embrace love without fear at all?

CHAPTER TWENTY-TWO

They were in Malcolm's car, driving back from his parents' house, when Josie asked, "Are you really thinking about changing careers?"

"I've been feeling like it's time for a change for a while now," he replied. "And then you gave me *Walden*, and that made me think about what I really want. It's been good to get back to work with my hands." He reached over to take hers. "And I've loved working with you."

"If I were still going to leave, would you still be making the same plans? Or is this because you're worried I won't be able to make this transition without your help?"

"I'm not the least bit worried about you," he replied. "You're resilient, you're smart, and there's that positive attitude of yours. Whatever situation is thrown at you, I have no doubt in my mind that you'll make it work."

"I know you're exactly the same," she said. "And it's not that I'm at all doubting that you'll make a success of any career change you want to make. I guess I'm just projecting some of my own fears onto you."

"What are you afraid of, Josie?"

"The correct answer is nothing," she said with a small smile. "But the honest answer is that sometimes it feels like I'm afraid of everything. But then I always remind myself I'm going to wake up in the morning, and the sun will hopefully be shining, and I'll realize that all those fears were just the darkness playing tricks on me."

"Late nights have a habit of messing with one's mind, that's true," he agreed. "But I suspect some of your concerns have to do with the way my family is reacting. It's almost like they can't believe I'm managing a real relationship, or that I've found someone as great as you are."

"They love you so much," she said, "and it's so obvious that they want you to be happy, despite their teasing. But at the same time, I know it's never easy when other people, especially family, critique your life and the decisions you've made along the way." She squeezed his hand. "It's a testament to your closeness that they feel they can speak so openly to you."

"Did you enjoy yourself this afternoon? Or did the Sullivans overwhelm you?"

"I loved every second of being with your family. They're wonderful. It makes perfect sense that you turned out so well." They had just parked and were getting out of the car when she said, "There's one other thing I wanted to talk about. Where I'm going to live."

He was shocked. "I insist that you stay on the houseboat with me."

She nodded. "That's a really lovely offer, but I can't help but wonder if this is all moving too fast."

"No." He stopped them on the path and pulled her into his arms. "When you know, you know. And I know." He stroked her cheek. "Don't you know too?" He could feel her heart beating through the pulse point just behind her earlobe.

"I do. I know that you're right for me and moving to London is right, but we don't have to move in together right away."

"There's nothing either of us needs to be afraid of." He lowered his mouth to hers to seal his words with a kiss. Now more than ever, he refused to let any of his doubts or that tightening in his chest rise to the surface.

"Are you nervous about Wednesday?" he asked when they got inside.

"A little," she admitted. "But mostly excited about my first reading retreat on Elderflower Island."

"I can't wait to walk over with you the first day." He pictured them hand in hand as they headed to the cottages, only this time she'd be there to welcome guests who would hopefully find their lives changed by the books Josie had chosen especially for them.

"You're going to walk me to work?" She laughed. "Are you afraid I'll get lost?"

"No. But I want to kiss you good luck on your first day, and I want to do it inside the cottages."

She put her arms around him, and the expression in her eyes made his heart swell. "I would love that."

★ ★ ★

After they'd both dealt with a few emails, they went to bed and made love. It was as wonderful as always, and Malcolm seemed even more tuned in to her pleasure, if that was possible. She shuddered to climax and heard him cry out her name as he came right behind her. Still trembling, heart pounding, she turned to kiss him, and he held her gaze, his eyes intense in the near dark.

"I love you," he said.

She felt like her whole heart turned over. He'd shown her in so many ways that he loved her, but this was the first time he'd said those all-important words.

"I love you too," she said.

And suddenly, all her fears seemed foolish. He loved her.

What could possibly go wrong?

★ ★ ★

Josie fell asleep in Malcolm's arms, but even though he loved the way her body curled around his, he couldn't sleep. There had been an email from Genevieve warning him that Kieran Taylor was becoming increasingly difficult. Malcolm knew this stage of the negotiations was always make-or-break. Damn, they'd worked long and hard on this project, and it could be one of the biggest deals of his career.

He calculated that it was midday on Monday in Christchurch. There was no harm in checking in, even if a little voice in the back of his head said he should stay out of it and let Genevieve handle things. But as Josie said—sometimes in the darkness your mind spiraled off, and the worries and the fears that you were able to push away during the day rose up.

He slid out of bed, wondering if Josie was right, and they were moving too fast. But he'd always made decisions quickly and stuck to them.

He was Malcolm Sullivan. Success was what he did. And no, he wasn't at all concerned about things moving too fast. The tightening in his gut be damned. It was unreasonable to expect that taking any leap would be simple, that he would just go with the flow. The way he'd been doing since the moment he picked up Josie at the airport and realized how much he liked being with her. Loved being with her. It was why he'd finally said those three little words.

I love you.

He'd never said that to any other woman. Only to Josie. And he meant it with his whole heart. He did love her. Loved her so much that he could no longer envision his life without her.

He took one last look at Josie lying in his bed, her hair spread out on the pillow, her skin still slightly flushed from their lovemaking. The copy of *Walden* she'd given him sat on the bed shelf, almost mocking him as though it knew he was about to check business emails late on a Sunday night. Thoreau would shake his wise head if he could see Malcolm now.

Gently, he pulled up the covers over Josie's shoulders and then crept out into the lounge. He opened his laptop. For so many years, this computer had been an appendage, his fingers always on it, never leaving his sight for too long. He'd thought he couldn't live without it, or his phone, but this week he'd learned to use them as the tools they were meant to be and not as his masters.

It was no wonder his family was so overwhelmed by the changes in him. He was like a new man. And all because of Josie.

Out the window, he could see moonlight on the river. A bat flitted over the glossy surface of the water, and he realized he was able to see things like this again. It wasn't that they hadn't happened while he'd been working all those years, it was simply that he'd stopped noticing because they had no bearing on his business deals.

Truthfully, he'd achieved everything he wanted to in his career. Once House in a Box was launched globally, he would step back.

He opened his email and, almost as though he'd known it would be there, found an email from Kieran Taylor, CEO and inventor of House in a Box.

Malcolm read the email... and then read it again more slowly. His gut clenched hard in frustration. Kieran had called a board meeting and invited his bankers to discuss moving forward with the global expansion. He was *inviting* Malcolm Sullivan to the board meeting, but made it clear that the meeting would happen anyway. Malcolm could read between the lines that Kieran was completely overwhelmed and suffering a massive anxiety attack over taking his product global.

But to get to a Wednesday meeting in New Zealand with time to meet the board and talk some sense into Kieran meant jumping on a plane from London ASAP. He grabbed his phone, went up to the roof deck so as not to disturb Josie, and called Kieran.

"Good to hear from you," Kieran said. "I hope you can make the board meeting. I really want to make sure we've got all our i's dotted and t's crossed. You understand."

What Malcolm understood was that Kieran was running scared, but he didn't say that. Instead, he reiterated all the good points of the deal he and Genevieve had worked so hard on.

"I know all that," Kieran replied. "But if you're asking me to commit everything to this global expansion, I need you to commit too."

"We are completely committed to making House in a Box a global brand," Malcolm assured him.

"Then I want you here, on the ground, running the operation. I can't do it. I'm stretched too thin as it is. If I have to ramp up production, I'll need you to run the business."

Malcolm was completely taken aback. He calculated rapidly. "But you're asking for at least a year."

"That's right, mate. If you believe in House in a Box the way you say you do, I need you here for a year."

In the silence, Malcolm heard the river lapping gently against *River Star*'s hull. Was this the change he needed? What if he took Kieran up on his demand and moved to New Zealand for a year? He thought of all the places he'd like to show Josie. The mountains and beaches, the charming cities and sheep ranches. Because he couldn't imagine a year without Josie.

They talked a little longer, and finally Kieran said

aloud what Malcolm had already figured out. "Your being here is a nonnegotiable." Kieran Taylor didn't make decisions as quickly as Malcolm did, but he'd discovered the young inventor was hard line when he finally did decide.

When Malcolm got off the phone, he went inside, poured himself a two fingers of whiskey, and downed the lot in one.

This was an impossible choice.

He couldn't ask Josie to come with him to New Zealand for a full year, the day after she'd committed to running reading retreats here on Elderflower Island.

A voice in his head said, *It's not impossible. Go. And if it's meant to be, she'll be waiting at the end of the year.*

He tried to shake the thought off. But it just kept playing inside his head, louder. *This is the deal you've been waiting for. Are you really going to blow it for a relationship that might not even work out?*

No, he was in love with her. She was in love with him. He'd asked her to move in with him.

The voice grew to a shout. *It's only a year.*

He could fly Josie out between reading retreats. They'd see each other.

If your relationship can't make it for a year, then how strong is it anyway?

Dammit, the voice seemed to be making sense.

CHAPTER TWENTY-THREE

Josie woke, surprised and more than a little disappointed to find that Malcolm was already out of bed. She loved waking up snuggled in his arms—and then everything that came after snuggling. A delicious shiver ran through her as she thought about getting up and grabbing him to take him back to bed. They could be a little later to the cottages today. After all, they were making great progress. And with the sun shining through the boat's windows, it was true that her fears had disappeared along with the night sky. There was no reason to be scared. They loved each other. And this time, she was certain that love was real. That it wasn't just a lie, like it had been with her ex.

Putting on a long-sleeved shirt of Malcolm's, she walked barefoot out into the living room. He was on his computer, typing quickly, an empty coffee cup beside him. He must have been up for a while. He looked a little guilty when he spotted her.

"Good morning. Did you sleep well?"

She nodded, moving over to his outstretched

hands. He pulled her onto his lap and kissed her. He tasted like freshly roasted coffee.

When he finally let her lips go, he said, "There's something I need to talk with you about this morning, once you've had a cup of coffee."

The tone of his voice was serious enough that she said, "Coffee can wait."

"You know that deal I told you about? House in a Box?"

That was all it took for her chest to clench. But there was no reason to freak out, she reminded herself. He was simply sharing some news.

"The CEO is panicking. I need to go to New Zealand to attend a board meeting. And I might need to stay on longer."

It was only through great force of will that she kept herself from jumping off his lap. She wasn't going to let her doubts win at the first small issue. "How long will you have to stay?" A few weeks without him would be manageable, even though she'd miss him.

"A year." He paused as she took the blow of his words. "Josie, I said yes."

"Oh." Now she did get off his lap. She walked over to the coffeepot on slightly shaky legs and poured herself a cup. She took a few sips without turning to face him, trying to figure out what this meant.

He moved behind her, putting his hands on her

shoulders and gently turning her so that he could look into her eyes. "I'll fly back as often as I can, and you can come and visit me between retreats. You'll love New Zealand."

"You're going to be busy." She wanted to be realistic about this, not create some sort of fantasy that would never happen. "And of course you should go. Of course you should take the deal. It's what you've been working on for so long, after all."

"Nothing will change for us," he insisted.

At last, she lost some of that tightly held control. "Of course it will. We're brand new, not even a week old. I know we care about each other—"

"We love each other."

She nodded, but couldn't quite bring herself to say the words. "But I'm going to be transitioning into a new job in a new country as well, and both of us are going to be busy. We shouldn't expect too much of our relationship."

"What are you saying? You don't want a long-distance relationship?"

"I don't know. Maybe we should play it by ear, see how things go in the first couple of months. And of course I'll move out of your houseboat."

"No! I want you to stay."

But she couldn't. Even when she'd thought he was going to stay on Elderflower Island, she'd felt moving in with him would be moving too fast. It had been one thing to stay temporarily on his boat for a couple of weeks, but to move in permanently? No, it was right that she find her own place. "How soon do you need to leave?"

He ran a hand over his hair in frustration. "Today."

The breath pushed out of her lungs.

"Genevieve and I are working on a presentation for a board meeting Wednesday. The CEO would like to hammer out all the last details in person, and then move immediately on the expansion plans."

"Do you already have your plane ticket?"

Something that looked like guilt crossed his face. "I do. I have to leave in a couple of hours. I'm sorry to miss walking you to the reading retreat for your first day, but I know you'll do an amazing job."

She took a deep breath, working to center herself before speaking again. "I'm happy for you, Malcolm. It's all your hard work that's given you this opportunity. And I want you to make the most of it, just like I know you want to. You've been so much help with the cottages this week, and I've loved every minute we've spent together."

"Why does it sound like you're saying good-bye? We still have phones, and we can talk over video, and you can fly to New Zealand too."

She nodded, not wanting to burst his bubble. "Yes,

all that's true. But promise me you won't let us, or thinking about my being here, hold you back."

"You're not holding me back. It's exactly the opposite, Josie. Ever since I've been with you, you've lifted me up."

She went to her tippy-toes and pressed a kiss to his lips. At that exact moment, his phone rang, and she could feel the tension already between them.

"Go ahead, it's okay. I know this is important. I'll just take a shower and get ready for work, and then I'll say good-bye before you have to leave for the airport."

In the shower, she was glad for the water pouring down her face. Because that way, she could lie to herself and say she wasn't crying.

CHAPTER TWENTY-FOUR

Malcolm had been in a thousand airports waiting for a thousand flights. But he'd never felt like this. He sat in the executive lounge with Genevieve, who was wired on coffee and still working on the presentation to House in a Box's board. But he could barely concentrate. Why the hell was he going to New Zealand?

It had been only an hour and a half since he'd been with Josie, and already he missed her. It was like an ache in the deepest part of him.

He couldn't stop rewinding back to their good-bye. She'd left first, heading for the cottages alone, when everything inside him longed to be going with her. She'd put on a brave face, but he was pretty sure she'd been crying. Still, she'd encouraged him to go with an understanding that amazed him. She got how important this deal was to him. Maybe when it was over, when the year in New Zealand was up...

But how much did it really mean to him? Okay, so he'd spent a couple of years courting Kieran Taylor. Umpteen hours with one big goal in mind. From a purely business standpoint, this was the ultimate success. This would go down as one of the greatest deals in the history of his company. And yet...

While he should be flying with excitement, he only felt numb when he thought about the business, the deal. He didn't *feel* anything. If he were subjected to a lie detector test right now and asked if he was happy about the deal, there was no way that he could say yes without the machine going crazy and labeling him a liar. But if he were asked whether he missed Josie with every fiber of his being, if he was haunted by the look in her eyes when he'd told her he was going to New Zealand for a year, any answer but yes would also be proven to be false.

Entwined with it all was the conversation he'd had with his father the day before. His father had thanked him for basically saving his life. Instead of asking why Malcolm had run away all those years ago, he'd told his son that he had done more for him than quite possibly anyone else. For the first time, Malcolm saw that he'd been a scared seventeen-year-old, and he'd done his best in a terrifying situation.

And then when his dad had said that he'd worried about Malcolm all these years, worried that he might have been badly impacted in an emotional way, but that now he knew everything was okay because of Malcolm's relationship with Josie...

Malcolm ran a hand through his hair. Should he have been honest with his father? Should he have said, *Yes, it did screw me up seeing you like that. It made me hellbent and determined to never ever be torn apart by anything that way. It's made me keep relationships on the surface and shut the door on passions that I otherwise might've pursued.* Should he have said, *I wasn't there for you. Yes, that night I helped you. But then I left.* Should he have admitted the guilt that he'd felt for so long?

So many questions swirled in Malcolm's head. About going to New Zealand, about his relationship with his father and, most of all, about Josie. He'd meant it when he told her he loved her. He'd never said those words to another woman and couldn't imagine ever saying them to someone else. Because no one else would be Josie. She was everything he hadn't known he wanted.

No, that wasn't true.

Even back in high school, she'd been special. And though he'd known her only from afar, their kiss had still been electrifying. Memorable for years afterward. Josie had been with him since he was seventeen, and it felt almost as though fate had brought her back into his life.

Fate was not something Malcolm Sullivan had ever believed in. He'd always believed that you got to where you were and ended up with the life you had because of focus, work, and attention. But there was no other reason that he could possibly think of for Josie to have shown up in his life again other than fate. Some cosmic force that wanted them to be together.

And then what did he do? His usual MO. He got the hell out of there. Told her he loved her and then said good-bye.

Oh sure, he'd said it would only be for a year, that they could have a long-distance relationship. But he hardly even believed himself. And he sure as hell knew she hadn't believed him.

She'd been kind enough to let him go without a big emotional explosion. But he wished that she had exploded. Because then maybe, *maybe* he would've changed his mind. Would have turned down the deal and stayed.

He owed her an apology. An apology he knew she'd never ask for. Because she would never emotionally manipulate him. It wasn't who she was. She was good, and sweet, and kind, and she'd let him go.

He'd be in New Zealand in a matter of hours. He'd get a few hours of sleep on the plane, and then he and Genevieve would head straight into an intense meeting where it would be on them to prove that House in a Box was ready for global success. Somehow he was going to have to pull it together. Somehow he was going to have to focus and do the work that he'd agreed to do. Somehow he was going to have to let his longing for Josie go. For now.

But even as he strategized with Genevieve, tried to focus on the plans for the global launch, he knew that would be impossible.

CHAPTER TWENTY-FIVE

Alice was already in the garden by the time Josie got there. Her good-bye with Malcolm had gone on until his driver had loaded Malcolm's luggage into the car. Neither of them had wanted to say good-bye. Neither had wanted to admit that this was likely a far bigger good-bye than they thought. In their heart of hearts, they both knew.

"Good morning!" Alice called. She was an early riser, and it was just as obvious that she absolutely loved her time in the garden. How wonderful that she had been able to make a career out of it.

"Good morning," Josie said in as bright a voice as she could muster, with as big a smile as she could paste on her face.

Fortunately, Alice was fighting with a rock that she was trying to get out of the soil, so she didn't notice just how strained Josie's response had been. "Is Malcolm coming along soon? I'm going to need his help later moving a tree."

Okay, this was it. This was when Josie had to start

letting everyone know that Malcolm had returned to normal.

"Actually, he is on a plane to New Zealand right now."

Alice's head whipped around. "What? He didn't say anything last night about going away."

"He was contacted by the CEO of a company in New Zealand overnight and it's basically the deal he's waited his entire career for. Of course he had to go." She didn't mean to sound like she was trying to convince Alice, even though she was trying to convince herself of the same thing.

"How long is he going to be there?" Alice had risen now and was walking over to Josie, frowning.

"A year." There was no way she could say that with a smile or in a chipper voice.

Alice dropped the stone in her hands so it made a soft *thud* on the earth. "That stupid sod. I can't believe he's just up and left like this. Is his head completely up his arse?"

Josie didn't know what to say. Privately, she thought he did have his head up his ass. But she also understood why he felt he needed to go. "This deal is important to him," she finally said. "And he has my full support."

Alice rolled her eyes. "You shouldn't need to give him your full support. He should know better. He's done plenty of business deals in his life, but he's never fallen in love before. If you ask me, he's deliberately sabotaging your relationship."

"Well, there's no way he could have planned for a business emergency," Josie pointed out.

"No, but he could have said no." She kicked at the rock she'd just dropped. "I'm going to call and leave him a message so it's the first thing he hears as soon as he lands."

Josie said quickly, "No, please don't. I don't want him to think I asked you to do that."

"I'll tell him it's entirely my opinion that he's being an idiot."

"I know you love him—I know all of you love him—but it's his life. And he should get to live it exactly the way he chooses."

Alice gave her a long, serious look. "Are you telling me you're okay with this?"

Josie hated lying to a woman who had so quickly become a friend. But she could barely admit how she felt to herself, so how could she admit the depth of her emotions to Malcolm's sister?

"I think if it's meant to be between us, it'll work out. And if it isn't—" She couldn't say the rest of the sentence, could barely hold back tears.

"I'm going to make you a cup of tea, and we're going to talk about anything except my brother." Alice glanced around the garden. "I really need his help. The garden looks okay, but I've found an old fountain that needs setting up too. I was counting on Malc to do it."

"A fountain sounds wonderful."

"Leave it with me," Alice said. "I'll have reinforcements here soon."

Alice wasn't kidding. By the time Josie finished her tea, Malcolm's mother and father, along with Tom and Fiona, were there. Owen was in London on Mathilda Westcott's business and couldn't come until later that afternoon, but Mathilda herself had walked over to join the family. Mari was alone in the bookshop. The only other person missing was—

"I can't believe my grandson has buggered off to New Zealand." Mathilda Westcott looked furious. "I'm tempted to get on a plane myself and give him a piece of my mind in person."

Josie hadn't had any compunction about asking Alice to leave Malcolm alone, but she didn't want to step on the older woman's toes. Still, she had to say, "I'm happy for him. It's a deal he's wanted for a long time. And now with your family here to help, I think we'll be fine on the timeline for the cottages."

Mathilda nodded. "Yes, I always have been a fan of a certain level of stoicism. I appreciate your backbone. I knew it was there from the start. Mark my words, he'll realize his mistake, even if none of us actually go read him the Riot Act."

But Josie didn't want to think about Malcolm anymore. She didn't want to talk about it. She just wanted to get to work. It was easier when she could just bury her thoughts under long to-do lists. One of those to-dos was finding somewhere else to live, because she didn't think she could stay on his boat for another night. She'd find a short-term vacation rental and go from there.

However, she wouldn't make the mistake of telling his family that she was leaving the houseboat.

Mathilda made an excuse to get Josie alone outside, where she said, "My dear, I don't like to interfere, but I was like you once. Very young. Very proud. I let the man I loved get away because I didn't ask him to stay." She looked off into the distance and smiled sadly. "I've regretted it my whole life."

"But—"

"Oh, I did marry, of course, and raised a wonderful family, but I let my true love get away."

Josie wondered if she was giving up too easily. Was she not fighting for the one thing worth fighting for?

In her silence, Mathilda spoke softly. "I checked Malcolm's flight. It's been delayed. I bet you could just make it if you left now."

She laughed then, glad for the sensation in a body and a heart that had been clenched so tightly all day.

"You mean race to the airport? Like in the movies?"

Mathilda's smile was warm and wise. "I think you deserve your happy ending, don't you?"

A tear escaped as Josie nodded. *Yes.*

"Tom," Mathilda called in her firm tone, "Josie needs a ride to the airport." When Tom appeared, car keys in hand, his grandmother added, "And step on it."

CHAPTER TWENTY-SIX

Josie had never done anything like this. Risked everything on love. Odds were that Malcolm's plane would have taken off by the time she got there. If so, she had her passport with her and a credit card. She'd buy a ticket on the next flight. That's what she'd do.

If he didn't feel the same way, she'd cope. On the way to the airport, she called Mari and explained the situation. "Mathilda said she could run one day of the reading retreat if you could do the others. I just really need to tell Malcolm how much I love him and that he needs to choose me over New Zealand."

But while the odds didn't seem to be in her favor, she'd never be able to live with herself if she didn't at least try. Try to show him how much he meant to her. That he had come, in such a short amount of time, to mean absolutely everything. Yes, she'd find a way to move on with her life if he didn't feel the same way. But her love for him would always be front and center. She knew that with utter certainty.

There would be no forgetting Malcolm Sullivan.

Not even the slightest chance.

Tom dropped her off at Departures and wished her luck. She nodded, too choked up to speak, then ran into the terminal.

Please let it not be too late.

She tried to call Malcolm, but his phone was off. No doubt he was already on the plane, flying away from her.

* * *

Malcolm felt the delay of his flight like a reprieve. For two more hours, he'd be in the same country as Josie. Even as he tried to refocus, he saw Genevieve quietly typing away. She'd created most of the slide deck with little input from him.

The words of Thoreau floated back to him. *Things do not change; we change. The cost of a thing is the amount of what I will call life which is required to be exchanged for it, immediately or in the long run.*

Everything Josie had been trying to tell him was right there. How much of his life had he exchanged for money, power, prestige, write-ups in the *Financial Times*? And how much was he going to keep giving away? Including Josie?

A sudden urgency bloomed in his chest. He'd hurt Josie this morning—he knew that. At the first test, he'd done what he'd vowed not to do. He'd run away from her. From *them*.

"Genevieve," he said, startling her. "I'm not going with you to New Zealand."

Her brows rose in understandable surprise, seeing as they were waiting for their flight to board.

"You're the one who's been managing this project," he said. "You can do this. You can see it through."

She looked gratified, but reminded him, "Kieran's expecting you."

"But when I tell him that you're the one who's been doing all the work on this, and when he sees your presentation at the board meeting, he'll know you're the better person for the job." He paused. "Is there anything I could say that would make you stay in New Zealand for a year?"

She gazed at him for a moment. "Make me an equity partner."

Just like that, he knew she was ready to take on the lead role in his business. She'd played a winning card and done it at exactly the right moment. He was proud of her.

"Done. We'll get the lawyers to work out an agreement." He held out his hand. "Partner."

She shook his firmly, keeping her smile in check. "Partner."

"Now I really have to go."

He jumped up and headed into the main terminal. He couldn't wait for his driver. He'd get a cab back to Elderflower Island. He couldn't wait to see Josie's face. He only hoped she didn't slap his.

He was racing through the airport when a bookshop caught his eye, and he detoured inside.

★ ★ ★

Josie didn't know what to do. The Departures display said that Malcolm's flight was boarding, and he still had his phone off. She'd been too late to buy a ticket for the flight. She'd have to buy a ticket for the next one. She might have her passport and credit card, but no way was she going to sit for hours on a plane without a book. She headed for the WHSmith and then stopped, gaping, as she nearly bumped into the man coming out of the bookstore.

"Malcolm?" she cried. Her mind must be playing tricks.

"Josie!" He looked as stunned as she felt.

"What are you doing here?" they both said at the same time.

"Coming to find you." Again, they spoke in unison.

She shook her head. "Let me go first. Otherwise, I'm afraid I might never get the chance to say what I need to say to you."

* * *

He stared into her eyes, drinking in the sight of her. The luminosity of her skin, the fullness of her lips. Every last inch of her was so beautiful. He nodded, and she took a deep breath, so deep that he could practically feel it in his own chest.

"I wasn't honest with you earlier," she said. "I didn't tell you the truth about how much I wished you would stay. I don't want a year of long-distance. There's already been so much time lost for us, all those years between high school and now. And I've never loved anyone the way I love you. I love you with everything I am, with everything I was and will be. I love you for your past, your present, and your future. And I want so badly to be able to see you every morning and every night. To let our love continue to deepen. To learn everything there is to know about you, from your childhood to the things that you're proud of as an adult, and even the things that you're not. I can't stand the thought of you resenting me for pulling you away from a world and a deal that has always meant so much to you, but I have to be honest. I love you, and please, don't go to New Zealand for a year. Please stay in England. Be my boyfriend. My proper relationship. And I promise you won't regret it. I'll never let you regret it."

At last, she seemed to run out of breath. As soon as she did, he had to kiss her. Had to capture her beautiful mouth, had to draw her lovely body against his and hold her tight. He kissed her as though it had been a year instead of a few hours since the last time.

Finally, he drew back to look into her eyes. "Do you know what I just did? I handed the deal over to Genevieve. It's hers now, and she's willing to stay in New Zealand for a year."

Josie's eyes widened. "But what if the CEO won't take the trade and insists on you?"

"I'm pretty sure Genevieve can handle him. And if not?" He stopped to imagine losing House in a Box. And he knew. "I really don't care."

"I'm so glad."

"I should never have said yes to it. You and what we're building between us mean so much more to me than any business deal ever could. The only project I'm interested in right now is you and me together, in London, as a proper couple."

"You're doing that for me?"

"For *us*. You don't know how much I admire you for coming here and being so honest. Honest in a way that I have not been with anyone since I was seventeen. I've always been too afraid of how they might respond to the truth inside me. To my fears. To my weaknesses. But you, Josie—you're not afraid of anything. I look at you and I know this is such a big part of why I couldn't help but fall in love with you. Because you're so damned brave. And yet, your heart is right there on your sleeve for everyone to see. I want to learn from you. Maybe after twenty or thirty years with you, I will no longer be afraid to be who I really am."

"You're amazing," she told him. "And you have never given yourself enough credit for that. The way your family loves you—that's not just because of blood ties. It's because of the man you are. And I hope it doesn't take twenty or thirty years for me to convince you that you are lovable exactly as you are."

This time, she was the one kissing him. Stealing his breath in the same way that she had completely stolen his heart.

"I love you, Josie. And I promise you I won't ever do this to you again. I won't run, even if everything inside of me is telling me that it's the safest thing to do. I'm going to count on you to help me face and deal with that voice inside me that tells me it's too risky to love. That it's too dangerous to devote myself to something I'm passionate about. And to know that it will be okay if something ever hurts me the way my father was hurt all those years ago."

"Anything you need from me, I want to give to you. And just like you, I know you will always support me when that little voice inside *my* head tries to tell me that I'm not good enough. That I'm not special enough."

"You are the most special, wonderful woman alive. I'm going to spend the rest of my life making sure that you never, ever forget that. Oh, and I bought you something."

He handed her a bag with a book inside. She pulled it out. *"Pride and Prejudice,"* she said aloud. Then she glanced up, puzzled. "How did you know this is my favorite book?"

"I didn't. But I remembered Mari saying it was about a man who had to let go of his pride in order to win the woman of his dreams. It seemed appropriate."

She hugged him to her. "It's perfect, and so are you."

EPILOGUE

Fiona Sullivan showed up at the informal family launch party of Elderflower Island Reading Retreats promptly at seven o'clock Tuesday night. The reading retreats started the next day, but Mari and Josie had decided to hold a little party to thank the family for pitching in to get the cottages ready in time. Secretly, they all wanted to see with their own eyes that Malcolm had learned his lesson and wouldn't be putting his heart at risk again anytime soon.

Malcolm and Josie couldn't seem to stop touching each other, glancing over with looks so full of love that Fiona felt she was intruding if she didn't glance away.

The cottages were beautiful, and she took a moment to take pride in the part she and her decorating eye had played. She'd even enjoyed working within a tight budget, sourcing secondhand designer curtains and cushions. Amazingly, she'd popped into a couple of charity shops, something she'd never done before and secretly enjoyed. She'd bought a couple of lamps, a side table that was also a bookshelf, and some book-themed prints for almost nothing.

Lewis demanded the best, and she'd learned early in their marriage that he equated cost with quality. Everything from their house to their furniture to their cars and clothes was top of the line. So she'd enjoyed a little holiday from buying the very best and gotten creative with cheaper finds. It had been surprisingly satisfying.

"You really should have become a professional decorator," Alice said, also gazing around at the comfortable room that looked like something between a country hotel and a private library.

Perhaps there were moments when she'd have liked a career, but Lewis needed her. They entertained his clients a great deal, and he expected her always to look her best, so she spent more time than she cared to admit on treadmills and in salons and high-end boutiques. She hired and managed the household staff, but always did her own cooking. Lewis liked a home-cooked meal, and she did love to cook. At one time, she'd imagined motherhood would take up a lot of her time, but that joy had been denied her.

Still, she was happy. Why wouldn't she be? She had everything she could ever want, like the diamond earrings Lewis had given her on their tenth wedding anniversary. He'd made sure she knew how much they cost, and the sum had made her eyes grow wide. She was glad they were insured, or she'd never be able to wear them outside of the house in case she lost one.

Glancing over at where Malcolm was sitting beside Josie, holding her hand as though he'd never let it go, she wondered if she'd ever been as happy as those two were.

For a moment, she wondered whether she might ask Josie to suggest some books she might read. Not that she had a problem, of course. Her life was perfect, but sometimes there was an ache inside her.

Could she explain that to Josie? And would the bibliotherapist be able to prescribe a course of books that would help her find contentment?

Her phone buzzed. Lewis hadn't been able to come tonight. He'd had a squash game with a client. Now he was on his way home and asking that she join him there for dinner.

It wasn't a command, of course. He worked very hard and understandably liked to find his wife home and dinner ready to serve when he returned after a long day at work. She had left homemade moussaka warming in the oven and a Greek salad in the fridge. All she had to do when she got home was warm the bread and pour the wine.

She rose, wished Josie well in her reading retreats, and left. When she glanced back, the windows were lit from within, and she heard the sound of happy laughter. For a moment, she was tempted to turn back.

Then she shook her head at her own foolishness and got into her late model Jaguar. She checked that her makeup was perfect and her hair in place. Lewis hated it when she didn't look her best, and even more when she was late.

★ ★ ★

ABOUT THE AUTHOR

Having sold more than 10 million books, Bella Andre's novels have been #1 bestsellers around the world and have appeared on the *New York Times* and *USA Today* bestseller lists 93 times. She has been the #1 Ranked Author on a top 10 list that included Nora Roberts, JK Rowling, James Patterson and Steven King.

Known for "sensual, empowered stories enveloped in heady romance" (Publishers Weekly), her books have been Cosmopolitan Magazine "Red Hot Reads" twice and have been translated into ten languages. She is a graduate of Stanford University and has won the Award of Excellence in romantic fiction. The Washington Post called her "One of the top writers in America" and she has been featured by Entertainment Weekly, NPR, USA Today, Forbes, The Wall Street Journal, and TIME Magazine.

Bella also writes the *New York Times* bestselling "Four Weddings and a Fiasco" series as Lucy Kevin. Her sweet contemporary romances also include the USA Today bestselling "Walker Island" and "Married in Malibu" series.

If not behind her computer, you can find her reading her favorite authors, hiking, swimming or laughing. Married with two children, Bella splits her time between the Northern California wine country, a log cabin in the Adirondack mountains of upstate New York, and a flat in London overlooking the Thames.

Sign up for Bella's New Release newsletter:
bellaandre.com/Newsletter
Join Bella Andre on Facebook:
facebook.com/authorbellaandre
Join Bella Andre's reader group:
bellaandre.com/readergroup
Follow Bella Andre on Instagram:
instagram.com/bellaandrebooks
Follow Bella Andre on Twitter:
twitter.com/bellaandre
Visit Bella's website for her complete booklist:
www.BellaAndre.com

Made in United States
Troutdale, OR
04/14/2025